IN ANOTHER TIME

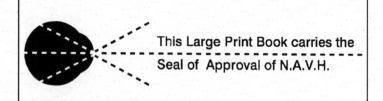
This Large Print Book carries the
Seal of Approval of N.A.V.H.

IN ANOTHER TIME

JILLIAN CANTOR

WHEELER PUBLISHING
A part of Gale, a Cengage Company

Farmington Hills, Mich • San Francisco • New York • Waterville, Maine
Meriden, Conn • Mason, Ohio • Chicago

Copyright © 2019 by Jillian Cantor.
Wheeler Publishing, a part of Gale, a Cengage Company.

ALL RIGHTS RESERVED
Wheeler Publishing Large Print Hardcover.
The text of this Large Print edition is unabridged.
Other aspects of the book may vary from the original edition.
Set in 16 pt. Plantin.

LIBRARY OF CONGRESS CIP DATA ON FILE.
CATALOGUING IN PUBLICATION FOR THIS BOOK
IS AVAILABLE FROM THE LIBRARY OF CONGRESS

ISBN-13: 978-1-4328-6496-5 (hardcover alk. paper)

Published in 2019 by arrangement with Harper Perennial, an imprint of HarperCollins Publishers

Printed in Mexico
1 2 3 4 5 6 7 23 22 21 20 19

For Gregg, the reason I write love stories

The time is out of joint: O cursèd spite,
That ever I was born to set it right!
— *Hamlet,* Act I, Scene V

PROLOGUE:
HANNA, 1958

I haven't told Stuart the whole truth about where I came from. Because for one thing, he wouldn't understand. How could he, when I don't really understand it for myself? And for another, even if I did tell him, he wouldn't believe it. He would frown, and his blue eyes would soften, crinkle just around the edges, illuminating both his age and his kindness. *Oh, my dear,* he might say, as Sister Louisa once did, after I'd stumbled into the last-standing church in Gutenstat, freezing cold and sick with thirst and hunger.

Sometimes, even now, I wonder if I made it all up. If Max, too, was just a dream, a figment of my imagination. Impossible, like all the rest of it.

You have been through a trauma, Sister Louisa reminded me, after I first saw the doctor in Berlin. *Your mind plays tricks to protect you.*

And it was a strange thing, but when Sister said it, I almost believed her. How could she be wrong, after all? This nun with her wrinkly face, pale as snow, and light gray eyes, with her habit and her soft smile. She wouldn't lie. Then she pointed to my violin in my hand. *Can I hear you play, my dear?*

She touched my Stradivari. I'd had it since my sixteenth birthday, an extravagant present from Zayde Moritz, just before he passed. I was holding it when I came to in the field. I'd held it playing for Max, in the bookshop once, too. And sometimes the only thing to me that still feels real, even now, is my violin.

I have played the violin since I was six years old, and it has always felt a part of me, another limb, one that is necessary and vital to my daily survival. My violin connects my present and my past, my dreams and my reality. My fingers move nimbly over the strings, my mind forgetting all I've lost or forgotten. There is only the music that is my constant companion. Nothing but the music. Not Stuart. Not Max. Not now. Not the past, either.

"Hanna," Stuart interrupts me today. I've etched the date, November 6, 1958, in pencil at the top of my music, so I know it is real, so I don't forget. I do this every single day and have since I was living in London with Julia. While I sometimes still forget how old I am now, my fingers do not move as they used to. Some days my knuckles swell, and I must cover them in bags of ice when I get home after practice. I hide this from Stuart, too, like so much else.

Today, I'm practicing at the conservatory, as I do every day after the group rehearsal. The orchestra will tour again in the spring. We'll go around Europe this time, playing Bach and Vivaldi and Holst. London, Paris, *Berlin*. As first chair violinist, I must play everything right, everything perfect. Though I already know all the music well, it is not enough. I have to breathe it, too. It has to sink into my skin, into my memory, so I will never ever forget it, a sweet perfume that lingers on and overtakes all my senses.

When Stuart walks in, I rest my violin on my knee and smile at him. Dear, sweet Stuart who brought me into the orchestra's fold five years ago. He's ten years older than I am and would like nothing more than to marry me. Which he has told me on more than one occasion. But I laugh and pretend as though I believe him to be joking, though we both know he's not. *You're an old soul,* he told me once, as if trying to explain away our age difference. It was only then that I'd thought: *Maybe Stuart really does know me?*

"Hanna," he says now. "You have a friend here to see you."

My world in New York City is a bubble. Rehearsal and practice. I live alone in a one-bedroom apartment in Greenwich Village, and though I am friendly with nearly everyone in the orchestra, I wouldn't call any of them dear friends. Only Stuart. And it's only because he thinks he loves me, thinks he understands me. "It must be some mistake," I tell him, bringing the violin back to my chin.

"No mistake," Stuart says. "He asked for Hanna. He said the 'girl who plays violin like fire.'" Stuart laughs. His eyes crinkle. He is both amused and stricken by the accuracy of the description.

Once, so many years ago, when I was insisting I would have to give it all up, that I had ruined everything, Max had told me that I would have other auditions. Other orchestras. *And you can't give up,* he'd told me. *You play the violin like fire, Hanna. You can't give up on your fire.*

MAX, 1931

Max heard Hanna before he saw her. Rather, he heard her violin as it pierced through the empty auditorium at the Lyceum: sharp and bright, passionate and enormous. He'd never heard a violin before other than maybe once on a record playing on his mother's phonograph when he was a boy. And the sound in real life, echoing in the large empty room, was so beautiful and intense that, for a moment, Max froze.

Max had opened the door to this particular auditorium quite by accident. He'd been looking for Herr Detweiler's lecture on economics, which, as it turned out, was taking place in a different auditorium, in a building across the green. The Lyceum in Gutenstat was large, sprawling. Max had read the schedule wrong and had reversed his course, landed himself exactly opposite where he'd intended, here, instead, where Hanna was practicing onstage.

13

He walked toward her, toward the music. Her eyes were closed, and she was small but her body swung with the notes she played, a force like a giant gust of wind that bowled her back and forth, and yet would never topple her. No. She was in control of the music, of the instrument. That much was clear to him. Even knowing nothing about music, about the violin. This woman possessed this music. Not the other way around.

She finished with one hard downward sweep of the bow, and then she opened her eyes, saw him standing there, not ten feet from the stage now, because he'd walked closer and closer as he'd been listening. She put her hand to her mouth. Shocked? Alarmed? Angry?

"I'm . . . I'm . . . sorry," he stammered. "I've gotten the wrong auditorium." He suddenly felt foolish for having invaded her space. It wasn't a performance; her music this morning had been meant to be private. And feeling like an intruder, he turned and ran out.

It wasn't until he was across the green, walking into the correct building, that he realized he should've introduced himself, that he should've asked her name. Because the sound of that violin, her violin, he could not get it out of his mind.

Max's father had owned a small bookshop in the center of Gutenstat, and when his heart stopped last spring, suddenly and all at once while he was in the middle of a conversation with a patron, Max had taken over the shop. His mother had died when Max was only ten, and so after his father's death, there was no one else. Max had no choice but to continue running the shop. Even if he had, he would've chosen what was handed to him: he loved his father's shop — the smell of the books, ink, paper, and binding glue, the patrons in the town who came in looking for stories and suggestions. Max felt a comfort in this life, the familiar town of Gutenstat where he'd grown up, just an hour train ride west from Berlin. But the bookshop was quieter than it had once been, and that was why Max had enrolled in Herr Detweiler's economics lecture. It had occurred to him more than once that he might not be able to run the bookshop forever, that he might need to learn something else. And an economics class had felt like a good place to start. At the very least it might give him some help in keeping the bookshop afloat.

He slipped into the correct auditorium in the middle of Detweiler's lecture, trying not to draw attention to himself now. Most of the seats were taken, and in the front of the room, Detweiler — an older, overweight balding man with spectacles — was talking animatedly, scribbling an equation on a chalkboard. People all around Max listened intently, took notes. And he tried to follow the lecture. It had been a few years since he'd been in school, and truth be told, he'd always enjoyed literature so much more than math and science. His mind drifted back to the woman across the green, playing the violin. If he went back, could he still catch her? He wanted to ask her name, ask her if she liked books, or coffee. Yes, he would invite her to coffee.

He slipped back out of the lecture, ran across the green and back into the auditorium where she'd been playing on the stage. But now the room was empty; Max had lost his chance.

Max lived a ten-minute train ride from the Lyceum on Hauptstrasse in Gutenstat, in a tiny three-room apartment above the bookshop. The apartment still contained many of his father's things and some of his mother's things as well, though she had been gone over ten years now. What was their life had become Max's life, with the exception of the dull ache of loneliness that came over him each evening. The bookshop was in the shopping district of Gutenstat and sat next to Feinstein's bakery shop and across the street from Herr Sokolov's *Fischmarkt.* Between the two he was never wanting for anything fresh to eat, though, since his father's passing, he was often wanting for company in which to eat it. His parents had never been alone here — first they'd had each other. Then his father had him. And though Max had friends in Gutenstat, it wasn't the same.

When he got home from the Lyceum that morning, Max searched through the closet in the bedroom until he found his mother's old phonograph and her records. It was dusty from lack of use, and he wasn't sure if the records would still play. He tried one, and out came an operatic voice, high and distant and scratchy. It was nothing at all like the violin music he'd heard. Not even close. And he felt it again in his stomach, an ache, an emptiness.

Max opened the bookshop at noon (as he did every day now but Sundays), and as he straightened up the shelves, still feeling quite lonely, he glanced again toward the closet at the back of the store. His father had hung a sign on the door and installed a lock years ago, cautioning patrons to stay out: ACHTUNG! The sign still hung there now, but it wasn't visible because Max had moved a bookshelf in front of the closet door a few months earlier.

He had opened the closet door only once, in June. It was just a month after his father had died. Max's heartache had felt so fresh and painful, and business in the shop was already slowing. The economy was bad, and people who were worried about buying food did not have enough money for books. On top of everything, his girlfriend, Etta, had just broken up with him, and he'd been feeling quite sorry for himself. He'd wondered: Is this it? Is this all he could expect for his life? *Or is there something else?*

The bell over the shop door chimed now, bringing Max's attention back to the front of the store. And much to his shock and delight, there she was, walking into his bookshop: the beautiful girl who'd been playing the violin at the Lyceum earlier.

He stared at her, his mouth slightly agape. She was taller than he'd thought from seeing her up onstage, only a head shorter than him. Her brown hair was in a knot behind her head, but wayward curls escaped in front and fell across her heart-shaped face in misdirected wisps. She pushed them back, absentmindedly.

"You left this," she said, her tone brusque. "When you were . . . what was it you were doing exactly this morning? Spying on me or something?" She held up a book, and it was only then that he remembered he'd had it in his hand earlier when he'd walked in on her playing violin. He'd taken it to read on the train. He must've put it down in the auditorium and he'd forgotten all about it until now. Like all the books they sold in the shop, this one, too, was stamped with the store's name and address in the very back, a way, his father had always said, to remind their patrons to return for more after they'd turned the very last page.

Max took the book back and thanked her. "I'm Max," he said. "Max Beissinger."

"Ah, so this is your store?" She ran her fingers across a row of spines on a shelf. *Beissinger Buchhandlung* — the words that had been stamped inside the back of the book were also painted on the shop's glass front window.

"Yes, it was my father's, but he recently passed."

She looked up from the bookshelf, and

her face softened. "Oh, I'm sorry." She walked toward him and held out her hand. "Hanna Ginsberg."

He took her hand, shook it. Her fingers were tiny, thin, but felt quite strong. "I didn't mean to intrude earlier. I stepped inside the wrong room by accident. But your violin playing . . . it's, it's so beautiful."

She smiled a little, pulled her hand away. "Well, that's very kind of you to say, but Herr Fruchtenwalder — he's my instructor at the Lyceum — says it's not good enough for the symphony yet."

"Not good enough? Is he mad?" Max said quickly.

She laughed. "And you are a violinist too?"

He shook his head. "But your playing . . . it's amazing. I've never heard anything like it before."

"There are hundreds of violinists in and around Berlin. There's nothing special about me," she said.

"I disagree," Max said. "I think you are special, Hanna Ginsberg."

She laughed again and then told him she had to go, she was late.

"Will I see you again?" he called after her, but she didn't answer. She held up a hand to wave behind her on the way out.

The bright butterfly pin she had in the back of her hair, holding her knot of curls together, caught the late afternoon sunlight and glinted, momentarily blinding him. He blinked, and then she was gone.

Hanna, 1946

When I opened my eyes, I was in a field.
The sky was black. A million stars glittered
above me, and my first thought was how
beautiful they were. How the night was
diamonds and Beethoven's Concerto in D
Major. And then I realized I was holding
my violin. I clutched it in my right hand,
my fingers numb and cold, and shaking. My
hands vibrated so much that the violin was
hitting my leg, the hard wood bruising my
kneecap.

"Max," I called out. "Max?" My voice
quivered, and the words echoed back at me.
No response. Only silence and night sky and
stars. *And my violin?*

I was just in the bookshop. I was playing
Mahler, and Max was sitting behind the
counter, reading a book. *Play me the fire,
Hanna.* And he looked at me that same way
he did when we were lying next to each
other in bed, his green eyes ablaze, like

music and desire were the same thing. *Fire.*

I'd smiled at him, closed my eyes to play, and the music had taken over me. But then there was that horrible sound: pounding against the glass. Men's voices. *The SA.* They were shouting to open up. Shouting that we had broken the law. *What had we done?*

The store was closed for the night; Max had the front door locked. But I liked the acoustics in the shop, so I often practiced there at night. The men rattled the door, pushing on it. The lock wouldn't hold out much longer.

You have to hide, Max said, running toward the back of the store.

More banging against the glass storefront, and I ran to where Max was standing. He grabbed me, pulled me close, and hugged me so hard.

And that was the last thing I remembered before now, the starry night, this field. How in the world had I gotten here? And where was *here,* exactly?

"Max," I cried out again, softer this time. Because the SA. What if they were still looking for me?

But the field was open, quiet; the night air, crisp and cool. I shivered. I heard an owl hooting somewhere in the distance, but that was all. I pinched myself on the arm, and it hurt, but nothing changed. I wasn't dreaming. I was here, wherever this was. And I was all alone.

I began walking. Because, what else could I do? I couldn't stay in this field, waiting for Max, or for those horrible SA who wanted to, what? Arrest me? *Murder me?* And what was my crime exactly? I shivered again, but I clutched my violin and kept walking.

I walked and I walked and I walked, and the sky began to turn from black to pearly gray to orange blue. In the distance, there was a cathedral. I saw the steeple first, rising above the hill, and as I got closer the structure looked vaguely familiar, like the cathedral I would see from the train window riding from Hauptstrasse toward the Lyceum. But that church was white; this one was brown. My legs were so tired, but I would just make it there, and surely someone inside could help me get back to the bookshop. And Max would know what happened. Max would remember. *Max.* What if something had happened to him?

I went over it again and again in my mind, retracing those last words, those last moments with Max, pushing myself to remember after that. But try as I might I still had no memory of getting to this field.

By the time I reached the church door, I was so thirsty and cold. And tired. My head ached, and something was terribly wrong. I knew it was. I just wasn't sure what, and my body was heavy with dread and exhaustion.

Had the SA broken down the door then, taken me, brought me here? Had I hit my head? Is that why I could not remember? Was I injured? I put my hand to my head, my face, but everything felt normal. No bumps. No blood. No pain.

I opened the door to the church and walked inside. It was filled with wooden pews, all empty. A large stained-glass window in front was partially boarded up, as if it had shattered and not yet been repaired. "Hello," I called out. "Is anyone here? Hello?"

No one answered back, and I was exhausted. It was much warmer inside the church, and I went to the closest pew, lay down on the hard wood bench, and hugged my violin tight to my chest. I would rest. Just for a little while. And maybe when I awoke, I would be back in the bookshop, back with Max.

"Are you all right, child?" A woman's voice brought me out of sleep. I'd been dreaming

25

of music, as I often did. Whatever I'd been practicing most of late, burned so deep into my mind, it almost haunted me in my dreams. I'd been dreaming Wagner. *But no, that wasn't right.* I'd been practicing Mahler in the bookshop. My fingers twitched against the fingerboard of the violin, restless, wanting. The woman placed her hand on my shoulder, and I jumped, opened my eyes. *The church. The field. Max?* I shrank away from her. "It's okay, you're safe here. I'm not going to harm you," the woman said gently. "I'm Sister Louisa."

"Where am I?" I asked her.

"Menchen's Dom, about twenty kilometers outside of Berlin." So this *was* the church I would see from the train. They must've painted it recently, and I hadn't noticed. Or had it always been brown? "And what brings you here, child?"

"I . . . I . . ." I wanted to answer her question. But I wasn't sure how. "I need to get back into Gutenstat," I told her. "Beissinger Buchhandlung. My . . . um . . ." I paused, remembering I couldn't say the truth about Max and me out loud without fear. "I just need to . . . visit the shop."

She shook her head and frowned. "That shop has been gone for many years, child. Since . . . before the war."

26

"No, I was just there last night. Many years after the Great War ended."

"The Great War?" She sat down next to me on the bench. "I don't know what has happened to you," she said. "And I am sorry for whatever it was, child . . . But you are safe now. All the camps have been liberated. Hitler is dead."

I despised Hitler with every fiber of my being. He'd stolen my mother and the symphony from me, and relief coursed through my body, just hearing that he was dead. But why couldn't I remember it happening? "If you could help me get to the train station nearby," I said, "I could take the train back into Gutenstat."

"The station was bombed," Sister Louisa said, sadly. "We're lucky to still be standing, with only minor damage remaining." She glanced toward the boarded-up window. "Come, why don't you let me get you some food and water, and we can go into Berlin, see a doctor."

"I don't need a doctor," I insisted.

But did I? My memory was blank, devoid of the moments that led me here. And then there were the events Sister Louisa insisted upon that I couldn't recall: Hitler was dead; the train station had been bombed. She said that the bookshop wasn't here any longer, though, and that couldn't be right. I was just there.

"I just need to find Max," I said, meekly. But if she was right, and something had happened to the bookshop, to Gutenstat, then where was Max?

I was not a religious person, and besides that a Jew, not a Catholic. But here in the cathedral I said a silent prayer to myself: *Please, please, God. Let Max be okay.*

Max, 1931

The next morning, Max went back to the Lyceum, even though he didn't have another lecture scheduled until the following week. He went straight to the auditorium where he'd walked in on Hanna practicing yesterday. On the train he'd rehearsed in his head what he'd say to her should she be in there again. How her teacher was wrong, how her music was the most special thing he had ever heard, and how he had dreamed of it last night long after she'd left his shop.

But today there was a young male pianist playing onstage, no Hanna in sight. Max waited for him to stop playing and when he finished, Max walked up to the stage and asked him if he knew of Hanna Ginsberg.

"I do," the young man said, gathering up his sheet music. He was about Max's age, but very thin, too thin. Always the story-teller, Max imagined he didn't have enough to eat, that he had only his piano to sustain

29

him these days, as so many people were struggling. Max was lucky that his father had left him a healthy nest egg, or he would not be able to keep the bookshop — or himself — afloat.

"Do you know where to find her?" Max asked him.

The thin pianist frowned. "And why would I tell you?"

"I'm . . . She came to my shop yesterday and I have a book she was looking for." It was only half a lie, since Hanna *had* come to his shop yesterday. Max held up the book in his hand as proof, though it was the book he himself had been reading on the train, poems by Erich Kästner.

"She's not at school today," the thin pianist finally said. "She's with her mother. At the apartments just south of here on Maulbeerstrasse. I'm not sure of the exact address. Do you know them?"

Max thanked him and set off. He knew, but only vaguely, that the area where he was going was a small Jewish community. He'd walked by it when he'd gotten off the train this morning, a cluster of buildings on a street lined with mulberry trees, between the station and the Lyceum. But as he walked closer to them again now, he realized there were many, many apartments in these buildings — maybe a hundred or so, and that he had no way to know which one was Hanna's.

He leaned against one of the four brick three-story buildings and sighed. He couldn't knock on every single door. People would think he was a madman. Maybe he *was* a madman? Chasing after this girl he didn't even know, and all because her violin had enchanted him yesterday?

Then he heard the faintest sound. Music? *Hanna's violin.* The muted notes came from the building across from where he was standing, out a half-open second-floor window, but it was unmistakably her.

He followed the music: across the courtyard, up a flight of stairs, to the door just under the open window where the sounds of her violin floated out, louder and brighter as Max got closer. He knocked on her door; the music stopped abruptly, midnote. As the door began to open, Max realized he had no idea what he was going to say.

"You?" Hanna said. She held her violin and bow in one hand and put the other hand to her hip. She frowned, clearly annoyed. "Are you following me?"

"I just wanted to . . . I thought maybe we could . . ." Max stammered, and he felt his cheeks burning. He sounded like an idiot.

He was used to feeling confident, well-spoken. In the shop he spoke to patrons and recommended books with ease. But Hanna was beautiful, consumed by her music, and so determined. It intimidated him. "I didn't mean to interrupt your practicing," he finally said. "I was just . . . in the area."

Hanna stepped outside onto the porch and shut the door behind her. "Listen, you can't be here." She spoke in a hushed tone. "My mother isn't feeling well. I can't have any visitors right now."

"I'm sorry to hear that." He thought of his own mother, who had wasted away to practically just skin and bones after months in bed. Until one morning, when she was gone.

"I don't need your pity." Hanna crossed her arms in front of her chest, violin and all, as if it were a part of her, a natural extension of her body.

"How about my friendship?" Max offered.

Hanna smiled wryly. "I have friends."

Max had friends too. He and Johann still grabbed an ale together on Saturday nights after he closed the shop. Johann was married now, and his Elsa was expecting their first child, so Max and Johann saw each other less frequently than they had when they were in school, but still, they met every single Saturday night to catch up, if not a weeknight or two as well. Before his father died there was Etta. But she'd given up on him once he'd devoted more and more time to the shop after his father's death, and he realized that he hadn't missed her all that much, which made him think maybe he hadn't loved her at all. Hanna was the first person who'd piqued his interest since. "We could go get a coffee?" Max persisted. "So we wouldn't disturb your mother."

Hanna frowned and leaned against the door. "I have to focus on my music right now. And I have to take care of my mother. I don't have time for anything else. And I don't need anything else," she added. "Or anyone."

"That sounds terribly lonely," Max said.

Hanna rolled her eyes at him. "If I'm ever in need of a book, I'll be sure to come to your shop," she said. "But I have to get back to practicing." She walked back inside and slammed the door before Max could protest. And he stood there for a few moments, his mouth hanging open, as the sounds of the violin began again. The music was mesmerizing, and it haunted him the whole train ride back to Hauptstrasse.

That afternoon, the bookshop was quiet, as

it had been often lately. Max had regular patrons that his father and he had had for years. Some people would always find money for books, and he also sometimes dealt in trade, taking back their old books in good condition in exchange for deep discounts on shiny new ones. But new customers had become more and more scarce as the economy worsened in Germany. The emergency spending cuts and tax hikes in the past year had left more and more people unemployed. Unemployed people did not buy books. Max was less worried about the money and more about the quiet. It was boring to sit alone in the shop waiting for patrons who came only infrequently. There were only so many hours he could spend sitting behind the counter reading by himself.

The only visitor to the shop today, just after five, was Johann, stopping in after work. Johann said he was coming by to pick up books for Elsa, who was growing larger and more uncomfortable by the week. But Max knew Johann was also checking up on him, as he had been making a point to do since his father had passed.

"Slow day?" Johann said, walking up to the counter now. He was dressed in a full suit, the tie loosened around the neck after a presumably long and busy day himself. Sometimes Max envied him, all the things he was *doing.* And then he had Elsa, and the baby who would soon be here too. Max had known Johann practically his whole life, and Elsa almost that long. He and Johann had gone to grade school together, and Johann had spent many afternoons in the bookshop with him after school, the two of them poring over stories. Johann's father had died when he was very young, and sometimes it had felt like Max's father was both of their fathers, like Max and Johann were something akin to brothers. Later, in secondary school, Johann fell in love with Elsa, and then Elsa became Max's friend too. Of course, now they were adults, and he didn't see them nearly as often. Johann was in school to become a lawyer and he worked part-time at a law firm in the city, trying to get his foot in the door for when school was over. And Max had . . . the shop.

"They're all slow nowadays," Max finally answered him.

He had a pile of new books, waiting behind the counter for Johann to take to Elsa. Pulp romances, Elsa's favorite, and he handed them across to Johann. "Thanks," Johann said. "Els will be happy to have these."

"Hey, Jo," Max called after him as he was walking out with the books. Johann stopped walking and turned back. Carrying the large pile of books, he looked weighed down, tired. "I'm trying to remember . . . How did you first get Elsa to notice you?"

"You mean aside from my unabashed good looks and impressive wit?"

"Yes." Max rolled his eyes. Johann was quite shy and somewhat plain looking, though he did have a good sense of humor. "Aside from all that."

"Your father . . . Didn't I ever tell you this?" Max shook his head. "I told him that I really liked this girl and she wouldn't give me the time of day. He gave me a book to give her. Said that was the way to any woman's heart worth having." Johann smiled a little at the memory, and Max smiled, too, picturing his father standing here, saying those words to Johann, choosing exactly the right book for Elsa. "I'll see you on Saturday," Johann said, walking out of the shop.

"Give my love to Elsa," Max called after him, and then he started searching the shelves, looking for the perfect book.

I said. My memory of the piece was as perfect and as clear as could be, as if it really had only been hours, not years, since I'd been practicing in the bookshop.

"Well, that is a very good sign," Herr Doctor said. "A very good sign indeed." He held up his hands. "But the mind is a curious thing. You may recover that time, or you may not." He stood up and put a hand on my shoulder. "But you are very lucky, Hanna. A Jew alive and so healthy in Berlin these days . . . it is a very rare thing."

I was silent as Sister Louisa drove us back to the cathedral, taking in the landscape of Berlin and the outskirts. Nothing was the same as it was in my mind. Whole blocks of the city, and buildings, were missing. As we got back to Gutenstat, I noticed that the apartments where I'd once lived on Maulbeerstrasse with Julia and Mamele before she died were no longer there. All that remained was the lower half of building *drei,* the roof completely gone as if a great storm had swept in and taken it all away.

"Herr Doctor says I've forgotten ten years," I told Sister as she pulled off the road by the cathedral. "Memory loss due to trauma." Sister Louisa nodded but seemed oddly unsurprised. "Where are all the

Jews?" I asked her quietly.

She turned her eyes away from me, looked straight ahead to the road, though the car was parked; she was no longer driving. "The lucky ones got out before the war," she said.

"Not the Great War?" I said.

She shook her head. "The Second War."

An entire war I couldn't remember? It was unfathomable really. My memory had always been meticulous, spectacular. I could play a short piece only once and step away from the music and play it again by heart. "What about the ones who weren't lucky?" I asked Sister Louisa.

She sighed, then cocked her head, trying to decide whether or not she should tell me. "They were all sent to forced labor camps," she said. Then she lowered her voice to almost a whisper. "And many were killed."

Her words were so hard to understand, and yet, I didn't disbelieve them. The current was there, the hatred for Jews, the boycott of Jewish shops and businesses, the Nazis' non-Aryan decrees. I knew of labor camps, for political prisoners. And in 1936 Jews were already banned from many things: health insurance, cultural unions, the military. The symphony. Even, love. But forced labor camps for all Jews? They were *killed*? Why hadn't anyone stopped them? How had all the good kind people I'd known in Gutenstat and Berlin allowed this to happen? Tears welled up in my eyes as I thought about all the Jews I'd known my entire life, and not just Doctor Wein and Herr Fruchtenwalder but my classmates at the Lyceum, my friend Gerta, who'd played violin with me in primary school, and her boyfriend, Hans, and her father, Herr Brichtman, the baker. Fritzie, the pianist, who accompanied me at my symphony audition. Were they all really *gone*?

My sister, Julia, had moved to London with her husband, Friedrich, just after Mamele died. She'd wanted me to come with her then. She was worried things wouldn't be safe for Jews much longer in Germany. But I had refused to leave my chance at the symphony and Max. I could still vividly remember the words we'd exchanged outside on the porch of our apartment on Maulbeerstrasse. *You will risk your life, your career, for what . . . music? This unreliable man?* That was how Julia saw Max, as *unreliable.* Not as I knew him: generous, handsome, brilliant. Julia and I had fought that afternoon and had lost touch for months. *She was right,* I thought now. Not about Max, but about the danger. But at least she hadn't been in Germany when it had happened.

But . . . *Max*? Max wasn't Jewish. But he also wasn't here, with me now. And I felt this cold hard icy truth in my chest. *Trauma to the psyche. The last time I was truly happy.* Had something horrible happened to Max, and my mind did not want me to remember it?

"You said the bookshop in Gutenstat was gone?" I asked Sister. "When? What happened to it?"

"It burned to the ground," Sister Louisa said, matter-of-factly. "The whole Hauptstrasse did in '38."

Burned to the ground? There was a large book bonfire in the streets of Berlin in '33, the smell of smoke I'd tried to ignore as I'd played with my quartet blocks away. We'd had barely anyone in the audience for our concert. And yet, thousands and thousands had come out to listen to Goebbels decree that Jewish intellectualism was dead as they burned books by Freud and others. Max feared that they would come for him, his books, his store. This was when Julia and Friedrich first started to talk about moving to London. Friedrich was a doctoral student in biology and he'd been writing his own book at the time of the burning.

44

But Max wasn't Jewish, and he'd made sure to display only German Aryan books in the shop after the bonfire. He kept the others, the forbidden ones, in the back, in a closet, and only went in to find them should a trusted customer ask. Had the soldiers found them? Had they ignored the ACHTUNG! sign on the closet door and barged in, found the contraband, then killed Max for his crimes and burned the bookshop, the entire street, down? I shivered at the thought, and deep down I couldn't believe it was true. If that had happened, I would remember it. I knew I would.

"Come on, let's go back inside, shall we?" It was chilly in the car, and Sister Louisa blew on her hands, then moved to open her car door and get out. And I did the same. Because I didn't know what else to do. *What else was I supposed to do?* If Julia was still in London, I could contact her. Maybe she had an idea of what had happened to me? And if she didn't, she must be worried sick. I had to let her know I was okay.

"Will you play your violin for us?" Sister Louisa asked as we walked toward the front of the cathedral.

I shook my head. "I don't have a bow." And besides, what was the point? The Lyceum was gone and Herr Fruchtenwalder could be dead. And Max. What had happened to Max? I tried so hard to come up with a memory after that night in the bookshop, when I was practicing Mahler. Max and I, running away, escaping together. Max and I being arrested. Something. Max wasn't tethered to one place the way I'd always been. Had we left Gutenstat before everything had gotten dangerous? Had I gotten my visa for Holland like I'd been hoping? Had we run to Julia? But then why was I here, now?

"Ah, the bow." Sister Louisa was still talking about the violin as we entered the church. "I asked Father Broving to go in search of one while we were out. Some sort of case for you, too, so you don't have to just carry that around like that." Sister Louisa stopped walking and put her hand on my shoulder. "Perhaps if you remember your music, you will remember other things?" she suggested. I was suddenly so touched by her kindness, I felt like I might cry.

"I will play, if Father finds a bow," I promised her. "Do you mind if I ask you for one more favor?"

"Anything, my child," she said.

"Can you take me to send a telegram to my sister in London?"

"Telegram?" Sister laughed a little. "Well, I can do better than that. We've just installed a telephone in the rectory."

The thought of my sister's voice, so close, just like that! It made me want to cry. No matter what disagreements we might have had in the past, Julia would know what to do; she would have answers for me.

MAX, 1931

Max waited to go back to the Lyceum until the following week, when he had Detweiler's lecture. As he got off the train and walked by the apartments on Maulbeerstrasse, all he could think of was Hanna. He'd found himself thinking about her at odd moments all week, daydreaming about her nimble fingers and her beautiful smile. Maybe he would catch her practicing in the auditorium as he had the week before? Or if not, he'd try at her apartment again on the way back toward the train. He'd brought her a book, a biography of Ludwig van Beethoven, which was the most musical choice he had found in his shop.

He walked to the auditorium first, and he listened outside the door. He heard a violin and felt certain it was her. She was practicing something different today. No less haunting or filled with passion, but last week's song had been slow, while this one was fast. He waited for a pause in the music, before he opened the door and walked into the auditorium.

Hanna was on the stage, wiping her violin with a cloth, and then she bent down to put it in her case. Max watched her from the back of the room; she hadn't noticed him yet, and for a second he hesitated. She'd been very clear that she hadn't wanted to be friends with him. But he'd taken his father's old advice to Johann; he'd brought her a book, and he wasn't going to be a chicken now.

"Hanna," he called out, as he approached the stage. She latched her case, picked it up, and stood. She looked at him and frowned. "I have a lecture just across the green," he said before she could yell at him for pestering her. "And I thought you might be here. I brought you a book." He held up the biography. She was still frowning so he kept talking. "When my mother was very ill, I used to read to her. It used to comfort her to listen to a story, to hear the sound of my voice." He had only been nine years old, but he'd been a good reader, and the memory was so tangible; it was still one of the clearest memories he had of his mother.

Her face softened a little, and she jumped down from the stage. She took the book from him. For a second their fingers touched, and Max felt a thrilling surge of energy up through his arm. "This was very kind of you," Hanna said. "Thank you." She looked at him for another moment, as if she wanted to say more. But then she began walking toward the door of the auditorium and Max jogged to keep up with her.

"Do you want to get a coffee?" Max asked her.

She stopped walking and turned to him. "I thought you had a lecture?"

"I could skip it," he said. It had been foolish to pay for the course if he wasn't going to attend, but at that moment he cared more about getting to know Hanna than about anything he'd learn in class.

"Well, I have a lesson now, anyway," she said. "And then I have to get back to my mother. My sister, Julia, is with her now and she has things to do." Hanna rolled her eyes. She held up the book. "But thank you for this. I'll return it to your store when I'm done."

"No need," Max told her. "You can keep it." She shrugged a little and started to walk out of the auditorium and then he wanted to kick himself. If she returned it to the shop, he would have the opportunity to see her again.

"Let me know if you like it," he called after her. "I have many others. Come into the shop anytime."

That afternoon in the bookshop, Max got two real paying customers — a near miracle these days. And he was feeling good as he readied the shop to close for the evening. Just as he was about to turn off the lights and walk upstairs to his apartment, he heard a knock on the glass storefront door, and when he turned to look, Hanna was there, standing on the other side. He couldn't believe she'd actually accepted his invitation and come by so soon.

"Sorry to come so late," Hanna said when he opened the door. "I didn't realize you'd be closed. I just couldn't get away till now."

He smiled. "No, I'm glad you're here. Come in." She walked inside the shop, and she seemed more at ease than she had earlier in the Lyceum, less on guard. Maybe it was that she didn't have her violin in her hand, and instead the book he'd brought her this morning. "You couldn't have finished it!" He was a fast reader but not *that* fast.

"No." She laughed. "To tell you the truth, I'd read it already." She smiled sheepishly. "I didn't want to tell you this morning because it was so thoughtful of you. It really was. It's been a long time since anyone has . . . well." She held the book out to him. "I felt bad keeping a book I already have when maybe you could sell it to someone else. Business must be hard these days."

Instead of taking the book from her, he put his hand on her arm, lightly. "You came all the way here for that?" he asked. She shrugged but didn't answer. Had she been eager to see him again, like he'd wanted to see her? "I know it's late," Max said. "But Feinstein's bakeshop next door is still open. We could get that coffee now?"

"I . . . I should get back," Hanna said. She put the book down on the display in front of him and began to back away toward the door.

"At least let me get you another book," he said. "One you haven't read." She stopped walking. "What do you like, something else about music? Or fiction? Poetry . . . ?"

"Maybe something hopeful, that I could read to Mamele, like you suggested. I think she might like that."

Hopeful. Nothing he had read of late was hopeful. Since the market had crashed in America none of the English writers were in a very good mood. Not that the German writers were either, as their economy had similarly withered. His eyes scanned the shelves looking for something, and he landed on Virginia Woolf. He pulled out *A Room of One's Own.* "Have you read this one?" She took it from him, examined it, turned it over, and shook her head. "I don't know if you'd call it hopeful, exactly. But I have a feeling you'll like it." Hanna and her violin reminded him of Woolf's argument about women writers, needing a space of their own to create their art.

She held the book up to her chest and smiled at him, and this was what he liked best about the bookshop, this was what he did best. Pairing books and people together. It was what his father had taught him, what he missed now that business was so much slower.

"I'm going to read this, and then I'll bring it back. I promise."

"No rush," he said, though he hoped she would, so he could see her again soon.

She stood up on her tiptoes, reached out, and wrapped her arms around him in a hug. The gesture surprised him so, that he stumbled backward a step, and he put his arms around her, too, and steadied himself. Up close she smelled like spring, like lemons and wildflowers, and something else he'd never smelled before . . . almost like molasses. He closed his eyes and inhaled. Her body was warm, and feeling her that close to him, he felt that same thrilling energy as when their fingers had touched.

He put his hand on her cheek. Her skin felt so soft, and she tilted her chin up to look at him. She smiled a little. And then as fast as she'd hugged him, she pulled away and walked out of the shop.

He stood there and watched her go, his mouth agape. He wanted to call after her, to tell her to stay here longer with him. He had almost kissed her. *If she had stayed another second.*

He put his hand to his mouth, his lips warm from the anticipation. And that was the moment he realized that he was going to fall in love with Hanna Ginsberg.

HANNA, 1946

It took Julia two weeks to come to Berlin after I telephoned her from the rectory. She had believed for nearly ten years that I was dead, and when she first heard my voice through the telephone, she screamed, and then she swore I was a ghost.

"I'm no ghost," I promised her. But everything about myself felt strange, detached. My fingers could play the violin as they always had — Father Broving had procured a bow and I'd spent hours playing in the church, much to the delight of the sisters. But my fingers felt like they didn't belong to my body anymore; they had a memory, a life, all their own.

"I don't understand," Julia repeated several times. "Where were you during the war? Where have you been all this time? How did you survive?"

"I wish I knew, but I don't remember anything," I said, and I could hear the disbelief in my sister's silence.

"Are you sure you're okay?" Julia finally asked, her tone softening.

"Yes," I assured her, though the truth was I didn't know whether I was okay or not.

"Well, I'm coming to get you," she said. "And don't argue with me about it." I didn't argue. What else was there for me to do?

She hesitated for a moment, and I thought she might ask me about Max, but then she said, "Oh, Hanni, I'll be so glad to see you again." She cleared her throat on the other end of the line. "I'll telephone you back when I know which train I can get on."

Sister Louisa told me that the station in Berlin had only been repaired enough in the last month to begin accepting some train service again. "Life is getting back to normal," she said, but she shook her head sadly, so that I wondered if for her, remembering every horrible thing that had happened around her over these last years, life would ever feel *normal* again. Was it better not to remember? *No.* That made it worse. I wasn't a ghost as Julia claimed, and yet I felt like a shadow of the woman I used to be. Nothing felt normal to me, either.

In my two weeks living at the rectory, I spent my days playing violin for the sisters, and I also walked around what remained of the Gutenstat I used to know, looking for any small piece that might trigger my memory. But nothing did. The Lyceum had closed down, and the building where the conservatory was housed had been damaged, most likely bombed. The roof was missing, the windows to the auditorium where I'd often practiced blown away. The door was boarded up so that I couldn't even walk inside.

I asked Sister Louisa to drive me to Hauptstrasse where the bookshop had been. She insisted that there was nothing much there to see but she drove down the road a few kilometers for me to see it with my own eyes.

And she was right. All the buildings on Hauptstrasse were burned to the ground. The space the bookshop used to occupy was unrecognizable from the café next door or the *Fischmarkt* that had once been across the street.

"It feels like I was just here," I said, staring out the car's window in shock. I felt paralyzed, breathless staring at the destruction. Even if I wanted to, I could not move, get out of the car, or walk around, examine the ashy mess of what had once been a street that felt like home to me. More than my apartment on Maulbeerstrasse ever had. Though, of course, that was gone too.

Back at the rectory I asked Sister if she minded if I used the telephone again to call the operator and ask for Max. I promised I would pay her back for any charges once Julia got here, though knowing Julia, she wouldn't be pleased, but I didn't care. "Of course, child," Sister said, and she left to give me privacy.

My voice shook as I spoke into the phone asking the operator for Max Beissinger, and though I was not surprised when she said she didn't have a listing for one, tears filled my eyes and ran down my cheeks. I couldn't stop them. Max had disappeared on me before, but this was different. I understood somehow, fractured memory and all, that it was. Then I asked the operator if she had a listing for Johann Wilhelm, Max's best friend.

"I'll connect you," she said.

And then again came a flood of hope. If anyone would know where Max was or what had happened to us, it would be Johann.

"Hello." Elsa picked up the line, and her voice rang through, so clear and familiar. Elsa, Johann, Max, and I had dinner together on Saturday nights sometimes, when Max was around and the two of us were together. And I'd come to consider Elsa my friend, too.

"Elsa," I said. "It's me. Hanna."

The other end of the line went silent for a moment, and then Elsa said, "Hanna Ginsberg? Is that really you?"

"It really is," I echoed back. I dreaded having to retell my unbelievable story, or nonstory as it was, again over the phone like I had to Julia, but I let it all out in a rush and then asked Elsa if she knew where Max was, what had happened to us.

"Well, I think you were arrested," Elsa said. "Do you remember that?"

I shook my head, forgetting she couldn't see me. Had the SA banging on the door arrested me? Is that what happened next? "And when was this?" I asked her, still not believing it.

"Oh my, well . . . years ago. Let's see. Before the war. Goodness, ten years ago, maybe?"

Ten years. "And where is Max now?" I asked, holding my breath. If I could talk to him, see him again, touch him, he could explain everything. He could fill in all the gaps in my memory, make me whole again, the way he always had when we were together.

Elsa hesitated for a moment. "I'm sorry. I

59

don't know, Hanna. We weren't exactly sure what had happened to you. We thought you'd been arrested, and he was looking for you. But then one night, he just disappeared himself. I haven't seen him in years. I mean, you know how he was . . ."

Though Max loved Germany, he was filled with wanderlust. He would disappear with no notice for weeks at a time whenever the whim struck him, which we fought about intensely. Not only because he didn't tell me where he was going, how long he'd truly be gone, but also because he never invited me to come along. And deep down that was the part that hurt me the most. I would've turned him down — I had violin and Mamele to keep me here. But still, I would've liked to have been asked.

"So you don't know what happened to him . . . during the war? Or me?" I asked Elsa now.

"No," Elsa said. "Johann and I have been hoping . . . But it has been many years."

"The shop burned down," I said matter-of-factly.

"Yes," Elsa said. "I think he was arrested that night. But Johann doesn't believe it . . . he likes to think Max ran away first. Maybe he is drinking wine and reading a book on an island off the south of Spain right now."

rolling down the curtains in the front window. Hanna let go of Max's hand, knocked on the glass, and when the older gentleman inside saw her, he smiled and waved them in.

"Herr Brichtman lives just down the way from me," Hanna explained. "His daughter Gerta plays violin, too. Or she used to, when we were younger. We're still close friends." He remembered what she'd told him that day on Maulbeerstrasse — she had friends; she didn't need more. "Come on." She pushed open the door. "I hope there's a strudel left."

"Hannalie, how are you *mein Mädchen?*" He grabbed her in a hug, then stepped back and eyed Max.

"This is . . . my friend, Max," Hanna said. "Max Beissinger. He owns the bookshop on Hauptstrasse."

Herr Brichtman extended his hand for Max to shake. "Any friend of Hannalie's is a friend of mine. I'll bring out your favorite strudel, two forks. Have a seat."

The inside of the bakery was tiny, just five small tables with chairs, but they were the only ones inside now. Hanna pulled out a chair and Max sat across the table from her. She rested her violin case on the floor by her feet and put the flowers on top of it, and a moment later, Herr Brichtman brought out a plate, filled with heaping apple strudel and two forks as promised. "I have some things to ready in the kitchen for tomorrow. You two enjoy." He patted Hanna affectionately on the shoulder and then walked toward the back of the shop.

Hanna took a fork and dug in, and Max did the same. The pastry was buttery and delicious, the apples and cinnamon melting against his tongue. "This is so good," he said. Herr Feinstein, who owned the bakeshop next door to him, specialized in bread, not pastry, and having such a sweet treat was a rarity for him.

Hanna took another bite and then looked at him and laughed. "You have some on your face." She reached across the table and touched his cheek, wiping away the piece of apple, her fingers lingering there a few seconds longer than they needed to. Her fingers were so small and soft — it amazed him how strong they must be to play the violin as she did.

She moved her hand back and smiled, shyly, and then without really thinking, he leaned across the table and he kissed her. Her lips were warm and she tasted liked strudel, and once his brain caught up, he thought she would pull back, she would push him away. But then she put her hand back on his cheek and kissed him back.

push him away. But they she put her hand
back on his cheek and kissed him back.

HANNA, 1946

When I first saw Julia again, she hugged me
and exclaimed that I hadn't changed one
bit. I said the same thing back to her,
though it was a lie. Her hair had turned half
gray since I'd seen her last. She looked not
only older, but also . . . lumpier around her
midsection. That was probably due to the
two sons she mentioned giving birth to.

"Boys," Julia said while we were on the
train back to London. "Two of them. Can
you believe that, Hannalie?" Really, I
couldn't. It was hard to picture Julia as a
mother, much less to boys. Julia despised
messes and loud noises, and I imagined she
had trained them to make neither somehow.
Either that, or they drove her crazy. Maybe
that explained the gray hairs.

"How old are they?" I asked. These two
little boys, *my nephews*, felt imaginary,
distant, unconnected to me. I clutched my
violin tightly to my chest and looked out

the train window. There was so much evidence of war, buildings and cities decimated by bombs and fires, all through Germany, and now into the Netherlands. Many of the stations were still closed and the conductor announced that there would not be stops except for in the major cities, where I assumed repairs had been made the fastest. I wanted to stop looking out the window, but I couldn't turn away. Where had I been during all this? How could I not remember?

"Well, Levin is nine, and Moritz is seven. Levin is named for Papa and Moritz for Zayde, of course." Papa died when I was a baby, and I knew him only in stories and pictures, but Zayde and I had been quite close. It was weird to think of a little boy, *my nephew,* with his same name.

My head had begun to throb, and as the train whistle blew, I felt an odd jolt, the sensation of being afraid, though I didn't know of what, and I wiped sweat away from my brow with the back of my hand.

"I mean I would've saved one for you, but I thought you were dead." Julia was still talking. "And maybe you'll have a girl and you can name her Hedy, for Mamele?"

"That's the last thing on my mind right now," I said.

Julia patted my arm. "I know, but we'll

get you settled in London, and then you'll see. Friedrich works in the laboratory at the hospital and he knows a lot of nice eligible men. Doctors." I shook my head. "You're thirty-four now, Hanna. You can't be picky." Was I really? Thirty-four? In my head I was still twenty-four, still in the bookshop with Max. If I closed my eyes, I could still feel him there, standing next to me, just before I played, the warmth of his hand on my arm, of his lips against my cheek.

"If you want to have children, you'll have to act quickly." Julia was *still* talking, and I sighed. Though she looked older, she really hadn't changed a bit. That old familiar annoyance crept up in my stomach, like I'd eaten something vile before we'd left Berlin. And I was feeling nauseated. But maybe that was just from the endless rocking of the train down the tracks, the continuing grip of fear. I didn't want to be on the train. I wanted to get up, to run off, but how else would I get to London? I should be relieved to be here, to have Julia now, someone, something, that I knew. But I wasn't. I didn't want her. I wanted Max.

I held tighter to my violin and turned away from the window. "What about the symphony?" I asked her. "Did it survive the war? Does it still exist?" I'd auditioned in

Berlin, twice. The second time I'd actually gotten in, too. Was I good enough now, all these years later, to try again?

Julia laughed a little. "I really don't know, Hanni. I don't keep up with the symphony." Of course she didn't. She reached out and touched my violin. "But aren't you too old for this nonsense now? Friedrich will get you a nice job with the Civil Service. Maybe in bookkeeping? You were always good with numbers."

"Bookkeeping?" I shook my head. "No thanks."

"There was a war, Hanni. People needed to eat. No one had time for music." She held up her hands, exasperated.

Julia had never had time for music, had never understood what the violin meant, how playing it for me was like breathing or sleeping or eating for her. Without it, I wouldn't exist. I used to think it was all I needed, all I would ever need. Until I met Max. And now, without him I felt only half, only partially here. But at least I had my violin. I could still play. No matter what Julia thought or said or wanted, I knew that as soon as I got to London I was going to search for a symphony to join.

London, too, looked broken, tired. Though

I'd never been before, I'd imagined the entire train ride that it would be untouched, that it would not look like the rest of the cities I'd seen from the train window, bombed, destroyed. Julia explained about the Blitz as we got off the train, but like everything else, it didn't feel real, and as I stepped out of the railcar, my legs felt unsteady, as if the ground were still moving beneath me and I was staying still.

Julia and Friedrich lived in a duplex in the West End, and their neighborhood looked strangely serene, brick buildings and cobblestone streets. "We were lucky," Julia said, as the taxi car pulled up in front of her home.

"It's beautiful," I said, taking in their three-storied brick home from the street.

"Friedrich works hard and has managed to do all right, even through the war," Julia said, matter-of-factly. "The fact is, the hospital only got busier."

I got out of the car and followed behind her, up the stairs to her red front door.

"I made up the guest room for you," she said. "You can stay as long as you like, until you get back on your feet." Before she put her key in the lock she turned back to look at me, and she grabbed me hard in a hug. Julia was never affectionate, and she hadn't hugged me back at the rectory in Berlin. The shock of it now nearly knocked me off balance.

She held on to me for only a moment, then inhaled, straightened the wrinkles out of her blue dress, and smiled. "The boys are excited to meet you. They've never had a *tante* before. Friedrich's sisters didn't . . . well. You are the only one left."

It was hard to take in the enormity of it. That I had two nephews I'd never met, that I was the only family, the only auntie, they had left.

I clutched my violin in my hand as I followed Julia inside her house. There was a large open parlor in the front, with high ceilings, marble floors. This was nice, much, much bigger and grander than our apartment on Maulbeerstrasse growing up. Julia inhabited a different life now, one I could barely imagine or dream of, one that felt far from everything else in my heart, Germany, the bookshop, Max.

Two boys, well dressed in matching navy knickers and pressed white shirts, ran down the stairs at the sound of the door. Julia scooped them up into a hug, and the older one, Levin, squirmed out quickly, while Moritz pressed himself against his mother. "Oh, I've missed you," Julia said. "Were you good for Papa?"

"I was," Levin said pointedly, staring at his brother. Moritz shrugged sheepishly and I liked him instantly.

"This is Tante Hanna," Julia said, looking from the boys to me. I held up my hand to wave.

"What's that?" Moritz pointed to my violin in my other hand.

"It's my violin," I told him. "And it's very special to me. Your great-grandfather gave it to me when I was sixteen. I believe you're named after him."

"Can you play it for us?" Moritz asked. His eyes widened a little, and I wondered if he'd ever heard live music before. The frown on Julia's face told me no.

"Not now," Julia said. "Tante's tired. It was a long trip."

But I ignored her, took my violin from its case. I put it up to my chin, closed my eyes. I could see the Mahler in my mind, all the perfect notes on the sheet music. The music had been with me that last night in the bookshop and my eyes had been closed then, too, as I'd played. The music already ingrained.

It was still there. Nothing else was left in my memory but the Mahler. And Max. With my eyes closed now, I could almost still feel

him, real and breathing and just out of
reach.

MAX, 1931

For the next few weeks all Max thought about was Hanna. He rode the train to the Lyceum each morning before opening the shop, bringing her books to read, lingering in the auditorium and listening while she practiced. And then he eagerly awaited those few times a week when she would finish the books and bring them back and they would talk about them.

She was reading Shakespeare now. She had missed it in school because she'd been taking violin lessons during the literature course. She'd recently finished *Romeo and Juliet,* and she'd hated it, telling Max the ending made no sense, that she would've liked it much better had Juliet decided to move on with her life rather than stabbing herself when she thought Romeo was dead.

He'd laughed. "They're star-crossed lovers," he told her. "That's what has to happen."

"Oh please." She rolled her eyes.

He'd asked her if she was done with Shakespeare then, but she told him she would give him another try. And now she had moved on to *Hamlet*.

On a Friday morning a few weeks after her recital, Hanna invited Max to go to a movie with her after the Sabbath ended on Saturday. He not only quickly agreed but also completely forgot about his standing date with Johann until he got back home after the movie and found a note on the door of his shop, saying Johann had come to meet him and had missed him.

Hope you're okay . . . I'm worried about you. — J

But Max's lips were still tingling from the good-night kiss he'd given Hanna as he'd left her in front of her apartment on Maulbeerstrasse, and he read Johann's note with only the smallest pang of guilt.

The next afternoon, though, Max walked the six blocks over to Johann and Elsa's. They lived in a small two-bedroom house near the train station, which Johann liked because of the convenience. The proximity to the train made it quite easy for him to get to school and to his job at the law firm in Berlin. Elsa, on the other hand, hated it because she said the noise of the trains woke her before dawn each morning.

"Max!" Elsa exclaimed when she opened the door. Her belly was so large and round that his eyes went to that first, not her swollen face. It still seemed strange to him that there was a person in there, a baby. Part Johann, part Elsa. "It's been a while. Come on in. I'm making *Gemüsesuppe*. There's plenty, if you want some."

"Thanks, Els." He leaned across her giant belly to kiss her cheek. "But I don't want to intrude on your Sunday supper."

"Nonsense, Max. You're never intruding. You're family." Elsa was a far better cook than he'd ever be. Most of the food he cooked for himself tasted bland. Sustenance, not a meal. So he was quite thrilled by her offer. "I'll set another bowl at the table. Johann's just getting changed from church. He'll be right out."

A moment later, Johann walked out from the bedroom. "I thought I heard your voice, Max." He smiled, grabbed two ales from the small icebox, and kissed Elsa quickly. "Max and I are going to go out on the porch," he said. And Max followed Johann out front.

They sat down on the stoop and Johann handed Max one of the ales. "Sorry about last night," Max told him. "I didn't mean to worry you."

Johann looked at him, then took a drink. "Everything okay?" he asked carefully.

"Yes," Max said. "Really. I just went to see a movie with someone, and I lost track of time."

Johann smiled. "Ahh. The girl you wanted to notice you. You're succeeding, I see. And what is her name?"

"Hanna." He broke into a smile at just the mention of her name. He couldn't help himself.

"Hanna," Johann repeated. "Well, I'm glad that's what it was and not . . ." Johann's voice trailed off, but Max knew exactly what he was thinking, why he was concerned. He had disappeared for a week in June, somewhat unintentionally, just after his father's death, worrying both Johann and Elsa. Especially Johann, who still remembered what had happened to him after his mother's death. And he wished he'd remembered to cancel with Johann beforehand, so this wouldn't have come up again.

But the truth was, he hadn't thought about the closet in the bookshop in a while, since he'd met Hanna. "I told you," Max said again. "You don't have to worry about me. I'm fine."

Johann took another sip of his ale. A train was coming, and the whistle grew louder and louder, until it reached the station and the brakes squealed. "When can I meet her?" Johann asked, and Max was happy he'd changed the subject back to Hanna.

"Meet who?" Elsa waddled out onto the porch. Then added, "Soup's ready."

Johann stood up and kissed Elsa on the top of her head. "Our Max has met someone."

"Oh, that's wonderful news." Elsa grabbed him in a hug, or she tried anyway. She was all belly, and she moved awkwardly. "Yes, we definitely need to meet her. Bring her over next weekend. I'll bake pfeffernüsse for the occasion."

Johann laughed and rubbed her stomach softly. "You can think it over, Max. Elsa's really making the cookies for this one in here."

She swatted his hand away. "Well, of course, he doesn't have to commit right now. But the offer stands. And you know my pfeffernüsse are the best on this side of Berlin."

Max left with a belly full of soup, his head reeling from all Elsa's questions about Hanna. Everything was new still. Could you really be in love with someone you had only known a month, had only been on one real date with (well, two if you counted the apple strudel and the bakery-shop kiss, which he did)? And it was strange, but Hanna almost didn't feel real to him when he wasn't with her. That someone so bright and beautiful and talented as her might want to be with him felt almost like a dream.

But it was real. He knew it was. As he headed back to the shop, his mind drifted to the dark auditorium where he'd watched the movie with Hanna the night before. The way he had put his arm around her and she had snuggled in close to him. He had stopped paying attention to the movie altogether and had spent the time enjoying being close to her. That was real.

"Herr Fruchtenwalder says maybe next year I can try for the symphony," she'd told him, on the walk back to her apartment. "But I will have to practice extra hard, even more." She let go of his hand, stopped walking, and turned to face him.

"Am I distracting you?" He said it lightly, joking. But he worried that was how she saw him, as a distraction, and she would decide he wasn't worth her limited time.

She shook her head. "No. You make me

want to work harder," she said. "You believe in me."

"Me and Herr Fruchtenwalder," he reminded her.

"He believes in all his students." But Max was pretty sure that wasn't true.

"You are destined for greatness, Hanna," he told her, and he truly believed that. Though he wondered when that greatness came, if she would leave him, just an ordinary shopkeeper, here, behind.

Max unlocked the shop and walked inside now. He didn't open to customers on Sundays, and he planned on choosing a book and going upstairs to his apartment to read it. He felt full and tired and vaguely happy. Maybe he would even take a nap.

But something was off inside the shop. He felt it right away. Something in the air that made the hairs on the back of his neck bristle. Something was different, out of place. The front door had been locked, so no one had broken in, and he tried to shake the feeling away. It was the feeling of happiness, the feeling that things now were too good. He was looking for something wrong, his mind playing tricks on him.

But then he saw what it was: the bookshelf he'd moved in front of the closet was pushed to the side, the door to the closet slightly ajar. The ACHTUNG! sign hung just a little crooked, having been somehow knocked askew while he was eating soup at Johann and Elsa's.

It suddenly was hard to breathe, and he sat down on the floor, forcing himself to inhale, exhale. Maybe he'd forgotten to lock it? Perhaps a great gust of wind had blown through the shop and pushed the bookshelf aside, the door ajar while he'd been out. But it wasn't windy outside. The cool December sun shone against the front windowpane, and the mulberry trees lining the street were perfectly still.

Hanna had just finished *Hamlet,* and they'd discussed it earlier this week. It was sitting there still on the counter where he'd left it, untouched. A line from it came to him now: *There are more things in Heaven and Earth, Horatio, / Than are dreamt of in your philosophy.*

"Hallo," he called out now into the dark shop. He felt a sudden, overwhelming longing for his father. The back of his neck tingled and he began to sweat. He switched on the light and walked around. But the shop was perfectly quiet, perfectly empty. No one was here but him.

He shut the closet door, fastened the lock,

and pushed the bookshelf back in front of it.

HANNA, 1946

"A woman? In my orchestra?" Maestro Philip pulled at the ends of his handlebar mustache and raised his bushy gray eyebrows like he thought I was insane. The Royal London Symphony was holding auditions — I saw the advertisement in the newspaper over breakfast this morning, and I'd come straight over to inquire about an audition of my own. Julia had been pestering me to go out and interview for a job, but this, of course, was not what she meant.

After staying with her for three months, Julia's patience — and mine — was wearing thin. Her only solace, and really mine, too, was that I picked Moritz and Levin up from school each day and spent time with them until supper while Julia ran out to do various errands. I loved my nephews, who were smart and funny, and especially Moritz, who enjoyed disobeying Julia at every turn. Zayde would've loved that about his namesake. He'd always teased Julia for being much too uptight.

"Well, why not?" I asked Maestro Philip now. "I made it into the symphony in Berlin before the war."

"That was a long time ago," he said. It was, though it didn't feel like it to me. It still felt like months, not years, and as hard as I tried, nothing about the ten years I'd lost would come back to me. But I practiced my violin each afternoon, giving performances for Moritz and Levin after school, and I felt confident that my playing was nearly as good as it had been then. That with more practice still, it could get even better.

"Just give me an audition," I implored him. "If you don't like my playing, you can say no." He frowned and pulled at his mustache again. "Come on, what have you got to lose?"

Friedrich had told me that the Royal Symphony had closed down during the war, after too many of their members left to go fight. "No one cared about music during the war," Friedrich had said, matter-of-factly. But to me it seemed that people would've needed music more than ever, and it depressed me to think of an entire city without it. Friedrich continued by explain-

90

ing that now, the orchestra was probably like so many other things in London, only half staffed, too many of the former members recovering from injuries and unable to play as they once had, or worse, dead. That must be why they were holding auditions. "But there are many things more important than the symphony," he'd said. "You do know thirty thousand people were killed here by bombings and a million buildings were destroyed. And that's not even counting the soldiers who were fighting."

Friedrich's numbers were enormous and terrifying, and I murmured that it was all very sad. But I was going to audition, no matter what. "We still need the symphony," I told him, and he had frowned.

London was so different from Berlin, or maybe it was just that the war had changed everyone but me? In Berlin, when I'd studied at the Lyceum and when I'd auditioned for the symphony, no one had cared much that I was a woman. They cared how well I could play, and then later on, that I was a Jew. But here, Maestro had no notice or care for my religion. It was that his orchestra was a boys' club, and I would break that tradition. Would it always be something? Religion, gender, wrong time, wrong place? Would I ever escape all these uncontrollable factors that would keep me from playing onstage, with a real orchestra? "Please," I begged him now. "If you don't think my playing is good enough, I'll leave you alone, I promise. But at least give me a chance to prove myself. Just give me an audition."

"All right," he finally said. "Tomorrow morning here, promptly at nine. But I'm not going to promise anything."

I waited for Moritz and Levin out on the sidewalk in front of the steps of Carnaby Academy at three o'clock, as I'd been doing for weeks. But today my mind was somewhere else. Back in the Lyceum with Herr Fruchtenwalder, debating which piece would be best for my first symphony audition. He'd wanted me to play Beethoven, the first movement of the Kreutzer Sonata, but I argued for something more daring, something that would make me stand out, Ravel's *Tzigane.* And in the end, as I was the one who'd had to perform it, my piece had won out. But Maestro Philip, who could not imagine a *woman* in his symphony, might not look so kindly on any act of daring. I would play the Beethoven.

Standing outside on the street, I hummed a few bars and closed my eyes. I could see the notes on the page in my mind, but it had been a long time since I'd held the music in my hand; I began to second-guess the nuances, the fortissimos and andantes. There was a music shop on Denmark Street, only a few blocks out of the way, and I could stop with the boys on the way home.

"Tante, you're singing to yourself." Moritz yanked on my hand, and I opened my eyes.

"You look like a twit," Levin said, his voice low. Other children swarmed out of the Academy and went to their mothers and nannies waiting on the sidewalk near me. I was embarrassing him. He was so much Julia's child.

Moritz punched his older brother in the forearm. "Lev, be quiet. Remember what Mother said." Lev rubbed his arm and looked sheepishly at his shoes. I could only imagine what Julia had told them about me.

I ignored the exchange and grabbed each of their tiny hands. "Boys, come on," I said. "Have you ever been into a music shop before?" They shook their heads. Of course they hadn't. Who would've taken them? "Well, we're going to one now. I need to buy some music." I had a few pounds in my handbag that Julia had given me in case of emergencies. This wasn't the kind of emergency she'd meant, of course. But I really needed the music to make sure my audition would go smoothly.

"You're going to pay money, for *music*?" Lev asked skeptically, sounding exactly like Julia.

"Yes," I told him and Moritz both. "Music is very special, very valuable."

"Like gold?" Moritz asked, his eyes wide with wonder. He would truly believe me if I told him music and gold were one and the same.

I laughed. "Not exactly. But after we buy the music, we'll go home and I'll play it for you so you can hear how wonderful it is. I'm going to go on a very important audition tomorrow morning. Don't you boys want to help me get ready?"

Lev shrugged, like he knew we were about to do something his mother wouldn't approve of and didn't want to commit to enjoying any part of it, and Moritz nodded eagerly and squeezed my hand.

In my bedroom at Julia's house later, I etched today's date on the top page of my music in pencil, not wanting to forget, to lose any more time. I had played through the first movement of the Kreutzer Sonata once for the boys before dinner. Moritz had told me my playing was more beautiful than gold, and I'd hugged him for his sweetness.

But it sounded and felt sloppy to me. After dinner, in my bedroom, I played it over and over again. I knew all the notes; I still remembered them all, but it wasn't enough. I had to make sure it would be perfect, that there would be no question in Maestro Philip's mind, that he could not say no to me. As a Jew, as a woman, I had to not just be better than any man or Christian, but I had to be the best.

As I played, I felt alive again. The fire that Max said I possessed came back to me in small bursts. When Julia knocked on my door, I put down my violin to answer her, feeling breathless, nearly giddy.

"Do you have any idea what time it is?" Julia frowned. I shook my head. I didn't. When I played, time escaped me; everything escaped me. I'd even forgotten about Max, though now with Julia standing here frowning at me, it all rushed back, and I felt his absence again, a weight in my chest. When I'd been practicing for my symphony audition in Berlin, I'd been playing in the bookshop, all hours of the night, Max listening, sometimes even bringing me cups of tea in the middle of the night to keep me awake and hydrated. "Half past ten," Julia said sternly. "And the boys are still awake. And Friedrich is annoyed. The whole neighborhood is probably annoyed. I'm surprised no one has called the police yet, all the ruckus you're making."

"I'm sorry," I said, and truly I was. I didn't want to keep Moritz and Levin — or the neighbors — from sleep. "Just ten more minutes. I can practice in the closet. It'll mute the sound. I didn't realize it was so late."

Julia shook her head. "Hanni, no. It's too late. No more playing." I opened my mouth to tell Julia about my audition in the morning, about Maestro Philip, but then she said, "We've been patient with you, but enough is enough." And I bit my lip. Julia never understood me, and all these years later, all these miles away from Berlin, nothing had changed. "Friedrich arranged an interview for you at the hospital. They have an opening in the records department. You're a good typist. It's only part-time, so that will still give you time to rest, and be with the boys."

I was not, in fact, a good typist, or even an efficient one. My fingers weren't made for the keys of the typewriter, but for the strings of the violin. But I nodded all the same. I would go to the audition tomorrow, and once Maestro Philip offered me a spot in his orchestra I would tell Julia then. Once she saw that I could be paid to play the

96

violin, perhaps she would appreciate it more.

"Now good night," she said, her voice softened. She reached out and tucked some wayward curls behind my ears. "Sleep tight, Hanni."

She switched off the light and shut the door, and I stood there in the darkness, my violin still in my hand. I lifted it back to my chin. I could finger through the music still, from memory, moving the bow silently through the air, hovering above the strings. I closed my eyes, and then I was back in Gutenstat, in the bookshop with Max.

Just play him the fire, Max said to me, once. *They'll have no choice but to put you in the orchestra.* Max put his hands on my shoulders, and my whole body felt lighter. His green eyes were filled with warmth, and he smiled, revealing his slightly crooked top front tooth. For a moment, nothing mattered but him. Not even the violin. I wanted to reach up, to run my fingers through his brown curls, to feel the light stubble on his cheek against my palm. But I'd been so angry with him for leaving, I'd shrugged him off, continued to play instead. Why hadn't I kissed him then? Why hadn't I held on to him?

Now the violin was all I had. I stood there

in the darkness for a long while, fingering through the music, until I could no longer force myself to stay awake. And then, in a restless sleep, I dreamed about myself auditioning, but I was being forced to play my violin for Hitler himself. And when I awoke, sweating, shaking, I had to stifle a scream.

I snuck out of the house just after sunrise the next morning, before Julia or Friedrich could wake up and say anything more to me. I didn't want to hear their voices, their doubts in my head while I auditioned. I stopped at the market on Carnaby Street near the boys' school, wanting some tea and breakfast, but I'd forgotten my ration coupons at home. It was still hard to remember that I needed them, that there had just been a war and that food was still in such short supply. I'd also gotten used to the sight of missing and bombed buildings, so that I barely even noticed the piles of rubble and ash anymore, tucked in among the beauty and the splendor of what still stood in the West End. That was just the way the world looked, here and now. Kind of how I felt myself: bombed out and broken and yet somehow still carrying myself through daily life.

But today was different. Today there was music, opportunity. And who needed breakfast anyway? As I walked toward my audition, slowly, I played through the piece in my mind. I felt confident I could play it well this morning. The question was whether Maestro Philip would care. *He had to care.* When I had played in Germany, people had always cared. As Mamele always used to tell me, my playing was my gift. And I knew it still was, whether Julia and Friedrich understood it or not.

The door to the auditorium was locked today when I arrived, but when I knocked once, Maestro Philip promptly opened it and ushered me inside. It was small, smaller than the auditoriums I'd played in in Berlin, even half the size of the one I used to practice in at the Lyceum. But this would be a real orchestra, a real paying job as a violinist. It was what I'd always wanted, even if I'd never envisioned it quite like this.

"Whenever you're ready," Maestro said dismissively, and he waved me toward the stage with his large hand. I walked onto the stage and breathed in the damp earthy smell of the auditorium. In my head I knew it had been ten years since I'd stood on a stage and played an audition like this one, but in my heart it felt as if it had been no time at all. This was home.

I put my violin up to my chin. I'd brought the music but I didn't need it, and I didn't bother to put it up on the stand. And then I closed my eyes, and I played. The music was fire and light, and my fingers moved as they knew how. My arms and my body moved with them. I was alive again. For the first time since I'd come to London, I felt vaguely happy.

When I finished, I was breathing hard, and I lowered the bow and opened my eyes. Maestro sat in the front row, his face expressionless, and I couldn't tell whether he'd liked the performance or not. "Well?" I said, anxiously.

"I'll be in touch," Maestro said.

"In touch?"

"Leave your contact information with my assistant at the door. I have many violinists coming in for an audition this week. A lot of interest."

Why had I assumed I was the only one? That my playing would immediately convince him the way I'd almost always been able to do in Berlin. First, to make it into the Lyceum as a music student, then to come under the tutelage of Herr Fruchtenwalder, who was the best teacher there. And then later still, when I auditioned for the symphony. "You'll let me know then?" My voice faltered a little.

"If you don't hear from me, you can assume I've chosen someone else," Maestro said.

MAX, 1932

Hanna brought her violin to dinner at Elsa
and Johann's the first time she came with
Max to meet them. Elsa had asked Max to
tell her to bring it, saying she'd heard so
much from Max about Hanna's playing, she
wanted to experience it for herself. But
when Max had mentioned it to Hanna
earlier in the week as they'd had coffee in
between Hanna's classes at the Lyceum, she
had argued against it. "I don't want to
perform for your friends," she said. "I want
to get to know them." Max had tried to
convince her she could do both, but he
wasn't sure she'd listened until she'd shown
up at his shop that afternoon, her violin in
hand.

"Come on in," Elsa said now, softly. She
wore the baby wrapped in a sheet across
her stomach. "This is the only way Emilia
will sleep." She smiled and ushered them
into the dining room. "Stew's almost ready."

Hanna offered to help in the kitchen, and she put her violin down by the fireplace and followed Elsa back, leaving Max and Johann to talk before dinner. "Let's go outside," Johann whispered. "Els will kill us if we wake the baby."

Max had been to see them only once since Emilia was born six weeks ago. Though she was tiny, little Emilia had disrupted everything. Johann complained he hadn't slept in weeks, and he and Max no longer met on Saturday nights for ale. But Max had been meeting Hanna after sundown each Saturday, and he realized now, somewhat guiltily, he'd barely noticed his friend's absence. Or the rather large black circles under his eyes.

"I'd offer you an ale," Johann whispered, "but I'm afraid to walk into the kitchen. And I don't think I could drink one. I'd fall asleep right here on the porch step."

Max smiled and shook his head. "I'm fine," he said. It was too cold to sit comfortably outside, but Johann didn't seem to notice the January chill, and Max buttoned up his coat and pulled on his hat.

It was already close to five, and on Sunday, the trains didn't run very late, so Hanna planned to sleep at his apartment for the first time tonight, to take the train to the Lyceum early tomorrow morning. She'd lied to her mother and sister, told them she was spending the night at her girlfriend Gerta's place, and Max felt nearly giddy at the thought of being with her all these many hours, this entire night, her sleeping next to him in his bed. It was hard to think of anything else, to listen to what Johann was saying about Emilia not wanting to sleep when it was dark outside.

"You want to hear something crazy?" Johann said now. Max blinked, shivered a little from the cold, and brought his attention back to his friend.

"What's that, Jo?"

"I thought I saw your father, on the train a few weeks ago."

"What?" Max's heart thudded in his chest at the mere idea of his father. How he would love for him to meet Hanna, and to just talk to him again about books and life.

Johann laughed. "I mean, that's how sleep deprived I am. I'm hallucinating now." He shook his head. "But I swore it was him. I even walked up to him, called out, Herr Beissinger!"

"And what did the man do?" Max thought of the closet door, open in the bookshop weeks earlier, and he felt light-headed. He forced himself to take a slow deep breath.

"What any sane man would do, run off at

the next stop and not look back. But, jeez, I swore it was him. It was the hat — remember the one he used to wear all the time when we were kids?"

Max nodded. "The brown bowler." His mother had bought his father that hat once, and after she died, he hadn't taken it off it seemed for months.

"Yes, that was the one. This fellow had the same hat," Johann said. "Els said it was my mind playing tricks . . . That your father was the only father I'd ever known, and here I was a father myself, with no idea what the hell I'm doing."

"You'll figure it out." Max put his hand on Johann's shoulder, trying to reassure his friend, though in a way he was also jealous. What he wouldn't give to see his father again. Even if it wasn't real.

"Stew's ready." Hanna peeked her head out of the door and interrupted their conversation. She shivered a little. "It's freezing out here. You boys will catch your death."

"Is it?" Johann asked.

"Yes." Max stood. "Come on, let's go inside. Elsa will kill me if I let you freeze."

Emilia slept wrapped and snuggled on Elsa's chest through the whole dinner, and the four of them ate their stew, talking in whispers, trying not to wake her. "We're really quite normal," Elsa whispered to Hanna. "I promise we're not always like this."

Hanna smiled and complimented Elsa on her stew, and Max felt a lightness bubbling up inside of him. Something felt right, whole. Him and Hanna. Johann and Elsa.

Emilia woke just as they were finishing dinner and as Elsa nursed her, Johann stood to clear the table. "Will you play for us?" Elsa asked Hanna.

"I don't want to disturb the baby," Hanna said.

Elsa shook her head. "Nonsense. She's eating now and won't even notice."

Hanna glanced at him, and Max smiled at her. He wanted Elsa and Johann to see Hanna, to hear Hanna, to understand how special she was, the way he already did. He was glad she'd brought her violin.

"All right, well, just a little," Hanna said. She stood and took her violin from the case, and she went and stood by the fireplace. She closed her eyes, and she played something soft and slow and sweet. Max's stomach was full from the soup, his skin warm from the fire.

"Like magic," Elsa said, as Hanna's music floated through her house.

■ ■ ■ ■

Later, inside his apartment, Max felt jittery with nerves. He and Hanna had been seeing each other for months. They'd gone to movies and met for coffees; Max had been to several recitals, more rehearsals. They'd kissed more times than he could count, quick kisses good-bye at the train station, slow passionate kisses that they savored in the darkness of the theater, which left him hungry for more. And though it had been left unspoken between them, they both knew that tonight could be something more, something bigger. At least, Max thought it could be, hoped it was what Hanna wanted.

Hanna had seemed jittery, too, as they walked up the stairs to his apartment. She let out a nervous laugh as she told him she had forgotten to bring something to sleep in. And Max walked to his closet, gave her one of his shirts.

She changed in the W.C. and brushed her teeth (she had remembered her toothbrush) and then she walked into his bedroom. His shirt was much too long on her — it hit at her knees, and she had rolled the sleeves up, but they still hit her wrists. "Hi," she said, shyly, looking down at her bare toes.

Then she looked up at him.

"Hi." He smiled at her, and she smiled back. They stood a few feet apart and neither one of them moved for a few moments. They had been spending a lot of time together. But this was different, and they both knew it. "We don't have to do . . . anything," he finally said, taking a step closer to her. "We can just go to sleep."

She reached out for his hand, laced her small fingers into his large ones, weaving them together. "I don't want to go to sleep," she said. "Unless you want to go to sleep?" She tugged his fingers lightly. She was teasing him. She knew he did not want to just go to sleep.

He unlaced his fingers and moved them to the buttons on her shirt, that she'd just buttoned up. He undid the top one and then she moved her hand up. "Let me," she said. Her fingers unfastened the buttons deftly, one by one, with precision, the same way they played the violin. With confidence, expertise.

She was completely naked underneath his shirt, and with the buttons undone, the curves of her breasts, her pale flat stomach, were exposed. She took his hand back and guided it to her bare skin, just below her breasts. And when he touched her, she shivered a little. "Are you cold?" he asked.

She shook her head. "No," she said. "I'm just so . . . alive."

And that was the way he felt, too, *alive.*

HANNA, 1946

A week went by, then two, and Maestro Philip did not call. At first I was waiting by the telephone in Julia's kitchen, but as the weeks went on, I began to understand it was never going to ring for me. I scoured the papers looking for news of other orchestras holding auditions, but that was the only one in London at the moment. And then I couldn't put Julia off any longer, and I finally went to interview for the job she wanted me to have typing up records in the hospital. My mind and body felt numb as I followed the directions Friedrich had given me to the hospital, walking down Carnaby Street in the rain. I was young still; there were many years ahead of me. And I pictured the rest of my life with no violin, no Max: a large empty void, filled with long boring days and sleepless nights. I could barely breathe.

The woman who interviewed me for the

job didn't ask too many questions, and if she noticed that my hair was a frizzy mess from the misty rain outside, or that I was, in general, a mess and altogether uninterested in the job, she pretended not to. "You can start first thing tomorrow, Miss Ginsberg," she told me. "Nine A.M. sharp."

"You look sad, Tante," Moritz said to me later that evening at supper. Julia and Lev looked up from their food, looked to him, then me, while Friedrich smoked his cigarette and read his paper, not bothering to listen. Lucky for him, cigarettes weren't rationed in London, because he seemed to smoke them an awful lot. I couldn't stand the smell. I didn't know how Julia could bear to kiss him.

"No," Julia said. "Tante isn't sad. In fact, she's very happy today because she got a new job."

"Playing in the orchestra?" Moritz's eyes widened, and Lev kicked him under the table. Moritz groaned and rubbed his leg.

"A real job," Julia said brightly, "at the hospital where Papa works."

"The hospital?" Moritz sounded almost as disappointed as I felt. "I can tell a joke to cheer you up," he offered.

"Darling, I told you." Julia's voice was

111

stretched thin. Moritz wore on her patience. "Tante is happy. She doesn't need jokes. Eat your supper."

"Roses are red, violets are blue," Moritz began, looking back at me, a mischievous grin on his face.

"Friedrich." Julia held her hands up, exasperated. "Can you do something about your son who doesn't understand how to behave like a gentleman at the supper table?" Friedrich took a puff of his cigarette and shrugged.

"A monkey like you." Moritz was still telling his joke, and he cast a sideways glance at Lev, the monkey in this rhyme. Lev was concentrating very hard on his food and pretending not to notice. "Belongs in a zoo." Moritz chuckled.

I smiled at Moritz, so he knew I appreciated the gesture, even if he was about to get sent to his room for it. Then I stood. "Excuse me." I felt suffocated in Julia's large house, with Julia's rules, Julia's family, Julia's idea of a real job, Friedrich's smoke hovering over the supper table. "I'm not very hungry tonight."

I stepped outside and breathed in deeply. The perpetual dampness of London still didn't feel like home to me, and I didn't think it ever would. I would give anything to be back in Gutenstat, in the bookshop with Max, at the Lyceum with Herr Fruchtenwalder, at the bakeshop with Gerta, or standing inside Elsa and Johann's tiny parlor admiring their adorable daughters. That it was all gone felt impossible, unbelievable. I was anesthetized and empty, and I didn't think I would ever feel alive again.

But you are free, I thought to myself, and then this feeling of relief washed over me. Though it immediately seemed an odd thing to think, an odd relief to feel.

The next morning at the hospital, I was given a pile of handwritten records and a typewriter. I plonked them out slowly, one letter at a time, finger by finger, nothing at all like the other women in the room who typed effortlessly, not even looking at their hands. They typed the way I played the violin.

It was hot inside the records room, and I began to feel nauseated. By ten thirty I was more than ready for a break and asked the shift supervisor, Mary, if I could take my thirty-minute allotted lunch. Mary was a tall blond-haired woman with a thick Irish accent, and though she frowned at my request she waved me off with her hand, and I assumed that meant yes. My position was, thankfully, only part-time and I would be finished for the day at two, in time to meet my nephews at the Academy and walk them home. But as the ninety minutes between nine and ten thirty had already felt interminable, I wasn't quite sure how I was going to make it.

I walked up a flight of stairs to the hospital cafeteria, and though I wasn't all that hungry, I appreciated that ration books weren't needed for food here and bought a biscuit and a cup of tea. I sat at a table in the corner and picked at the biscuit with my fingers, not really eating any of it, feeling guilty as I remembered Julia yelling at me that people were still starving. So I forced a few bites down.

"Excuse me." A man's voice startled me, and I looked up. I'd never seen him before. He was middle-aged, with a shock of red hair and freckles, wearing a white lab coat with *Dr. Childs* embroidered across the chest in blue writing. "You're Friedrich's sister-in-law, aren't you?"

I wasn't used to being identified in relation to Friedrich, as someone's sister-in-law even. I was Hanna Ginsberg, the violinist. But I supposed here in London, in the

hospital, I was just Friedrich's sister-in-law.
I nodded.

"I'm Henry Childs." He held out his hand
to shake but I didn't take it, not sure what
he wanted with me, and not in the mood to
make friends. He lowered his arm back to
his side. "Sorry to interrupt your lunch," he
said, glancing at my mostly uneaten biscuit
in crumbles on my napkin. "Friedrich told
me about what . . . happened to you."

"Which part?" I said curtly.

"All of it . . . I think?" He pulled out the
other chair at the table. "May I sit?" He
didn't wait for me to answer before sitting
down, and I sighed, not really wanting to
talk to him, or anyone. "My speciality is the
mind. My research is in memory to be
exact. We've had a lot of soldiers come back
from the war, missing pieces of time. Even
those who don't seem to have a physical
injury." I remembered what Herr Doctor
said to me in Berlin: *not a physical trauma.*
But something else, something that had
made my mind retreat back to that night
with Max in the bookshop. I bit my lip to
keep the tears from welling up. "And, well,
I was hoping you'd want to talk to me about
what happened," he said.

"There's nothing to say." I stood and
wrapped my biscuit crumbs in the napkin,

looking around for the trash. Henry Childs stood, too, took the napkin from my hand, and walked it to the trash can himself. I walked toward the exit of the cafeteria. I did not want to talk to him about what happened, about everything I'd had once in Germany that had been stolen from me. I didn't care what his specialty was, and I was annoyed with Friedrich for talking about my personal matters with his colleagues, behind my back.

"I've developed some methods . . ." he called after me. "Some have even recovered their memories."

I stopped walking. Did I even want to recover my memory?

What I wanted was to have it all back, Max, my violin, my life with him in Gutenstat. But I didn't know where Max was now, and if I remembered something, maybe it would lead me to him. But what if what I remembered was too awful to imagine? What if there was a reason for forgetting?

"If you ever want to stop by my office before work . . . I come in early. I'm on the fourth floor," Dr. Childs called out.

I resumed walking, pretending that I didn't hear him calling after me.

The truth was, I would think about Henry

Childs a lot over the next few weeks and months, and yet I hadn't been able to bring myself to actually go to his office on the fourth floor.

I was caught between feeling stifled in this new life, desperately wanting Max and my violin and that feeling of belonging, that feeling I once had of being in love and beautiful and alive. Between that and . . . this: Julia and my nephews and the stupid typing job. I developed a routine, a new normal. But I walked through each day dazed and numb. I began to understand that if I was ever going to feel anything again, I was going to have to accept all this as my new reality. I was going to have to find a new way to experience love and joy.

But the thing was, I couldn't accept it. At night after Julia and the boys went to sleep, I'd take out my violin in the darkness of my bedroom, finger through pieces, hearing them in my mind, feeling them in my heart. It was the only way I kept from going insane, really, remembering that there was that fire within me, feeling it, however briefly and silently.

I would finger through pieces until I was too tired to keep my eyes open, and then I would fall into a restless sleep, where I would dream again about my violin, but many times the dreams turned into night-mares, and I would wake up terrified, not remembering who or what I was scared of, only feeling that in my dream I had been fighting for my life.

I dreamed a lot of Max, too. I'd be so happy when I'd go back to the bookshop in my sleep, and deeply sad when I'd wake up and it would all be gone, again and again and again. I'd spent so many nights there that the bookshop was like my home. Max was my home. And when I dreamed myself there it was all so real again, so close. I could smell the books, could feel Max's strong hands on my face, my skin. I kissed him, and I could feel his tall, lean body against mine, like it was for real.

But the dreams often ended ugly, like all the others. The door to the shop would break open, the SA would be there, men in their ugly brown uniforms, commanding me to play violin for them. I would wake sweating again, Max's name on my lips.

"Max," I'd call out into the darkness, to no one. I knew I was safe, in London, in Julia's house. But I no longer felt truly safe.

By December I was utterly exhausted, barely sleeping, barely eating. Not truly playing violin. I was a hollow version of myself.

Mamele had believed so deeply in my talent for violin; she had encouraged me since I was a young girl, and after she died, Max had believed in me. But now I had only myself, and I was exhausted and I didn't know what to believe in anymore. I didn't want to live my life feeling sad and empty all the time, but I didn't know how to stop feeling this way.

Could Henry Childs really help me? I began to wonder.

I had to try something. I had to talk to someone. And one very chilly morning in December, I stepped out of Julia's house before dawn, made my way to the hospital and up to the fourth floor, and I knocked on Henry Childs's door.

MAX, 1932

Hanna began spending most Saturday nights staying over at his apartment, inventing excuses about why she suddenly needed to stay at Gerta's so much. Max had yet to meet her mother, or her sister, Julia, and when he asked her when he might, she simply shook her head and made a face.

"Are you ashamed of me?" he asked her.

"You?" She put her small hand on his cheek. "No. Never," she said. "Julia is awful sometimes. And my mother's illness can be . . . unpredictable." Hanna's mother had something wrong with her heart, and sometimes it would cause her to be extraordinarily tired, and other times it would cause her lungs to fill up with fluid and, Hanna had told him with a shudder, result in a terrible cough.

But if their relationship was going to be serious, forever, as Max already hoped it would, he was going to have to meet her

It had been a while since he'd been to Maulbeerstrasse, or near it. And the first thing he noticed after he got off the train was the Nazi symbol, the broken cross, Hakenkreuz, painted large and red and ugly on the side of building *zwei,* Hanna's building. Was this new, or had Hanna just decided not to mention it to him when he'd told her how he'd begun to worry about the climate now in Germany?

Jews have been hated since the beginning of time, she'd told him.

But staring at the ugly symbol defacing the side of her building he felt anger rising up inside of him, and he thought: *not quite like this.*

The inside of Hanna's apartment was roomier than he'd pictured from seeing it on the outside. There was a large parlor in the front where Frau Ginsberg sat on the sofa, a crocheted green blanket covering her legs, and empty chairs on the side where Julia, Hanna's sister, invited him to sit. She'd been cooking in the kitchen, and she wiped her hands on her apron before shaking his hand. "Friedrich will be here soon," she said, as way of introduction as if she had no use for Max, but Friedrich might. He handed her the flowers, and she thanked

125

him. Then she walked back to the kitchen, taking the flowers with her. She looked a lot like Hanna, a little taller, a little older, her hair pulled back a little tighter. But she didn't seem *awful* as Hanna had said, just busy cooking, and not all that interested in him.

Hanna sat down at the end of the sofa and tightened the blanket around her mother's legs. "Get me a cup of tea, would you, *meine Liebling*?" Hanna's mother asked her. Hanna glanced at Max and hesitated a little. "Go ahead," her mother said. "We can talk. Get to know each other." Max smiled at Frau Ginsberg, wanting to seem agreeable, wanting her to like him, so badly.

Hanna stood. Her face looked funny, her features tight. When she played the violin, when she kissed him, her eyes were bright, her face animated. There was a darkness to her now, a shadow, that he hadn't seen before. He smiled at her, to reassure her, though he was a little nervous about being left alone with her mother. But then Hanna turned and went into the kitchen to make her mother tea.

"So," Frau Ginsberg said, lowering her voice a little. "What are your intentions with my daughter?" She was to the point, he would give her that.

126

"I . . ." Hanna had said that she'd told her mother he was a friend. Should he lie or tell her the truth? He quickly decided he would share his feelings. "I love Hanna very much," he said.

"Love?" She grimaced and began to cough. Her cough sounded terrible, but neither Hanna nor Julia ran in. It was sad to think this must be normal for her. "Excuse me," she said, putting her hand to her throat.

"Can I get you something?" he asked.

She shook her head, waved away his offer with her hand. She wheezed a little more, then gathered her composure. "Beissinger," she finally said. "What kind of name is that?"

He wasn't sure how to answer her in a way that would make her happy, but she kept staring at him, waiting. "My great-grandfather was one of the founders of Gutenstat," he finally said. "My grandfather opened our bookshop there and ran it until he died. Then my father ran it, and now, since he's passed, it's my shop."

She nodded. "Businessmen, yes? But they were not Jews, no?"

"No," he said. "The Beissingers were Protestants. My mother was Catholic. I'm not a practicing anything," he said. "I wasn't raised religious."

"Eh." She waved her hand in the air, as if being a nonpracticing Christian were even worse than being a practicing one.

Did she think that because he wasn't Jewish he might support Hitler and the NSDAP ideas about Jews? "I don't think a person's religion matters," he said quickly. "I mean, it doesn't matter to me. I love Jews." His cheeks burned as he spoke, the words sounding all wrong.

And Hanna rushed in from the kitchen with a steaming cup of tea. The look on her face told Max she'd caught the tail end of their conversation. He clamped his mouth shut. "Here you go, Mamele. Nice and hot. Let it cool down before you sip." She placed it on the end table next to her mother and sat back down on the couch.

"On second thought," her mother said. "I'm feeling very tired. Help me to bed, *meine Liebling.*"

"But the Sabbath dinner . . . Julia has made a lot of food. We even splurged on a brisket for our company."

"I'm not very hungry. And Friedrich is on his way. You'll have two men here to eat all the food. Help me up and go fetch my sweater. I'm quite cold."

Hanna frowned but didn't protest further.

She walked into the other room to get the sweater, then put it over her mother's shoulders and helped her stand. Frau Ginsberg walked slowly over to Max and held out her hand to shake. "It was nice to meet you, Herr Beissinger," she said, and before he could tell her to call him Max, that Herr Beissinger was his father, she leaned in closer and lowered her voice a little. "You're wasting your time, though," she said. "My Hanna needs to concentrate on her violin right now. And besides, she will only ever love and marry a Jewish man."

Though Frau Ginsberg went back to bed and didn't reappear for the rest of the night, Max thought about her words all through dinner. He heard them in Julia's polite but distant conversation with him — her offerings for second and third helpings, Friedrich's questions about business in the bookshop these days. In the prayer he didn't understand, and in the rich challah bread they broke. And he saw it on Hanna's pinched expressions as she glanced between him and her sister the whole night. He tried to grab her hand under the table, just before dessert, but she quickly pulled away as she stood and helped her sister clear the table.

After dessert, Hanna walked him out to

the porch and shut the front door behind them, so it was only the two of them out there, in the darkness. Max wrapped his arms around her, kissed the top of her head, inhaled the scent of lemons in her hair and the molasses scent of rosin on her skin. He'd never smelled rosin before he met Hanna and now the scent *was* her. "Come with me," he whispered into her hair. "Come sleep at my place tonight."

"You know I can't," she said, pulling back a little. "It's the Sabbath."

"Tomorrow night?"

"I'll try," she said.

"Promise," he said.

She stood on her tiptoes and kissed him quickly on the mouth. He pulled her toward him, not wanting to let her go, but she broke away. "I have to get back inside," she said brusquely. He wanted to call after her, ask her to wait, to kiss him one more time, or to reassure him that nothing would change between them now that he'd met her family. But he had this horrible sinking feeling that it was too late, that it already had.

The next evening he stared anxiously at the shop door, still thinking about Frau Ginsberg's words. What had she said to Hanna after he'd left? He felt awful that her mamele had clearly disliked him, all because of his religion. It wasn't right and it wasn't fair. This was how his country was becoming. Things were black and white; you were a Jew or you weren't. Why was he beginning to feel like he was the only one who didn't care about those divisions?

And when sundown came and went that evening and Hanna didn't appear at his shop, he began to worry that she never would come again. That her mother had convinced her that he wasn't right, good enough for her. Just as he was about to go crazy worrying, the shop door opened and the bell chimed, and Hanna was there before him, a little breathless. He ran to her and hugged her.

"Sorry I'm late," she said. "I couldn't get away." She felt so good to hold, and he sighed with relief. He'd been silly to worry. He felt it in their hug, the intensity that was always there between them. He kissed her, then reached for the top button of her dress. But she pulled back. "I can't stay tonight."

"What? Why not?" He couldn't hide his disappointment.

"Mamele and Julia weren't believing I was staying at Gerta's now that they've met you . . . I mean it was pretty obvious that I was coming here."

"So? Tell them the truth," Max said.

"I can't do that. Mamele is old-fashioned. She doesn't even think it proper for a man and a woman to be in a room alone together if they're not married. Much less, well . . ." Her voice trailed off, and she blushed a little, as if thinking of all the things they had done together upstairs in his bed.

"Let's get married then," he said quickly.

"What?" Her eyes widened; the idea had never occurred to her, but he ignored her surprise and kept on talking.

"Yes. Marry me, and then we can be together every night." His words tumbled out in a rush, and as he said them, his enthusiasm grew. He realized they weren't empty words, but what he wanted. Hanna to be his wife, to be with him, every night, all the time.

But she frowned. "You know I can't."

"Why not?" he asked. "You can practice as many hours as you like. I never get tired of hearing you play. And when you get into the symphony and you're touring, I'll go with you."

She didn't answer and she looked at her shoes, shuffling her feet from side to side across the wooden floor. "It's not because of my violin," she said.

"Because I'm not Jewish." Frau Ginsberg's

words and her rattling cough haunted him. "But Hanna," he said. "I'm not even religious. I don't care what religion you are."

"But I am," she insisted. "I do."

She did or her mother did? What had everything been between them if she'd never had any intention of it lasting? "So what does that mean?" he asked her, unable to keep the sting of hurt and anger from his voice.

"I don't know," she said softly. "Maybe we should take a little break. I have to practice anyway, and I don't have time for . . ." Her voice broke and she didn't finish her sentence.

"A break?" Now that Max had Hanna in his life, he couldn't imagine his world without her. "This doesn't make any sense," Max said. "I love you."

She took a step back so there was distance between them now. "It's getting late. I have to get the train back."

"Please don't go," he said, his anger softening. He couldn't lose her. If she walked out right now, he was going to lose her. "Not like this."

"I have to," she said. "Good-bye, Max." And she turned and ran out.

Every part of Max's body felt numb after

Hanna ran out, and he sat behind the counter, stunned. He pulled out the scotch his father had kept on a high shelf for emergencies and took a sip, straight from the bottle. It burned his throat and somehow made him feel more, not less. His eyes went to the closet, in the back of the bookshop, and he stared at it, then took another swig of scotch.

If Hanna didn't want him, if Hanna wouldn't love him, then there was nothing for him here. He had nothing left.

HANNA, 1947

I began working with Henry Childs once a week, and at first, all we did was talk about my former life, everything I actually did remember from Gutenstat: all my days practicing and performing at the Lyceum, growing up with Mamele and Julia, meeting Max and falling in love with him. Then, Henry (he told me to call him Henry, not the more formal *Doctor Childs* as they did in Britain, so that I might feel more comfortable) reviewed historical events with me, hoping they might ignite my memory. He read a passage about Kristallnacht in 1938 from an old newspaper clipping, his account of Berlin so precise that I felt a physical sensation of homesickness, a shooting pain in my stomach. The descriptions of loss and destruction — the fire, the broken glass. I imagined all that happening in my beautiful Gutenstat, too, and it brought me to tears. But I had absolutely no memory, no personal recollection of the terrifying events he read about. "Anything?" he asked gently, as I wiped my eyes with the back of my hand. He kindly handed me his handkerchief. And I shook my head.

"Reichstag Fire, 1933." He read another passage, and this time, I nodded, and clutched his handkerchief tightly, twisting it between my fingers. Just after Julia and Friedrich's wedding, I told him. The Parliament burned. The government blamed Communists, and then there was the Reichstag Fire Decree, which took away all our freedoms, which the government said would protect us from harm, and which my mother, even in her very sick state, had decried was the end of Germany. She was wrong, though. It was still far from the end.

"That must have been quite scary," Henry said.

"At the time, it wasn't," I told him. "I guess it sounds crazy now, but we mostly went on with our normal lives. I had school and my violin and Max, and my mother was sick, and it all felt strangely far away. Like something that wouldn't actually touch me." Only Max believed it would. Max was so worried for my safety. He had wanted us to leave, but it seemed such a ridiculous notion to me at the time. How could you just

136

pick up and leave your entire life?

"Ahh," Henry said. "That's what the war was like here for a while. Until the air raid sirens started going off at night and bombs would just . . . rain from the sky."

It was the first time I thought about what it must've been like here, during the war, or how scary it would've been for Julia and the boys to have bombs falling all around them. Every day when I walked outside, I saw the aftermath, the rubble, the destruction, but that had become commonplace in my mind. What had it felt like to actually live through it, and to remember it all now? "I'm so sorry," I told him. "That must have been terrifying."

"To tell you the truth, it was," he said. "There were a few nights I really believed we were all going to die."

I thought about the high numbers Friedrich had rattled off at breakfast a few months ago, all the people killed and injured in London during the war, and the many buildings gone. "I know a lot of people died, or lost everything," I said. "You probably think it's selfish of me to be so wrapped up in myself . . . in what I can't remember."

Henry shook his head. "Not at all, Hanna. You've lost something very precious, too. You should not feel bad for wanting to recover it, all right?" He stared at me, waiting for an answer. His eyes were a bright green and filled with kindness.

"All right," I finally said.

"Good." He glanced at his pocket watch, then back at me and smiled. "Shall we continue next week at the same time?"

Henry and I met once a week for the next few months. We continued to talk about everything I did remember and everything I didn't. Anything from before 1936 was still so vivid to me. I could tell Henry exactly where I was, what I was doing, even what piece I'd been practicing when. But everything after 1936 was a blank, no matter how many news articles or details Henry read to me.

I also told Henry about my dreams, the one I'd now had several times about Hitler himself commanding me to play my violin, and there was always a faceless Nazi insisting I do it, at gunpoint. And how I would wake up terrified, most nights, so it had become hard to sleep at all.

Henry always listened carefully when I spoke. That was what I liked most about him. He didn't ever look at me like I was insane or insist that I shouldn't dwell on the past the way Julia sometimes did. He listened, jotted it all down in his notebook. When I got frustrated, he reassured me that we would keep talking, keep pushing, and that eventually we would get there. I would remember. People usually do, he promised me. But after months with no progress at all, I wasn't hopeful.

"What about your violin?" he asked me one morning, as I recounted my first and second symphony auditions for him in great detail. "Are you still playing now, Hanna?"

I shrugged, unwilling to admit both that I was still fingering through pieces in secret at night and also that I'd given up on playing for real. "A little," I said. "Not really."

"You should immerse yourself in it again," Henry suggested. "Anything familiar to your old life could bring the memories back. The violin would be a very good place to start."

A few days later, I saw in the newspaper that the Royal Symphony would be holding their first postwar concert the following Saturday afternoon. *Immerse yourself,* Henry had said. And I knew I had to go. Though I was bitter and angry still at not being chosen in the audition, I also wanted to see whom Maestro Philip had picked over me. And besides, every violinist knew that one audition did not define you, that you would fail sometimes. But you picked yourself up, kept on going. How had I let that one audition define me in London?

As kids Julia and I had always kept the Sabbath with our mother, but in London Julia's family didn't, and so I had stopped too. I'd felt guilty about it at first, but on this particular Saturday I was just happy that it wouldn't keep me from the symphony. I was bursting with excitement at the very thought of going to the concert, hearing a live orchestra again. And perhaps that was the best thing to come out of working with Henry, his reminder that I needed to still be the person that I always was. That my violin and the music I played were still important.

I didn't tell Julia or the boys where I was going, though I might have liked to have taken Lev and Moritz with me, especially Moritz. I imagined his little green eyes would light up at the music. But I didn't want Julia to try to stop me or talk me out of going, or even upset me with some vague negative comment she would most likely make. Julia believed I'd settled into my life as a part-time typist. Recently she'd mentioned a few men she might like to set me up on dates with, and I'd flatly refused, and she had so far let it go, happy enough that I was earning my keep with a practical job.

And so I snuck out after lunch, set out for the symphony alone. The sun was even shining today! As I walked there I felt more excited than I had in weeks, or maybe months. Or possibly years. If only I could remember them.

I slipped into the small auditorium and sat in the back row, not wanting to be noticed by Maestro Philip, and I prepared myself to be annoyed, critical of the violins. But as the music played, instead it left me wanting, longing. The orchestra wasn't spectacular. Certainly not as good as the symphony in Berlin had been once, when I'd auditioned. The cellists were a bit out of tune. The first viola missed his entrance on the second piece, one I knew well from having played it with a chamber group at the Lyceum. But the first chair violinist, Stuart Beckham, the program told me, was actually quite good. I watched him throughout with fascination, then with reverence. Was it possible Maestro Philip had chosen him because he was better than I was, not just because he was a man?

Afterward I hung around at the back exit to the auditorium, where the musicians came out. It had started misting again. (The sun was so short-lived in London.) I could

141

feel my curls wild around my face and I tried to smooth them down with my fingers as I waited. Finally, I saw Stuart Beckham, walking out of the back door to the stage, and I called out to him. He turned, surprised to hear his name.

"Hello." I held out my hand. He shifted his violin case into his left hand and took my hand. "You don't know me. I'm Hanna Ginsberg. I auditioned for your seat but obviously wasn't chosen."

"Have you come here to kill me for it?" His voice was deep and he had a thick British accent.

"What? No!"

He laughed a little. He was joking, but he held up his hand, and I realized I still hadn't let go of our handshake. I blushed and pulled away quickly. "I was just wondering if you gave lessons." I made only a little money at the hospital, and I'd been saving it up to get my own place. But I could live with Julia awhile longer and use my salary to pay for lessons instead. *Immerse yourself,* Henry had said. If I played again, I knew I would feel alive, whether I remembered anything from my past or not.

"Lessons?" Stuart raised his eyebrows. The prospect surprised him.

"I can pay you. Not that much," I added.

"What would you charge?"

"You're not from here," Stuart said, ignoring my question. "Your accent . . ."

Stuart was the first person I'd talked to in months who didn't know my story. Or, my nonstory. Everyone at the hospital knew via Friedrich, and all of them, but Henry, looked at me like I was crazy or broken or both. Stuart looked at me only with curiosity. "I grew up near Berlin," I said. "I studied violin there when I was younger. I moved here to be with my sister after the war, and I miss playing." All of that was true, and I didn't elaborate on the rest. Stuart nodded, satisfied with my answer.

"God knows I could use the money," Stuart finally said. "What if we said two pounds? And would Wednesday evening work for you? We don't rehearse that night."

"Yes," I said, though two pounds was almost all I earned in a week at the hospital. I didn't even care. "Wednesday evening would be perfect."

"Do you have a pen and paper?" he asked. I searched my pocketbook and came up with only a felt pen, no paper. I handed it to him, and he took my hand, gently flattened it over. "Do you mind?" he asked, holding the tip of the pen to my palm. I shook my head. He wrote lightly, the pen

143

tickling my skin, and my hand warmed as he wrote. "Now you have my address," he said. "Just don't wash your hand before you write it down. Shall we say seven P.M.?"

I glanced at the address, committed it to memory. I wouldn't forget it now. Or at least, the old Hanna wouldn't have in 1936. I would certainly write it down as soon as I got back to Julia's. "I'll see you Wednesday," I said and walked away feeling lighter and giddier than I had in months.

MAX, 1932

The truth was, Max had known about the closet in the bookshop in a vague sort of way for many years. He'd overheard his parents talking about it once, when he was a boy. Arguing about it, in fact.

It was a few weeks after his mother had gotten sick, and his father had been away for a while. His father used to travel all the time before his mother's illness overcame them. He was off, buying books, finding new things for the shop. Sometimes his parents would travel together and Max would be sent to stay with Johann and his mother for a few days. But then Max's mother got sick, and everything changed.

She was bedridden, quite suddenly. Or at least it had felt that way to Max, at nine years old. One day she'd been dancing around the kitchen, as her phonograph had played, laughing with his father as she cooked soup on the stove. And then the next, she couldn't get out of bed. Herr Doctor came from Berlin, and he told them there was nothing he could do. Nothing anyone could do. "Make her comfortable," Herr Doctor had said to Max's father. And to Max, suddenly, death and comfort were one and the same.

The next morning he heard his parents arguing. "You cannot go anymore," his mother had said. "It is too risky. Who will take care of Max if you don't make it back?"

"But what if we could all go?" his father had argued. "Maybe there is a cure for you in another time."

"Or maybe that's what is killing me," she'd said. "You can't go. We have a child to think about, Heinrich."

In another time. Max thought about those words a lot after his mother died. And when he'd asked his father what he'd meant by it, his father had frowned and hadn't answered at first.

"Like H. G. Wells?" he'd asked his father one afternoon in the shop. Max had just come back home after he'd been hospitalized in the city for months. The loss of his mother manifested itself into an unknowing, unyielding physical sickness that came on in fits, making it nearly impossible for him to breathe.

"Do you have a time machine?" he'd asked his father. It was hard to fathom, unbelievable even as he said it. But the idea fascinated him with little-boy wonder, a little boy who already lost himself in books and stories. His lungs had been gasping for air for months, but it had not been hard to keep on reading books and imagining, even in his sickest state.

His father hadn't answered for a little while still, and then he'd simply said: "H. G. Wells is fiction, Max." He knew. "Time machines aren't real." He paused a few moments before continuing. "But time isn't always linear. There are . . . gaps." He had walked over to the closet in the back of the shop, the one with the ACHTUNG! sign on the door, a lock on the handle that only he had the key to. "But it is extraordinarily dangerous, Max," he'd said. "And you must promise me you will never go in there. No matter what."

Max had promised. And he had kept that promise, until last June, nearly a year ago now when he had very briefly unlocked the closet door with the key he'd inherited upon his father's death and walked inside. With both his parents dead, with the bookshop floundering, with the feeling of loneliness creeping up inside of him, and with his lungs again threatening to refuse to pull the air in and out, the tightness lingering in his chest, he had thought: *Why not? What have I got to lose?*

When he had walked inside last June, the closet was long and deep, and he had walked farther and farther back, until suddenly everything changed, brightened with a light so intense he was momentarily blinded. Then all he could see was fire and smoke so thick, he really couldn't breathe. He coughed and gasped for breath and turned back around, running through the closet the way he'd come in.

Back inside the bookshop, the street out front had looked quiet and calm; there had been no smoke or fire. In fact, it was night, and he would later learn, it was not that same night, but a week later than he thought. Johann had come in frantically searching for him the following morning.

"Grief will make you do funny things," Elsa told him, when he tried to explain to her and Johann what had happened, where he had been. They had exchanged knowing glances, over his head. But Max knew what he'd experienced walking into the closet was different from grief. He'd suspected for a long time. He just hadn't been able to put his finger on it until he'd actually gone inside himself.

Elsa had patted him kindly on the shoulder. "But you don't have to lie to us, Max. If you need to get away for a little while, just tell us so we don't worry next time, all right?"

And now, here he was, nearly ten months later, drinking his father's scotch and eyeing the closet again.

He couldn't go to bed after Hanna left. He would never fall asleep, and the thought of his bed, without her, or that she would never stay here with him again, never kiss him again . . . It was all too much to bear.

His throat burned from the scotch, and he nearly gagged, coughing in a way that reminded him of Hanna's sick mother and her awful words to him. He ignored the coughing, the burning, and he took another sip. And another. And another. Until his body grew hot, and the words Hanna had spoken to him felt dull, far away.

If Hanna didn't want to be with him, would never marry him, then what was there for him here? Business was so slow, and Johann and Elsa had Emilia now. Germany was changing rapidly with many people voting for Hitler. He couldn't sit here day in and day out, bored and lonely.

And angry. And tired. He suddenly felt so tired.

He eyed the closet again. What if he went in it now? The future could be brighter, better than this. And what did he have to lose now, really?

He stood, wobbled a little, and steadied himself by holding on to the counter and catching his breath. He moved the bookshelf out of the way, and then before he could change his mind he unlocked the door, opened it, and stepped inside.

HANNA, 1947

Stuart lived in a small loft, just a fifteen-minute tube ride from the station near Julia's house. Still, I lied about where I was going on Wednesday night, having told only Henry where I'd planned to spend my weekly salary from now on, and only because I knew he'd approve. I told Julia that I had joined a small group of women I'd befriended at the hospital who also played instruments, and she'd clucked her tongue approvingly, as now she believed me to be making friends with coworkers and playing only as a hobby. In truth, I barely spoke to the women I worked with. Aside from Henry and Friedrich, of course, I barely even knew anyone at the hospital, a fact that Friedrich might have known if he bothered to pay attention, but I was pretty sure he didn't. His interest in me spanned only as far as making my sister happy, and that ended at having secured me the part-time job.

It was lightly raining when I walked up from the tube, and the buildings here were not as nicely kept up as on Julia's street. Many of the buildings surrounding Stuart's had been flattened, and a small neighborhood of prefabs, set up after the war to deal with the housing shortage, and what Julia called, with an upturned nose, *eyesores,* sat just behind his building. Julia would have been appalled by where Stuart lived.

I shielded my violin case under my coat to prevent it from getting wet, and I walked the three flights of steps up to Stuart's apartment. By the time I knocked on the door I was breathing hard, and I suddenly felt a little nervous. I didn't really know Stuart, after all, and here I was completely alone, having told no one where I was going.

"Ah, you came," he said, when he opened the door, as if I'd surprised him by showing up at the time we'd agreed upon. "Come on in." He smiled kindly, and my nervousness subsided.

I walked inside and took off my coat. His apartment was small. I was only steps from the kitchen and his bed, in the living area, where he had a couch, two chairs, and a music stand. The symphony, unsurprisingly, must not be paying him well.

"Have a seat." He gestured to one of the wooden chairs, and I sat down and took my violin from the case.

He let out a low whistle. "Is that a Strad?" He held out his hands, wanting to examine my instrument, and I hesitated for a moment before passing it to him. He caressed the wood gently with his fingertips. "She's beautiful," he said, though in truth, she had sustained a bit of wear in the ten years I couldn't remember and was in somewhat desperate need of a tune-up and cleanup. I wasn't sure there was anyone left in London after the war who could do it, though. Not that I could afford it anyway. "How did you ever get her?" Stuart was asking.

"My *zayde.*" He looked confused. "Grandfather," I corrected myself with the more English term. "He used to play himself, when he was younger. He was the whole reason why I picked up a violin in the first place, and he gave this to me for my sixteenth birthday." I smiled a little, remembering how Zayde had presented her to me, wrapped with a red ribbon, and how excited Mamele had been for me to finally have a good instrument to play on. "I don't know how he afforded it or where he got it, honestly. I didn't ask. I was just so excited to have it." That was before everything: before he died, before Mamele got sick, before Germany began to change into something ugly. And Julia had been spitting mad with jealousy. Zayde had given her a small heart necklace when she'd turned sixteen years earlier, which was lovely but not nearly as extravagant as my violin.

Stuart handed my violin back to me. "Play something," he said. "I want to see where you're at before we get started."

I put my violin to my chin, lifted the bow, and closed my eyes. I didn't think about what I was going to play but just began, letting my fingers move on the strings, the bow moving my arm where it needed to go. Mozart came out. Sonata no. 21. My favorite one. I'd played it at the Lyceum once, and Max had come. He'd told me he was going to, and as I'd walked onstage I'd searched the crowd for him. He'd been in the back, holding on to a bouquet of flowers. *Fire lilies.* My heart had lurched a little in a way it never had before, and though I'd closed my eyes and performed the sonata perfectly, my head had been in the back row of the auditorium with the sweet man who had brought me lilies, who'd actually wanted to hear me play.

I finished the piece now, put my bow down. I opened my eyes and I realized my cheeks were wet; I'd been crying. I wiped the tears away quickly, hoping Stuart hadn't noticed. He stared at me, his mouth agape. "You're quite good," he said, sounding shocked. He hadn't expected me to be. Because I was a woman? Or because he'd won the seat over me?

"I used to be," I said. "Back in Berlin."

"No," he said, adamantly. "You still are. I mean your technique is a little sloppy, but you play with passion. I can feel it."

My cheeks burned with the compliment and the criticism. I *was* sloppy because I hadn't practiced, really practiced in months, or maybe, years. He wasn't wrong about that. Herr Fruchtenwalder would've said the same thing. "So you will teach me then?" I asked. I took the two pounds out of my pocket and held them out to him.

He hesitated for a moment and then pushed the money back to me. "We will teach each other," he said. "I can correct you on your technique. You will help me to learn to play with more passion."

Could passion, *fire,* as Max called it, be taught? Deep down I felt that you were either born with it or you weren't. But I pressed my lips together tightly. If Stuart was willing to teach me, for free, I would play along.

He stood and went to the bookshelf behind the couch, skimmed across it with his fingers. "Here," he said, and I had the sudden vision of Max, standing in his shop in Gutenstat, trying so hard to find something for me to read, something I would love that would keep me coming back to the shop. Virginia Woolf had bored me, Shakespeare had annoyed me, William Faulkner's American books had intrigued me . . . But Max's earnestness was so sweet. I had returned for that much more than any books.

"My favorite book of scales," Stuart said now, pulling a thin volume from his shelf. "You can take it and practice this week." I knew all my scales by heart and had since I'd first started taking lessons at age eight, but I took the book. "Should we play through a few now, together?" Stuart asked. He took his own violin out of its case — not a Stradivari or a Guarneri or even a Willhelm. In fact, I didn't recognize it as any particular instrument of significance and so I didn't ask him where he'd gotten it. He raised his bow and I raised mine, and we began playing through the exercises in unison.

"Wait." I stopped him. He put his bow

down and turned to me. "You don't really need the book. Close your eyes."

"But how will I . . . ?"

"You should feel the music in here." I put my hand on his chest, over his heart. "Not on here." I pointed to the notes on the page.

"Shall we play number six again?" Stuart asked. I nodded. He closed his eyes and then I did the same. He counted to three, and we played D Major again, with arpeggios, in unison.

I felt almost giddy as I left Stuart's apartment. I took the scales book with me, promising him I'd practice with the music this week, while he promised me he'd practice without.

I skipped to the tube, and when I got back to Julia's, all the lights were out. Everyone was already asleep. In my bedroom, I lit a candle, and I fingered through the scales in Stuart's book until I was so tired I couldn't keep my eyes open anymore.

I blew the candle out and lay down in bed, my violin still in my hand. And when I closed my eyes, I put my hand over my heart, the way I had with Stuart's earlier, feeling it beat slow and steady beneath my palm. The beholder of all my passion, just like I'd told Stuart.

Since I'd come to London I'd thought maybe my fire was gone. That without Max, without a way to play violin, without my memory, I would be dead inside. But now, tonight, I was alive again. I felt warm from within and vaguely happy.

Run away with me. I heard Max's voice in my head as I was drifting off to sleep. His name was on my lips; he was so close. I could almost touch him. But in an instant, everything changed, grew dark. *Run!* Max was screaming now.

And then there was the man with the gun, the cold barrel against my forehead commanding me to play my violin, louder, faster, better, again.

Play like your life depends on it. It does.

Max, 1932

Max awoke the next morning, his head aching, feeling foggy, his sheets damp with sweat. It took a moment, but then he remembered why he felt so awful: Hanna coming to the shop, saying she wanted *a break,* drinking too much scotch, walking into the closet. *Oh, the closet.* Why had he done that? He moaned and pulled the pillow over his head. His head ached so badly that it was hard to think. What had happened after he'd walked into the closet? Where had he gone?

It came to him first in feelings: fear and loneliness and despair. And then in brief flashes of memory: he had walked outside of the bookshop, and everything had been . . . different. Soldiers had been marching on Hauptstrasse, shouting *Heil Hitler,* over and over again, but not *Reichswehr.* Judging from their bright red armbands with the broken cross, they were SA, Sturmabteilung. In fact, the broken cross had been everywhere, hanging up in every storefront.

Herr Feinstein next door had been standing outside his shop, sweeping the sidewalk, and he'd been very upset. Something bad had happened to his wife, and Max was trying to ask him if he was okay. But then he'd seen an SA, holding on to Hanna. No, dragging her out of his shop, arresting her. And he had been powerless to stop it. *Hanna was in terrible danger.*

He jumped out of bed, put his hand to his throbbing forehead in an attempt to quell the ache, found his shoes, and ran down the steps, out of the shop, and toward the train station. It was Sunday, and he expected the streets would be empty, but they weren't.

The train, too, was bustling and busy. And as he sat on the packed train car, it occurred to him that maybe it wasn't Sunday after all. The time he'd walked into the closet, in June, Johann and Elsa said he'd been gone for a week. Had he lost time again?

The man next to him on the train was reading the newspaper, and Max sat up a bit, glanced over the man's shoulder trying to catch the date. *Friday, April 15, 1932.* That would be . . . two weeks since he'd been to Hanna's apartment for the Sabbath dinner.

Two weeks? He had missed the runoff election. Had Hitler done the impossible and won? Is that why the soldiers had been shouting *Heil Hitler* in the street? He broke into a cold sweat. Where had he gone, or rather, *when* had he gone?

The train finally stopped at Maulbeerstrasse, and Max stood, steadied himself. He got off and gulped the fresh cool air. It was a pleasant spring morning, the sky a crystal blue, the sun shining brightly, illuminating the mulberry trees that lined the path from the station to the street. He stumbled past them, barely noticing, barely breathing. If it was a Friday morning, not a Sunday, then Hanna would not be at home; she would be at the Lyceum, finishing up her lesson, and he ran there, across the green, past the auditorium, where Herr Fruchtenwalder held his lessons. He waited outside, and when Hanna walked out a few minutes later, he ran to her, grabbed her in a hug, so relieved to see her, to feel her, to know that she was okay.

"You're safe," he whispered into her hair.

"Max?" She pushed him away and took a step back. "What's wrong with you? Have you been drinking? You smell like a tavern."

"Listen," he said, and then he hesitated, not wanting to shout it all out here, in the

161

middle of the green, which was teeming with students. "Can we go to Herr Bricht-man's bakeshop to talk?"

She shook her head. "I have to get home. It's my turn to make dinner." She started walking, briskly, and he had to run to keep up with her.

"Hanna, wait," he called. "I'm worried you're in danger."

She stopped walking, spun around quickly, her violin like a weapon that almost hit him. He jumped back. "You disappeared for two weeks. I looked everywhere for you. I was worried you were dead. And now you're here, worried for *my* safety? I don't think so."

"You were worried?" Last they'd left it, he wasn't sure if Hanna would ever want to see him or talk to him again. "But I thought you wanted a break?"

She sat down on the bench at the edge of the green. He sat down next to her, put his hand gently on her leg, and she didn't pull away this time. "I couldn't sleep all that night. I came back to your shop in the morning to apologize and tell you I was wrong, but you were gone. I saw the bottle of scotch. You'd obviously had too much to drink and just . . . decided to leave town. I didn't know if you were ever coming back."

162

He opened his mouth to correct her, then shut it again. If he told her about the closet, she would think he was crazy. And maybe, he was. "I'm sorry," he said, thinking it better to apologize. "I was so upset after you left. I . . . I had to get away. I needed to think."

She put her hand on top of his. "I'm sorry too," she said. "But don't ever do that again. You scared me half to death."

He laced his fingers with hers. "Now that Hitler has won, things are going to get bad. We should get out of Germany . . . Run away with me."

She pulled her hand away, narrowed her eyes, and tilted her head. "Hitler didn't win," she said.

He could still hear the chants of the Sturmabteilung on Hauptstrasse. *Heil Hitler. Heil Hitler. Heil Hitler.* And the Hakenkreuz was everywhere. "Are you sure?"

"Of course I'm sure. Everyone knew he couldn't win, and he didn't. Where did you go that you didn't hear the news?"

And what could he tell her? She would never believe him if he told her the truth. He barely believed it himself. Whatever he had seen, whatever danger Hanna was in, was not here, not now. It was in another time. And as long as he could be with her, he would keep her safe, protect her from it. "Never mind," he said.

Hanna squeezed his hand. "Promise me you'll never leave me like that again," she implored him. She squeezed tighter. "Promise."

"I promise," he said. And right then, it was an easy promise to make. His head throbbed; his body felt so sore and weak. What he had seen had terrified him, and how did he know it was even real? He had no desire to ever go back inside the closet. Ever.

Max walked Hanna as far as Maulbeerstrasse, then kissed her good-bye. It felt so good to kiss her, to hold her. He didn't want to let her go. But she pulled away, insisted that she had to get home and get preparations for the Sabbath dinner under way. She promised that she would come to his shop tomorrow night, after sundown.

"What about your mother?" he asked her.

"I'll think of something," Hanna said and kissed him one last quick time. He watched her walk away; the butterfly clip she always wore in her hair caught the sunlight just so and glinted. He suddenly saw a flash: men dragging her on Hauptstrasse, her screaming, the butterfly clip flying from her hair as if it were a real butterfly, suspended in the air for a moment, before crashing into the street and breaking.

But that hadn't happened. Not yet. And now it wouldn't. He would make sure of it.

He got off the train back on Hauptstrasse and decided to stop by Elsa and Johann's on the way home. Realizing it was Friday, and not Sunday, he knew he should be at the store, that he should have it open. But he doubted anyone would notice the difference. Or if they did, surely they would return tomorrow. If he had been missing for two weeks, Johann had probably gotten worried too.

"Max," Elsa whispered when she opened the door, then stepped out onto the porch and shut the screen behind her. "What are you doing here in the middle of the day?" She still spoke in a low tone. "Emilia is sleeping," she explained.

"I just . . . I wanted to let Jo know I was back."

"Where'd you go this time?" She sat down on the porch step, and he sat next to her. "Tell me it was somewhere warm, and beautiful. That you swam in the sea." She smiled a little, and he noticed the big black circles under her eyes. There was no way he was going to tell her the truth.

"Emilia still not sleeping through the night?" he asked instead.

She shook her head. "Everyone says it'll get easier, but it's getting harder to believe it."

"It will get easier," Max said, though he had no bearing, no experience of his own with babies or children. Elsa, understanding that, just laughed and shook her head a little. "Els, can I ask you a question? What happened with the election?"

"The election? Oh, Max, do you think I've had the energy to follow politics?" She had probably been the wrong person to ask, but she was also too tired to question him too much, as Hanna had. "Hindenburg won like everyone knew he would, I know that much. But, oh . . ." She stood up. "I do have all the papers still from the past week. I haven't had a chance to read them yet. Do you want to take them?"

"If you don't mind?" he said.

"No, hold on, I'll get them." She returned a few minutes later with a stack of newspapers and placed them into his arms. "I hate to cut our visit short, but I need to try to nap while Em is sleeping."

"Of course." He leaned down and kissed

her cheek. "Tell Jo I'm back and that I stopped by, would you?"

Back at the bookshop he pored over the papers Elsa had given him, catching up on what he missed. Hindenburg *had* won, but Hitler had also increased his popular vote to almost 37 percent. That felt like an impossibly large percentage of Germany, of his country. How long until it reached 50 percent or more?

How long until what he'd seen would not be out of the realm of possibility at all?

Not long enough. He knew it; he could feel time spooling out in front of him. And though it was warm inside the shop now, his head still ached something awful, and he began to shiver.

HANNA, 1948

Wednesday nights with Stuart quickly became my favorite moments of the week. I looked forward to them with fervor, and I practiced the lessons he had for me each day after I picked the boys up from school and before Julia got home. Had I been paying more attention, I might have wondered where Julia went each afternoon between three and five. She did not have a job, after all. Friedrich was still at work, and she had hired a girl, Betsy, to clean and cook dinner for us each weeknight. But selfishly, I only cared that she was gone, that I could have the two hours to practice. I swore the boys to secrecy, and Lev and Moritz would listen to me play while they did their schoolwork, clapping once I perfected an exercise.

Each Wednesday night, Stuart had another book of scales or technical exercises or a piece he would pick out to challenge me. And each week, at my lesson, we would play what he had chosen together, side by side, me with my eyes wide open, him with his eyes squeezed tightly shut.

I still went to talk to Henry sometimes before work. But I went with less urgency, not every week, more like every other week now. Not because I'd forgotten about Max, or wanted to know what happened to him — or me — any less, but because talking to Henry truly wasn't working. It made me feel stuck in the past. And when I played violin with Stuart, I started thinking about the future. Wherever Max was, I knew he would be happy I was playing again. Happy I was alive again. My violin began to consume me, as it once had, and for a little while, the nightmares ceased, and I even began sleeping through the night.

One Wednesday that spring, I arrived at Stuart's and found he didn't have his violin or music out for us like he usually did. "Oh, I'm quite sorry," he said, sounding and looking flustered when he opened the door, as if he'd forgotten all about our lesson.

He let me in and then continued what he'd been doing before I'd knocked, rushing around the apartment, gathering things to put into a suitcase that was sitting on the coffee table.

"You're going on a trip?" I asked, surprised he hadn't mentioned it last week.

"My mum is sick, and I have to get back to Wales straightaway."

"Oh, Stuart." I touched his arm lightly. "I'm so sorry. Is there anything I can do?"

He stopped moving for a second and looked at me. Stuart had dark hair, nearly the color of the ripe mulberries that used to fall from the trees that lined Maulbeerstrasse, but now standing closer than I usually did, I noticed how peppered it was with silver. It was the first time it occurred to me that Stuart was older than me, probably more like Henry's age, which made sense, as Henry had mentioned once he'd been just a bit too old to be conscripted in the war, and Stuart must've been too. "Actually, there is something . . ." he was saying now.

"What?" I asked. Stuart had quickly become my favorite person in London, after my nephews, and I would do anything to help him.

"Well, we have a performance on Saturday and I won't be back in time. Sit in for me?"

"Sit in for you?" I repeated the words back, and they didn't even sound real as I said them. Play? In a real orchestra. In front of an audience? It had been my dream for so long, and I had been so close before. And yet, it had never happened for me. I had come to believe it probably never would. "But Maestro Philip won't —"

"I'll ring him," Stuart said. "He'll be lucky to have you. You play with such passion." He reached for a folder of music on the coffee table and handed it to me. "Here's what we're playing. Just learn the pieces and he'll be thrilled."

I took the music and thumbed through: it was a concert for springtime, "Spring" from *The Four Seasons* by Vivaldi, and *Vårsång* by Sibelius, both of which I'd played before. *Appalachian Spring* by a composer named Copland whom I'd never heard of, the music completely new to me. Could I learn it in just a few days? I swallowed hard.

"You can do it, Hanna," Stuart said to me, as if he could see doubt written across my face. "Just close your eyes." He smiled, and I noticed how blue his eyes looked, reflecting off the overhead light in his flat.

I put my hand on his arm. "Don't worry about me. Just go be with your mother."

He moved his hand and impulsively swept away the curl that had fallen in front of my right eye. For a moment I thought he might lean down and hug me. But then he stepped back. "Leave me your sister's number. I'll ring you as soon as I'm back. Rehearsal starts tomorrow morning promptly at nine A.M. Don't be late. Maestro despises it when people are late."

"I won't be late," I said. "Promise."

Though the house was quiet and dark when I got back to Julia's, I knew I had to practice. I couldn't show up at Maestro Philip's rehearsal tomorrow without having ever played through *Appalachian Spring.* I turned on the light in my bedroom, took my violin out, and fingered through the piece. But it wasn't enough. I moved the bow across the strings ever so lightly, hoping the noise wouldn't wake Julia or the boys, and not a moment later Moritz wandered into my room. "What are you playing, Tante?"

"Did I wake you?" I asked. He jumped up on my bed, lay down, and yawned. "I'm sorry, *meine Liebling.* I'm going to play in a real live orchestra this weekend," I told him. "And I need to practice."

"Can I come watch you?" he asked.

"We'll have to ask your mother, but yes, I'm hoping you'll all come." Julia had never come to recitals or concerts when I was at the Lyceum. She'd been dragged by our mother when we were younger, and by the time I was serious, she was already dating

172

Friedrich, and neither of them had any interest in music. I doubted they would feel any differently now, but I didn't want to disappoint Moritz.

The next morning I was groggy, having only gotten a few hours of sleep, tucked into bed next to a snoring Moritz. Still, I woke up with the sun, the way I always have, and I tiptoed downstairs, hoping I'd be the first one awake. I needed to call the hospital and let them know I would be taking the rest of the week off so I could attend the rehearsals in Stuart's place. The telephone was in the kitchen, and I didn't want Julia or Friedrich to criticize. Luckily I was the first one down, and I placed the call before even making a cup of tea, asking the operator to connect me to the third floor. Mary, my shift supervisor, came in at seven each day, and she was the one who picked up the call. I quickly identified myself and told her I'd have to be out the rest of this week, and maybe some of next, not sure how long Stuart would be gone.

"Out?" Mary laughed. She had a thick Irish accent, and that coupled with her disbelief made it sound more like *Ooot*? "Unless yer dying I expect you at work. Yer not dying, are ya?"

I considered just lying and saying that I was to get myself off the hook, but I couldn't do that. "No," I said. "I just have a . . . something personal to take care of."

"Look, if yer not gonna come in this week, don't bother coming back. I'll have another girl doing yer work by week's end, I will."

"Please, I hope you'll reconsider," I said. I didn't want to lose my job. Or, rather, I didn't want Julia and Friedrich to get upset with me if I lost my job, and I didn't want to have to rely on them for money again, either. I didn't care one bit about the stupid typing and I dreaded every minute I spent in the hot windowless room on the third floor of the hospital.

"Get into work on time today and we won't have any problem," Mary said. She hung up the telephone, and I still held on to my end, waiting for something other than the static.

I'd promised Stuart I would not be late for rehearsal this morning. And that was a promise I intended to keep. But not only that, if ever in my life there had been a competition between my violin and something else, my violin had always won. That had been true all my life in Gutenstat, even with Max. And it was not any less true now.

It was such a strange feeling to have lost

so many years, to not remember where I'd been, what had happened. But I was still the same person, no matter what I had been through. And I didn't care who was mad at me — Mary, Julia, Friedrich — I was going to rehearsal this morning.

I arrived at the auditorium at a quarter till nine, and when I walked in, most of the rest of the orchestra — all men, of course — were already there. Everyone stopped what they were doing — tuning, fiddling with music — to stare at me. I heard a few snickers. Maestro Philip caught my eye and nodded a little. So Stuart had telephoned him as promised.

"All right, everyone." Maestro raised his arms to quiet them. "Stuart had an emergency and Hanna will be filling in this weekend." The snickers stopped and I felt everyone's eyes on me. I held my head up, jutted out my chin, as if all the confidence in the world were mine. But inwardly I felt like I might throw up. The room was silent, and I imagined they could all hear my heart pounding in my chest the way I could.

"Over here, Hanna," the second chair violinist called out. I didn't know his name, but he moved into Stuart's empty seat, and then pointed that I should sit second, next

175

to him. I gave Maestro a little nod back and walked over there. The tuning noises started again, the eyes off me, and I exhaled as I sat in the empty chair and opened my violin case.

"Charles Wentworth." The second chair violinist held out his hand. I shook it. "Stuart said you were . . ."

"What?" I was surprised Stuart had spoken to Charles about me at all, but I hoped it was to compliment my playing.

But Charles just shook his head and didn't finish the thought. "Maestro is a terrible conductor," he said instead. "We always follow Stuart instead. So you'll have to follow me now."

"Got it," I said softly, trying to breathe as I raised my violin to my chin and tuned. I closed my eyes and listened to the cacophony of the instruments noodling. *I could do this.* It was what I'd wanted my entire life, and no matter what else had happened, what I'd lost, I had this.

Walking back toward Julia's after an eight-hour rehearsal day, every part of my body was sore, and I was breathless, as if I'd just run for hours. My fingers and my shoulders ached, but it was a glorious feeling.

"Hanna!" Julia yelled at me the second I

walked in the door. Had Mary telephoned her? That seemed like too much effort for her, and the thought hadn't even crossed my mind until now. "Where were you?"

"I was —"

But she didn't give me a chance to answer before she ripped into me. "You didn't pick up the boys. They walked all the way home by themselves. And then I was so worried — I called the hospital to see what happened to you but they said you'd quit."

Oh no. The boys! I'd completely forgotten about our daily 3 P.M. routine. "I'm sorry, I just was . . ." I searched my brain for a suitable lie, and then I just told her the truth, all of it. My Wednesday nights with Stuart, how Henry said to immerse myself in violin again, and how the only thing that would ever make me happy was going to be to play, and not just as a hobby but as if my life depended on it. It did.

"So, what?" Julia threw her hands up in the air. "You quit your job for some silly orchestra that isn't even going to pay you?"

"Yes," I said. "You know if it hadn't been for Hitler, I would've been in the symphony in Berlin. This would *be* my life."

"If it hadn't been for Hitler . . . a lot of things," Julia said, exasperated. I thought of her very short wedding, but then she said, lowering her voice so the boys wouldn't hear, "Friedrich's sisters would still be alive. They were both murdered in a camp, Hanna."

"I'm so sorry," I said. I hadn't known Friedrich's sisters well. They were twins, only two years older than me, and the three of us had been bridesmaids together in Julia and Friedrich's wedding. *Genevie and Aliza.* Thinking of them again now, *murdered,* I felt like I was going to be sick. And I didn't want to argue with Julia. Despite our differences, I was grateful to her for giving me a home here in London, grateful that we were both still here. "I have to play in the concert on Saturday," I said. "It might be the only concert I ever play in." Though even as I said it, I hoped that wasn't true. "And I'd really, really like you all to come hear me."

Julia put her head in her hands and sighed. "Oh, Hanna. Of course, we'll come hear you. We're your family." I blinked back tears — it might've been the kindest thing my sister had ever said to me. "But on Monday morning you're going back to the hospital and begging Mary for your job back."

178

Max, 1932

For a few months, everything felt perfect. It was as if Hanna had never told him she wanted a break or admitted that she would never be able to marry him because of her religion. Deep down, he knew that might probably still be true. Nothing had changed, not really. Hanna still kept the Sabbath with her mother and sister each Friday and Saturday. And Max still wasn't Jewish. But they didn't talk about it.

Hanna started taking the train to his shop a few nights a week, not just Saturdays. She told her mother and Julia she was attending practice for a small, made-up string quartet, and that since practice was over late, she was sleeping at the made-up cellist's house, and riding the train with her to school in the morning. Max guessed her mother and Julia likely knew the truth. But Hanna said if no one spoke it aloud, then it wasn't happening. *That's just the way my family works,* she said with a nonchalant shrug. And Max let it all go, happy that Hanna was here, with him.

Each time Hanna walked into his shop, it was like a light came with her. The bell chimed over the door when she walked in, and without even looking up, he would know immediately, it was her. He could feel her energy from across the room.

She'd often come in breathless, as if she'd run the entire way from the train, as if she couldn't wait to see him, as much as he couldn't wait to see her. She'd run up behind the counter and kiss him, and whether it had only been a few hours, or a few days, Max would pull her toward him, hold on to her, close his eyes, and just for a moment feel that everything was all right with the world.

Then he would close down the shop, and she would take out her violin and she would play. He knew she was practicing songs for school and for Herr Fruchtenwalder, but when she played there in his shop, it felt like she was giving a concert just for him. Playing love songs that only he got to hear.

After she practiced for a few hours, they'd go upstairs and eat a light supper together that he would prepare for her so she could rest her fingers. And then they'd get into his bed.

Every time they were together, every time he touched her warm skin, felt her naked body, he felt so much, he wanted so much. It was still so new and wonderful that it felt like the first time. But it also felt like they had been together forever. That their bodies knew each other, fit each other. He could barely remember that his life had existed without her, without this.

But then he would wake up sometimes in the middle of the night, Hanna's leg entwined with his, her sleeping soundly next to him. He would wake up in a sweat, breathing hard, and it would hit him all over again, all at once. *She was in danger, in another time.* They couldn't stay here like this forever, no matter how much he wanted to. The world would move on, time would move forward.

In November there was another election, and the Nazi Party vote shrunk from the previous spring. "See," Hanna told him pointedly when they heard the results come in on the radio. "You worry too much." He was still somewhat frequently telling her how concerned he was about the anti-Semitic sentiment in Germany, about Hitler

181

getting elected. About what that would mean for Hanna and her family.

But it was also getting easier and easier to believe that what he'd seen wasn't real. Easier to believe that he'd dreamed it or had simply drunk too much scotch or that time, in the closet, was no more than an illusion. Because the alternative was believing that his city, his country, his home would soon turn into something terrible, something beyond belief. A place where Hanna wasn't safe. That everything they had and knew, everything he loved, was about to be taken from him.

Life went on and on each day, as it always had: the seasons changed; he unlocked his shop each morning and smelled the aroma of Herr Feinstein baking bread next door; there was fresh fish on ice in the window of the *Fischmarkt* across the street. Emilia even started sleeping through the night, and Max grabbed an ale with Johann on Saturdays again before sundown, when Hanna came to see him.

Elsa and Johann invited them over for Christmas Day brunch, and though Hanna said she had never once celebrated Christmas before, Max bought her a present, a gold violin pin he'd seen in the window of the jeweler's, down the block. He wrapped it up neatly in silver foil with a green ribbon and had it waiting on the counter for her when she arrived that afternoon.

The bookshop was closed for the holiday, and the train was running on a slow and intermittent schedule. It was bitterly cold outside, but not snowing as he'd hoped it would. When Hanna arrived, she knocked against the locked door with a mittened hand. For once, she did not have her violin with her.

"You look incomplete," he teased her when he opened the door, kissed her cold forehead, and drew her into the warmth of the heated shop.

"Incomplete?"

"No violin."

She smiled, took off her hat and mittens, and placed them on the counter; her eyes caught on his silver-foil-wrapped box. "What's this?" she asked.

He pushed the box toward her. "Open it," he said.

"Oh, Max," she said, shaking her head a little.

"It's okay," he said. "You didn't have to get anything for me. And just so you know, it's not a Christmas present. It's a Hanukkah present." Max had never bought anyone a Hanukkah present before, but he knew the holiday was happening this week, too, that gifts were given and a menorah was lit. He imagined Frau Ginsberg and Julia and Friedrich and Hanna standing around the flames each night and he wanted Hanna to see that he could do that too. That he could be a part of her world and learn her religion if she wanted him to.

She laughed and put her hands into the pockets of her coat. "Well, actually I did get you something. Merry Christmas." She pulled her hands out, held them up, and showed him she was holding a thick cream-colored envelope. She handed it to him. "Julia and Friedrich are getting married in February." He took the envelope from her, opened it up. An invitation, to the wedding. For him? "I want you to come with me."

He hadn't seen her mother or her sister since that Sabbath dinner at their apartment last spring. And neither he nor Hanna had mentioned any words like *wedding, marriage,* or *family* lately. It was easier if it was only the two of them. If they pretended everyone and everything else didn't exist. "But won't your mother be upset?" he asked her, turning the invitation over in his hand. The wedding was at the Hotel Adlon, a beautiful historied hotel in Mitte, Berlin.

She shrugged. "I love you, and I want to bring you with me. Friedrich's family has money and they're making it into a grand affair. Dancing and champagne, and Friedrich's sisters are both bridesmaids with me and are both bringing dates. I'm going to bring one, too," she said, somewhat defiantly.

"Okay." He leaned over and kissed the top of her head. Then he took the silver-foiled box off the counter. "Now you open mine."

She unwrapped the ribbon slowly, precisely, her strong, small fingers undoing the bow, neatly undoing the wrapping paper. Then she opened the box underneath, saw the gold violin pin, and gasped a little. "Oh, Max," she said. "It's stunning." She took it out of the box, fastened it on the lapel of her dress. "What do you think?" she asked. He smiled. "I'll wear it always," she said.

HANNA, 1948

I used to have this exquisite gold violin pin that Max gave me. I'd wear it when I auditioned or when I performed, and I'd started to believe, however foolishly, that it gave me luck. That I needed it to do well. The superstition started a year or so after Max gave me the pin, the first time I auditioned for the symphony in Berlin. I didn't wear the pin to the audition, wanting to show up looking austere, dressed in black, no jewelry as Herr Fruchtenwalder suggested. Also, I was furious at Max then; I didn't want to wear a pin he'd given me, didn't want to think about him at all. I was focused on the audition. And then I completely blew it in a way I hadn't even imagined possible beforehand.

I'd played the Ravel piece that I'd insisted upon: *Tzigane.* I'd rehearsed it hundreds of times, maybe even thousands, perfectly. I knew it by heart. My fingers could move on the strings without the music, gliding through with muscle memory. And then in the middle of the audition, halfway through the piece, they fumbled. My fingers slipped off the fingerboard, I played a wrong note, and I did the worst possible thing: I stopped. I could've kept on going — one wrong note wasn't the end of the world. But I froze, opened my eyes, and could not for the life of me remember the next note or the next or the next. The sheet music sat in front of me on a stand, but I hadn't been following along — I'd been playing the music by memory. I couldn't place where I was, where exactly I'd stopped. I stood there on-stage completely silent. "Are you finished?" the maestro had asked, sounding surprised. And I honestly hadn't known what to do — I'd never messed up in that way before, and the only thing I could think to do was to run off the stage.

"It was the pin," I told Max later, as he'd brushed my tears back with his thumbs, trying to console me. I'd given my anger a rest and run to him after the audition because who else was going to comfort me and understand? Certainly not Julia, who hadn't wanted me to audition in the first place. I couldn't bear the thought of telling Mamele, imagining the disappointment would hurt her heart even more. Or Herr Fruchtenwalder. I had already begun concocting a lie in my head about there just being someone better there auditioning. "The pin brings me good luck. I should've worn it. Why didn't I wear it?" I'd moaned and rolled over in Max's bed. He'd stroked my back.

"It's going to be okay," he told me. "You will have another chance. There will be other auditions, other orchestras."

"Other orchestras?" I was incredulous. "There are no other orchestras worth playing in in Berlin. This is it. This is the symphony. I may as well just give up violin forever." My eyes hurt from crying, but other than that I felt numb. Everything I'd worked so hard for my entire life was gone. Just like that.

"You're not going to give up the violin." He moved his hand up, brushed my hair back. "I promise you, Hanna, there will be other auditions. Other orchestras." He was trying to be kind, trying to make me feel better. But what did he know? "And you can't give up," he'd told me. "You play the violin like fire, Hanna. You can't give up on your fire."

I thought of that night, Max's words, sitting

onstage with the Royal Symphony, waiting for the curtain to open. I didn't have my violin pin now, of course. God knows what happened to it when I didn't even know what happened to myself. I wore it the next time I auditioned for the symphony and it had brought me all the luck I'd needed; my audition had been perfect. But then of course no luck, no pin, could've stopped Hitler.

But somehow I had gotten here, without the pin. By chance or by luck. Or, as Max surely would've corrected me, by my own talent. My *fire*. How I wished Max could be here now, to see me on the stage, finally. I closed my eyes for a second and wished for him to bring me luck, wherever he may be.

The curtain opened, I held my violin under my chin. Maestro Philip raised his arms and my bow went into the air, ready to strike. I didn't look out into the audience for Julia and Friedrich and the boys, and I didn't look at my music, either. I had memorized it, practicing this week. When Maestro's arms went down, I closed my eyes again and I played.

"You were very good," Moritz told me after the concert was over. He handed me a bouquet of flowers that he proudly told me he had picked himself — albeit without his mother's permission — from their tiny backyard garden. Julia sighed as he handed them over to me. And I kissed him on the top of the head and thanked him.

"What did you think, Lev?" I asked.

"It was very . . . long?" Lev said. His voice was sweet, like he was searching for a compliment and couldn't quite find one.

"Yes." I kissed his head, too, and being a little older than Moritz, he squirmed away embarrassed.

"It was very nice," Julia said. She'd come without Friedrich, just her and the boys, and I didn't ask where he was. I didn't care. I was thrilled that the three of them had come to see me.

We began to walk toward home, and the boys skipped ahead of us. Julia and I hung back a little, and Julia linked her arm with mine. "You know, you looked beautiful up there," she said. That was hardly the point, and somewhat insulting. I didn't want to *look* beautiful onstage. I wanted to sound beautiful — I wanted people in the audience to hear me, not see me. But she was trying to be kind, and I thanked her.

We were having a nice moment, so rare for us, that I actually blurted out what I was thinking. "I wish Max had been here to see me. He always believed in me."

"Oh, Hanni." She opened her mouth like she wanted to say more but she didn't for a moment. We kept walking. "I know you loved him," she said. "I know you did. But you were so young. So much has happened since then."

Everyone kept telling me that. But it still didn't feel that way to me. "He could still be alive," I told her. "I am."

"Yes," Julia said. "But he could be married to someone else. He could be anywhere in the world. It's been twelve years since you remember seeing him last. Do you really think he's fixated on you like you are on him?"

I shrugged, not sure what to say. What was easier to believe, that he might be dead? Or that he might've forgotten about me, moved on?

"You would not be hard to find. He knew where I lived." Julia was still talking. "That hasn't changed in all this time." I swallowed hard, not wanting to admit out loud that Julia was right. So I didn't answer her. I looked straight ahead, let go of Julia's arm, and walked faster. Julia ran to keep up.

"Hanni, don't be angry," Julia said. "I just want you to move on. Be happy again."

"I am happy." I stopped walking and spun

to face her. "Today, playing with the orchestra. That's what makes me happy."

She nodded like she understood, though she never had. "But what kind of life is that, Hanni? You will play and play and play your violin, and then what will you have to show for it?" Her eyes wandered ahead of us to her boys, and though I loved my nephews with all my heart, I had no yearning for children of my own. Especially not without Max.

Later that night, I couldn't sleep. The music still played in my mind. I could feel it in my pulse, and my fingers twitched wanting more, wanting to play again. I didn't know when Stuart would return, and of course I wanted his mother to be okay, but now that I had a taste of playing again, doing what I always dreamed, I couldn't let it go, either.

There will be other orchestras, Max had promised me once. And he had been right.

You will play and play and play your violin, and then what will you have to show for it? Julia had said.

And it occurred to me for the first time that I did not have to stay in London. That I could leave and audition somewhere else. That an entire world was open to me. I had no one or nothing to hold me back. Except for maybe money.

But if I did what Julia wanted, begged Mary for my job back on Monday and continued saving my weekly salary? Eventually I'd have enough saved up to find another orchestra, to move somewhere else. And with that thought, I finally fell asleep.

Stuart telephoned Monday evening in the middle of supper, much to Julia's annoyance. Now that she knew the truth about where I'd been going on Wednesday nights, she didn't at all like the idea of me being alone with a *strange man in his flat.* I told her that there was nothing going on between Stuart and me, that it was purely about playing the violin, and that I would not betray Max that way. That had only made her frown more. *Still,* she'd said. *It's improper . . .* Sounding exactly like Mamele when she'd learned I was spending nights at Max's.

But I didn't wait for her to respond when Stuart's call came in on Monday. And I didn't even finish my meal before grabbing my violin and running to catch the tube to his apartment.

"How's your mum?" I asked when he answered the door.

He shrugged a little. "Not great," he said.

"She's quite weak and not remembering things so well. But my brother and his wife are nearby and they're making sure she takes her medicines, eats her supper, and all that."

"Well, it's good she has them." I'd had no idea that Stuart had a brother before he said that. I actually knew surprisingly little about Stuart, considering how many Wednesday nights we'd spent playing together, moments that had felt oddly intimate to me. But they had only given me the illusion that I'd known him. Playing a duet with someone was like that. In a way, it was almost like making love with a stranger.

"How did the performance go?" Stuart asked.

"Great," I said.

"That's what Maestro said too." I felt a little hurt that he'd asked Maestro first, as if he trusted his opinion more than mine. But then he added, "He said you can fill in anytime. For any of us."

"Oh, okay." The performance had gone well, but I was surprised about Maestro's enthusiasm, given his skepticism over a woman even auditioning for his orchestra just last year. I didn't want to fill in, of course. I wanted to play all the time, every day. But I supposed filling in was better than nothing . . . for now. I had begged Mary for my job back this morning, and she had said she'd give me another chance. Next time, she wouldn't. So I wasn't sure how feasible filling in would be anyway. "I want more than that," I admitted to Stuart. "I need more than that."

"I know," he said, kindly. "And you'll get it. I know you will." *There will be other orchestras.*

Stuart reached down and took his violin from his case. "Shall we play?" he asked.

I sat next to him, took my violin out of its case, too. We both closed our eyes, and we played for an hour together without saying another word.

MAX, 1933

January of the new year was very cold in Gutenstat, the winter a harsh one. And Max was spending more money on coal to heat the shop than he was bringing in from selling books.

Next door Herr Feinstein was having only a little bit better luck, as people needed bread much more than they needed books. Feinstein confided he'd had to lower his prices to attract enough customers, to keep his shop afloat; he said he was barely getting by. But from Max's viewpoint, the bakeshop looked busy. Some mornings Feinstein would even have a line out the door.

One morning near the middle of the month, Max was sitting behind the counter in his shop, reading a book, when he suddenly heard a large crash, the sound of breaking glass, and screams from the street. He stood up and ran outside. Shards of glass littered the sidewalk, a few in front of his shop, many more in front of Feinstein's, where there was a large gaping hole in the front glass window.

"What happened?" Max asked a stunned-looking man standing on the street.

"A brick just went flying through the window, straight out of nowhere," the man said. He held up his hands and backed away from the shop. "I'll get my bread in the city today." He walked away, and the rest of the line dispersed as well.

Feinstein walked out of the shop and surveyed the damage. Gutenstat was a safe place, and aside from the occasional theft or teenage prank, they had no crime to speak of like there was in Berlin. Max was too flummoxed for a moment to speak.

"Are you all right?" Max asked when he recovered. "Is anybody hurt?"

Feinstein shook his head. He held the brick up in his hand so Max could see. Someone had written on it, in black ink, *unmenschlich.* Subhuman. The message was quite clear. Whoever had thrown the brick didn't like that Feinstein and his family were Jewish. "Damn Nazis," Feinstein said. "Can you believe these little pishers?"

He sounded angry, and he had every right to be. Max recalled a flash of Herr Fein-

stein as he'd seen him in the future: terrified, sick over something awful that had
happened to his wife. He felt overwhelm-
ingly sad for his next-door neighbor. Herr
Feinstein had been friends with his father
since Max was a little boy, and they'd always
exchanged bread for books a few times a
month. Max had been doing the same, since
his father's death. "Have you ever thought
of leaving?" Max asked him. "You and Frau
Feinstein, packing up and going somewhere
else in Europe?"

Herr Feinstein looked down at his worn
black boots, then back up at Max. "I've
been running this shop for thirty-three
years," he said, his voice unwavering. "If
they think one little brick is going to drive
me out . . ."

It was more than one little brick. They
both knew it was. But Max held out his
hand. "Give it to me," he said. "I'll get rid
of it. And I'll get a broom, help you clean
up this mess."

They boarded up the window and Herr
Feinstein replaced the glass at the end of
the month. But that didn't change anything.
And as news of the brick spread through
Gutenstat, Feinstein's shop grew nearly as
empty as Max's in the weeks that followed.

Then came the news that Hindenburg had appointed Hitler as *Reichskanzler,* and Adolf Hitler was now officially the chancellor of Germany. The morning paper on the first day of February proclaimed that Nazis were celebrating in the streets. *"Machtergreifung"* — the headline read. "Seizure of Power." Though Max did not witness any such celebrations in Gutenstat. In fact, Hauptstrasse was empty, even more quiet than it had been.

Immediately after the so-called celebration, Hitler banned political demonstrations, and so it at least appeared that his seizure of power had gone off unprotested in Germany, that everyone supported him and what his party believed in. All the shops on Hauptstrasse were ordered to hang the Nazi flag bearing the horrible broken cross, and all the shopkeepers, Max included, obliged. Not because they wanted to, but because they were afraid not to.

"It's so ugly," Hanna whispered to him in bed late one night. "I hate seeing the stupid flag when I walk in your front door. I want to burn it."

Max kissed her head, pushed back her hair. "It doesn't mean anything," he said. Though he knew even as he said it that it was a lie. It meant everything.

■ ■ ■ ■

On Sunday, a small group of riots erupted in Berlin, and they heard on the radio that many people were injured; one person was even killed. But then at least they knew that the entire country hadn't gone insane. Flags outside or no, there were still many people who did not agree with Hitler, or the Nazis, even if they were mostly afraid to speak up.

"Unbelievable," Johann said, shaking his head, when Max met up with him on the following Saturday evening for an ale. "None of the lawyers like it." Johann had finally gotten his degree and had been hired on as a lawyer at a firm in the city. He shrugged. "I mean, it's disgusting to think this man and the people he stands with have power in our country."

Max agreed with everything Johann was saying, but Johann's worry sounded distant, on principle. "I'm very worried for Hanna," Max said, taking a swig of his ale.

"You want some legal advice?" Johann said. "You should marry her."

"Legal advice?" Max laughed. There was nothing he'd like more than to marry Hanna, but since that night when they'd almost ended everything, he hadn't brought this desire up again. Things were good between them now, and he'd rather have Hanna like he did now than not at all.

"No, I mean it," Johann said. "If things get much worse . . . she'd be better off as your wife, legally speaking. Married to a Christian man, with a Christian man's last name."

Max finished off the last of his ale and stood, clapping Johann on the shoulder. "Next week I'll have to cancel," he reminded him. "Speaking of marriage . . . it's Hanna's sister's wedding."

"Have a good time. Think about what I said, though, okay? I'm being completely serious, Max."

Max knew that he was, and he promised him he would take it to heart.

Hanna was already waiting for him in front of his shop when he got back. Sundown was early this time of year and he'd lingered a little too long with Johann. He didn't like the idea of Hanna waiting out on the dark street, all alone, and made a mental note that he would give her a key so that she could let herself in from now on if she needed to. Feinstein's glass window was fixed, but the police hadn't caught the person who'd thrown the brick. Max didn't think they'd tried very hard.

He unlocked the door, and Hanna entered in front of him, lighting the coal stove so she could warm herself. She shivered a little, and Max wrapped his arms around her, trying to warm her himself. He thought about what Johann had said, but he bit his tongue. Johann may be right, but it wasn't the time or the place or the way to ask her right now. Besides, he wanted to marry her because he loved her, and the next time he asked — and he would ask again — he wanted it to be special. Instead he asked her about Julia's wedding.

"Well, it's all going on as planned, if that's what you mean," Hanna said. "Julia and Friedrich aren't going to let some stupid man and his stupid horrible ideas stop them from getting married at the Adlon." Having a Jewish wedding at one of the fanciest hotels in Berlin felt almost ridiculously dangerous now, and Max was glad to have been invited, as he would've been worried sick about Hanna being there without him.

"And what about us?" Max said softly, kissing her shoulder. "What if you auditioned for an orchestra in Paris or Rome instead and we moved away from Berlin entirely?"

She laughed. "It's not that simple, silly.

I'm only getting this audition because the principal is about to retire *and* because Herr Fruchtenwalder knows the maestro and he'll put in a good word for me."

"But surely Herr Fruchtenwalder must know someone, somewhere else," Max said.

"He doesn't," Hanna said. "And besides, even if he did, I wouldn't go. Mamele is too sick to move anywhere, and I would never leave her."

He couldn't argue with that. If his mother were still alive, if she were sick, he would never want to leave her, either, no matter what was going on in Germany or what it might mean for his future. And the fact that Hanna loved her mother so much only made him love her more.

But no matter Johann's legal advice or what Max wanted, he also knew deep down that Hanna would never agree to marry him while her mother was still alive.

HANNA, 1948

I told myself I would leave London, audition elsewhere, but so far it was proving impossible. I'd written letters to the maestros of ten different orchestras, in ten different cities in Europe, and had yet to receive even one reply. Never mind having the money saved up to leave London and start over somewhere else. If I couldn't even get an audition, then what would it matter? Stuart said that some orchestras weren't even functioning fully yet after the war, that recovery had been quite slow all through Europe, and he was sure that was why I was having trouble. And maybe he was right.

It was strange, but now that I barely met with Henry any longer, I kept forgetting about the war. It was still obvious everywhere you walked in London, so many damaged buildings, and there were still the food shortages and rations, so that most of what we ate was for sustenance, not for taste, without enough sugar or eggs. Even clothing was still rationed, so the few dresses I had were old ones of Julia's. But I couldn't remember any of the war, so all this became my normal. In my mind it was almost as if it had never happened, as if London had always been broken this way. Food had always tasted bland. And every time someone else brought the war up, it shocked me all over again.

"Guess what, Tante?" Moritz said at supper one Wednesday night in June. I hadn't been paying attention to the table conversation, my mind already in Stuart's apartment, thinking about the music we would play through together later tonight. It was only Julia and me and the boys tonight. Friedrich was working late, as he had been doing more and more lately.

"Mmm, what?" I murmured. I took a bite of my biscuit, and it tasted stale, though I supposed I was lucky to have one at all. That's what Julia told the boys, that we were the lucky ones, with enough money to live so nicely these days.

"Did you know the Olympics are coming to London next month? The first games since I was born. Mummy says we can go!"

"I said *maybe* we can go," Julia said. "If

the tickets aren't too expensive."

If there was anything Julia cared less about than music, it was athletic competitions, and I bit my lip to keep from laughing. In 1936 the Olympics were in Berlin. But even if Moritz had been alive, he wouldn't have been able to go, as a Jew, of course. Max's friends Johann and Elsa had gotten tickets from Johann's law firm, and Max and I had watched Emilia and Grace while they went. For a second, the memory swept me up: Max kissing my cheek, just near my ear, as we sat on the couch in Johann and Elsa's small house, having just put the kids to bed. We'd talked about how maybe we would have two little girls of our own one day. How we could take them to the Olympics the next time they came to Germany, when everything went back to normal, the way it used to be. I had still firmly believed it would, that someone would stop Hitler before it got any worse.

"I'll take them," I said to Julia now. "If the tickets aren't too expensive and you want to buy them. I wouldn't mind going myself." Julia shrugged to say, *Suit yourself.* She'd left Berlin before 1936, so she didn't remember like I did what it was like not to be allowed to go.

"Thank you, Tante." Moritz squeezed my arm and even Lev smiled enthusiastically.

I was still feeling pretty good about my nephews' excitement as I got off the tube and walked toward Stuart's flat. And at first I didn't notice that he looked upset when he opened the door to let me in.

"Have you heard about the Olympics?" I asked Stuart, sitting down, taking out my violin. It was a silly question. Of course he had. You couldn't walk down the street without hearing someone talking about it. But Stuart didn't answer, and he didn't sit down next to me either. That's when I looked up and saw his face. He was very pale. "Are you all right?" I asked him. "Is it your mother?"

He shook his head, sat down next to me, and didn't say anything for a moment. Then he held up his left hand, slowly extended his fingers, but his ring finger stayed bent and didn't move at all. "It's frozen like that," he said. "I haven't been able to move it all day. I had to leave rehearsal."

"Did you go to see a doctor?" I asked.

Stuart shook his head. "I hate doctors."

He still held his hand in the air. I rested my violin in its case and took his hand in mine. I stroked his palm gently, ran my forefinger over his bent finger. "Does it hurt?" I asked, wondering if he injured it somehow.

"No, it doesn't hurt at all. I just can't make it move." Panic rose in his voice, and his hand tensed up in mine. I kneaded his palm softly with my fingers until his hand relaxed again. But his ring finger stayed bent.

"I'm sure it's nothing," I said. "You overused it this week. Practiced too hard. Injured it a little."

"Do you really think so?"

I was no doctor, and nothing like this had ever happened to me, no matter how hard or long I'd practiced. My fingers swelled or ached sometimes; I iced them, had soaked them in a hot tub of water warmed over the coal stove in Max's shop. But never something like this. "I do think so," I said, trying to reassure him. I could feel his alarm, a clamminess on his skin, and see the pallor on his face. "But I do think it also couldn't hurt to see a doctor. You could come into the hospital tomorrow morning and I could get my brother-in-law to set you up with someone good." I didn't actually know if Friedrich would do this for me or not, but I was pretty sure Henry Childs would.

Stuart wouldn't meet my eyes. "The violin

is everything to me," he said. "Who would I be if I couldn't play?"

I understood Stuart so completely in that moment; I ached for him, a physical pang in my chest. "I promise you that's not going to happen," I said, though I had no right to promise him any such thing.

He looked up, smiled a half smile. He put his good hand on my arm. "Will you sit with me for a little while, even though I can't play tonight?"

"Of course," I said.

"You're the only one who understands," he said softly, moving his hand from my arm, to my face, stroking my cheek with his thumb. "The only one," he repeated.

It wasn't until he leaned his face in, until his lips were almost on mine that I realized what he was doing. I heard myself gasp a little, and then his lips touched mine, softly, slowly. I knew that I should pull away, but for a moment, I didn't. I kissed him back. He felt nothing like Max. Kissing Stuart was like eating a slice of Black Forest cake, sweet and rich and satisfying. But kissing Max was like dancing too close to the fire. *Max . . . oh God, Max.* What was I doing?

I abruptly pulled back, dropped Stuart's hand, put my hand to my lips. "I can't," I said. Stuart tilted his head to the side, confused. It wasn't his fault. I'd never told him about my past, never told him about Max. "There's someone else. I'm in love with someone else," I said.

Stuart's mouth dropped open, surprised. "I'm so very sorry," he said. And for a second I thought he meant he was sorry that I had someone else. And then I realized he meant he was sorry that he kissed me. I didn't want him to be. I stood up, hastily packed up my violin. "I have to go," I said.

"Hanna, wait," he called after me. His voice sounded so forlorn, and oh, his poor bent finger, and I'd promised I'd sit with him. But I felt sick. I'd kissed him. *I'd wanted to kiss him.* It was a betrayal to Max, and to myself, and I was angry, and at the same time I wanted to kiss him again.

"Just come find me at the hospital tomorrow morning," I called as I ran out. "I'm on the third floor."

I couldn't breathe until I reached the street, and even then I was sweating, breathing hard as if I'd just been running for miles and miles.

MAX, 1933

On the evening of Julia's wedding, Max took the train the hour into Berlin. He was meeting Hanna and her family there at the Adlon, as Hanna said they needed to be at the hotel early to get dressed and set up. It had been a while since he'd been into the city. He expected it to look different, to feel different somehow, now that Hitler was chancellor. It had been only two weeks since riots erupted on a Sunday and many Jews were injured — a Communist was even killed. But when Max stepped off the train, the city was as it always had been — busy. Well-dressed men and women sat inside glass-windowed cafés enjoying Saturday night dates; the streets were crowded with cars and taxicabs, the sidewalks with people bundled in coats, talking, laughing even. Everything appeared oddly the same; everything felt shockingly normal, except for the Nazi flags hanging up in the storefronts.

He crossed through the Brandenburg Gate, onto Unter den Linden. The Adlon, up ahead, was aglow and bustling; the cigar peddler out front had a line of men waiting to buy a Saturday night treat. The hotel itself had been named for Kaiser Adlon who had been such a monarchist that he didn't believe any cars would ever cross here but his and thus didn't look when crossing the street. That resulted in him being hit by a car in this exact spot, twice, a few years apart, the second time killing him. But the hotel, and his name, lived on right here. And even though Germany had changed, the politics had changed, Berlin had changed, it all looked just exactly the same as it always had.

Max looked both ways before crossing the street, always remembering the cautionary tale his father had told him about Kaiser Adlon whenever he stood in this exact spot, and then walked inside the hotel.

Hanna was waiting for him inside the sweeping lobby. He noticed her before she saw him, and he stopped for a moment just to look at her. She was stunning. Even more than usual. She wore a lilac dress, and her hair down, which she hardly ever did, the curls like waterfalls over her shoulders. She turned, saw him, and her face lit up into a smile. God, she was beautiful. "Max, over here." She waved, and he walked toward her, swept her up in a hug. She laughed as her feet lifted off the ground, and he went in to kiss her cheek. "Don't mess up my makeup," she said, pulling back just as his lips were about to touch her skin. "Julia will kill me."

He'd never heard Hanna mention her makeup before, but he didn't want Julia to get mad, so he reluctantly let her go, kissing her only gently on the hand instead. After the riots, he'd wanted to reserve a room at the hotel for them to stay the night, not liking the idea of Hanna out in Berlin, making her way back to the train and home in Gutenstat so late after the wedding. But Hanna had said no, that someone would have to make sure her mother got home safely. And besides, she said, *Mamele would have a fit if I were staying in a hotel room with you, and there'd be no fibbing about that one.*

"Come on!" Hanna grabbed his arm. "Come get a seat in the drawing room for the ceremony. I have to go back and walk out with Julia." She squeezed his hand and ushered him through a door to a room with a sign that said GINSBERG/WEINER WEDDING. "I'll find you after the ceremony," she said, touching his arm lightly, and then she disappeared to rejoin Julia.

Rows and rows of chairs were set up, many of them already filled, and he didn't know a single soul in the room, so he sat toward the back. As he looked around, all the men were wearing those flat little pancake hats that he had seen Jews wearing walking out of the temple in Gutenstat on Saturdays. The fact that he was out of place here felt even more obvious, as he did not have a hat. All the unfamiliar eyes rested on his head, then the guests seemed to frown, collectively.

But then the door to the room opened, and all eyes turned toward the back. The room was completely silent as Julia walked in on Hanna's and Frau Ginsberg's arms. Everyone was watching the bride. But if someone had asked Max later what Julia had looked like at her wedding, he would not have been able to say. His eyes went to Hanna, only to Hanna. She smiled at him as she walked by his row, and he imagined how it might feel if she were walking down the aisle toward him, to marry him.

After the ceremony, the guests moved to the winter-garden hall, crowded with tables and flowers, drinks and dinner and dancing. And Max found Hanna again. She stood on her tiptoes and kissed him fully on the mouth, with all the passion she normally reserved for when they were alone. She was holding a half-empty glass of champagne, and she was no longer worried about her makeup or how scandalous they might appear. He was completely sober, but he couldn't help himself; he kissed her back, a long, slow, deep kiss. The band stopped, and then they began a new, slower song.

"Dance with me," she said, impulsively, finishing off her champagne, putting the empty flute down on a table. She held out her hand, and Max took it. Maybe it was the alcohol; maybe it was the energy of the wedding, but Hanna didn't seem to care what anyone else in the room thought, who saw the two of them together. So he wasn't Jewish and she was. So what? They loved each other. They were going to be together.

He allowed himself to be pulled onto the dance floor, and he took Hanna in his arms, leaned his chin on top of her curls, and they swayed together to the music, as the band played.

"The trumpet is flat," Hanna whispered to him, and she giggled a little, amused. He heard only a slow dance song that allowed him to hold her close, in public. She heard the actual music.

Frau Ginsberg sat at a table at the edge of the dance floor, watching them dancing, frowning. But Max looked away, closed his eyes, and breathed in the lemon scent of Hanna's hair.

He could've danced with Hanna forever, held on to Hanna forever. But after two songs like that, the music abruptly stopped. He opened his eyes; Hanna took a step back. People murmured and looked around. A gentleman in a suit was standing by the five-piece band, talking to them, and then he turned and raised his arms, faced the wedding guests. "I'm sorry," he said. "We will have to end early tonight."

"Early?" Friedrich's father, whom Max had never met, but who had walked Friedrich up to the altar along with his mother earlier at the ceremony, pushed his way through the crowd. "But I have paid for the room until midnight."

"I'm sorry," the man said again. "Some guests have been complaining about the noise."

"The noise?" Hanna whispered, her hands on her hips now, incredulous. It was ridiculous. All weddings made the noise of music, chatter, and dancing. It wasn't *the noise.* Every single person in the room knew it wasn't the noise, and the room grew so quiet, it was almost laughable they were talking about noise. Just then Frau Ginsberg coughed, and the sound echoed so loudly it felt painful to hear.

"But I have paid for the whole night," Herr Weiner tried again.

The man shrugged, turned back toward the crowd. "I'd appreciate you all leaving without disturbing the other guests. I don't want to have to call the police."

The police? To a wedding? Max thought of the riots that had happened just two weeks earlier, how the police had injured and killed those speaking up, like it was nothing. But this was different. This wasn't a riot. It was a wedding, for heaven's sake.

But at that, the man walked out of the room, ignoring Herr Weiner's continued protests. The guests looked at one another for a moment, as if they weren't quite sure what to do. Then one couple walked out, followed by another, and another, until the room was almost empty.

Julia was standing just across the dance floor from them, and now she was crying, Friedrich holding on to her shoulders. *"Scheisse,"* Hanna cursed under her breath, let go of Max's hand, and ran to her sister. Frau Ginsberg continued to cough, louder and harder, the spasms shaking her entire body.

Max went to Frau Ginsberg, and she somehow managed to glare at him, even through coughs. But he sat down next to her, anyway, handed her a glass of water from the table. She took it, sipped it slowly, and her coughs began to subside.

"I know you don't like me," he said to her. "But we both want the same thing, you and I, for your daughter to be happy and safe."

Frau Ginsberg didn't say anything for a moment, took another sip of water. Then she said, "Will you walk us home? I don't like the streets after dark without a man. I tell Hannalie that all the time, and yet she insists on taking the trains to see friends and play in orchestras late at night."

Max knew exactly what she was saying, that if he wanted Hanna to be safe, he wouldn't want her to come see him, to come be with him at night. But he didn't want to argue with her. He held out his arm to help her up. "Of course I'll walk you home," he said.

On the way out, Max saw the sign that he'd noticed at first walking in: GINSBERG/ WEINER WEDDING. Only someone had, during the ceremony or during the shortest wedding party ever, defaced it. The slash between the names had been turned into a Nazi Hakenkreuz in bright blue ink.

The three of them walked out onto the street, and the night somehow was still bustling. The entire breath of the city moved on, oblivious and uncaring to what it had taken.

Two days later their parliament building, the Reichstag, was set on fire by an arsonist, Communists trying to overthrow the government. And by Tuesday, Chancellor Hitler passed new laws suspending freedom of expression, freedom of press, the right to public assembly, the secrecy of post and telephone. The papers called the fire a great act of terrorism against Germans and claimed that Hitler's Reichstag Fire Decree, giving the government more powers to arrest and incarcerate and suppress, would keep them all safe.

And then Hanna rode the train to his shop after her lesson at the Lyceum. She walked inside, holding her violin, just as she always had.

He hadn't seen her since he'd walked her home from the wedding, and somehow their entire world had changed since then. Germany had changed. The Parliament had burned and Hitler had taken away so many of their freedoms, *to keep them all safe.* The injustice of it all made his stomach roil.

He opened his mouth to speak to Hanna about it, but she put her finger to her lips, took her violin out of her case, and began to play, to practice as she always had. The sound of her violin floated through the air of his shop, passionate, fierce, angry: her music expressing everything she felt.

There was still music, he thought. *And they still had each other.*

Hanna, 1948

Stuart's finger did not improve, not even after seeing three different doctors at the hospital whom Henry connected us with. None of them agreed on a diagnosis or whether his ailment would be permanent or temporary. The third doctor suggested more tests — perhaps it was a rare form of arthritis? — but Stuart told me he didn't want any more tests.

"What's the point?" he said, sounding completely defeated. "Who cares *why* it's happening? It's happening, and I can't play."

"But if they figured out why," I said, "maybe they could fix it?" My voice faltered a little because I didn't really believe the words, even as I said them. Neither Henry Childs nor Herr Doctor in Berlin had been able to *fix* me, after all. My memory of those ten years was still completely blank; my faith in doctors was not very strong these days. Of course, Stuart didn't know about any of that, and when I considered it, I felt worse for Stuart than myself. At least I could still play; at least I still had my violin. Music was breath, and life, and joy. My future. Without it who would I be?

In one stroke of luck, Stuart's ailment coincided with the orchestra's summer break, so he was not expected back at rehearsal until September. But as the summer went on, he became increasingly frustrated and more certain that he would have to tell Maestro Philip that he would need to fill his seat.

Of course, it did occur to me, if Stuart couldn't play, that maybe Maestro would offer the seat to me. It's not at all how I wanted to join the orchestra. I genuinely wanted Stuart to heal; he was my closest friend, after all. And I did everything I could to cheer him up, still showing up at his apartment every Wednesday night, though after a few weeks I stopped bringing my violin. Instead I brought cakes that I'd bake with the boys in the afternoons after they got home from summer camp, and I'd sit with him and we'd listen to records. Stuart had a nice collection of European orchestra recordings, all prewar, as even now, many of the orchestras had just gotten back together, just started recording again. I was both relieved and disappointed that he had nothing in his collection from Berlin. But maybe it was for the best. I was already still in prewar Berlin in my mind; I wasn't sure I could bear to listen to the music from there, too. Or face all the emotions, the longings for a different life, that I knew that music might conjure in me.

After that one time, Stuart did not try to kiss me again. We sat there listening to music together in his flat, only as friends, never touching. When I would think about it sometimes later, when I was back in my bed at Julia's, in the dark, I would feel both relieved and disappointed about that, too.

In the beginning of August, Lev, Moritz, and I had tickets to watch the Olympic sprinters, and, boy, were we cheering for Fanny Blankers-Koen, the "Flying Housewife" from Holland, who could run so fast that people almost forgot she was a thirty-year-old mother of two. I stood up and screamed with my nephews, and for just the smallest moment, I had a glimpse of Max, sitting with me on Johann and Elsa's couch in Gutenstat, praying that by the next Olympics, everything would be different. And oh, how it was.

But I pushed the thought away, not wanting to be lost in old memories, wanting to enjoy my time making new memories with Lev and Moritz. And I did. By the time we left, I was hoarse from cheering so loud.

"She's quite fast for a girl," Lev said contemplatively as we made our way home on the tube after watching Fanny win a gold medal.

"She's quite fast, period," I told him. "I'd like to see *you* run that fast." Moritz laughed, picturing his older brother racing a woman and losing, no doubt. "Girls can do everything boys can, and sometimes better," I told them. And as I said it, I felt heat rising on the back of my neck. Was I really talking about the Flying Housewife now, or was I talking about myself, playing the violin?

"We already know that," Lev said, matter-of-factly.

"Of course you do." I ruffled his hair a little, and he pulled away, embarrassed. "You are going to make a great husband someday," I told him, and he began to blush.

"Tante, stop," he begged me.

Moritz broke into a hysterical fit of giggles, imagining his older brother as someone's husband.

As we got off the tube and walked back to Julia's I thought about how lucky they were, to have been born in England, to be living now, after the war, where you didn't have to be afraid to be Jewish, and everything was being rebuilt, not destroyed. How they would have the opportunity to be anything they wanted to be. Maybe I was lucky too. If Fanny could win a gold medal in the Olympics, while being thirty and having children, then why couldn't I get a job with an orchestra somewhere? There was still time for me yet.

I arrived at Stuart's the next evening with a plate full of lopsided cookies Moritz and Lev and I had baked, excited to tell him about Fanny, and all the energy and noise of the crowd cheering for her. Our baking was not the best, neither in appearance nor taste, which I blamed on the rations still. In Germany, I'd baked with so much more sugar and eggs, and here it was hard to know what I was doing with the ingredients we could get. But Stuart hadn't noticed, or at least hadn't complained.

I forgot about the cookies I brought when Stuart opened the door for me. All his furniture was gone. The room was completely empty. And I gasped. "Have you been robbed?"

"Robbed?" Stuart shook his head sadly,

took my plate of cookies with his good hand, and placed them on the counter. "No, Hanna, I'm moving back to Wales for a while. I need a break from the city, from . . . life. I should've told you last week, but I couldn't bring myself to say it out loud yet."

"You're not giving up," I insisted, trying not to stare at his awkwardly bent finger. I knew how badly Stuart wanted to play, how badly he wanted to make his fingers move as they always had. It wasn't his fault he couldn't. "Maybe you just need to give it more time?"

"I will," he said, sadly. "But not here." He looked at me; our eyes locked and he opened his mouth to speak, then hesitated. "I mean it would be different if you and I were . . . but you're . . ." I nodded, understanding what he was trying to say. Stuart and I were just friends, connected by the violin, and now that he couldn't play, what did we have? Even if our friendship transcended playing violin together, I was not a reason for him to stay. Still, I didn't want him to leave. "I let Maestro know yesterday," he said. "I suggested you as my replacement."

"Oh, Stuart," I said.

"I don't know if he'll listen to me. He should. But Maestro Philip doesn't appreciate passion as much as he appreciates technique," Stuart said.

The truth was, and we both knew it, Maestro still probably would not want a woman in his orchestra, and certainly not in a permanent position, and as first chair violin. Not that I wasn't going to go speak to him first thing tomorrow — I was. But you could not draw blood from a turnip as Julia was fond of saying.

I leaned against the wall and put my head in my hands. Stuart was leaving and with him my best chance at playing violin on any regular basis in London. But, of course, that wasn't the only thing that upset me. I was going to miss seeing him every week; there were few people who understood me like Stuart. "You'll come back, though?" I finally said. "When your hand is better."

Stuart pressed his lips tightly together and didn't respond at first. "I'll write," he said. "You'll write me back?" He held out his good hand to shake mine, but instead I impulsively grabbed him in a hug. He didn't move for a moment, but then he hugged me back, just briefly, before he pulled away. "Don't give up, okay?" he said. "You have a true gift."

I felt so heavy as I walked out of Stuart's flat for the last time. I had lost so many things, and those losses had become a part of me. Who I was. Playing the violin was who I would still become, who I would always be. Or at least, I hoped. My weekly playing time with Stuart had kept that hope burning inside of me, had kept me alive.

Outside it was dark and the air was sticky, wet. There were raindrops hitting my cheeks, as I walked toward the tube, or maybe they were tears.

MAX, 1933

The wildflowers bloomed in the long fields that stretched between Gutenstat and Berlin, a blur of yellow and orange and pink outside the train window, like every spring before it. But Germany was changing fast; it was hard to keep up with the news, hard to understand how springtime looked exactly as it always had when everything else was different.

Max became obsessed with reading the papers each morning in his shop, trying to digest everything that occurred. And each day he kept a record of what was happening, reading the newspapers in the morning, listening to the radio broadcasts at night, then writing it all down in a notebook, as if it might be evidence he would present to Hanna at a later date, to convince her how dangerous Germany was truly getting.

The Nazi Party was winning a majority now, taking almost three hundred seats in

Parliament in the March election, and Hitler had pushed through a new amendment to the Weimar Constitution, the Enabling Act, that decreed him dictator for the next four years. A special court was set up to deal with political dissidents, and people who opposed Hitler's Reichstag could be sent to a prison camp, just opened in Dachau. Max wrote this all down in his notebook, his list growing longer and longer by the day.

Everyone else around him took a different tact, though — they ignored it. Elsa and Johann had Emilia to worry about. And Johann began working longer hours at the law firm after some of the Jewish lawyers had been let go. And Hanna said she didn't have time to worry about the things she couldn't change, that politics would be politics. Her mother was growing sicker; she had her biggest audition coming up in just a few months. *And besides,* she would say, what did it matter for them if they just kept quiet and continued about their normal lives? It seemed to Max that Hanna, and everyone around him, was in a strange sort of denial. As if they believed Hitler and the growing anti-Semitism would simply fade away if they all kept quiet, ignored it, and went about their daily lives.

And that is what everyone did. Each morning the shops on Hauptstrasse opened and closed as they always had. Sometimes, people came into his shop in search of books, and the only difference was, now if they saluted him with the *Hitlergruss* when they walked in, Max was sure to salute back, as he had heard rumors of the SA beating up some shopkeepers who refused. Feinstein still had a line for bread, albeit a little shorter than it once had been. Even as the jeweler down the block hung a sign in the window that Jews were no longer welcome there, most people in Gutenstat still wanted Feinstein's bread. Their country was being dismantled, day by day, piece by piece, and yet life still mostly moved like it always had.

But Max could not forget what he'd seen when he'd gone into the closet, the flashes of memory returning to him time after time. He felt this incessant need to pay attention, to look closely, keep track of everything, so that if or when it came time, he would be there to save Hanna. He would change the future he saw for her and protect her.

In April the SA declared a boycott of all Jewish shops and businesses, and Max thought for sure everyone else around him would finally take notice.

"Hitler can say whatever he wants," Elsa said, sounding more flabbergasted than alarmed. "But I've always bought my bread from Feinstein. Where else would I get it from?"

And most people agreed with Elsa. The boycott only lasted one day because the German citizens, the people Max had known all his life, did not want to follow such a thing.

"See," Hanna said to him, the following evening. "We're still more powerful than one man. Us Germans are not going to let anything terrible happen like you keep saying."

Then she tucked her violin under her chin and she closed her eyes and played. The music echoed through his shop in a way that felt natural now. When Hanna wasn't there, the shop was too quiet; he missed the sound of her music, almost as much as he missed her.

"How's Frau Feinstein?" Max asked Herr Feinstein when he walked outside to unlock his shop the next morning, and Feinstein was out front of his own shop, sweeping the sidewalk. Max asked after Frau Feinstein every time he saw Herr Feinstein on Hauptstrasse these days, a question that Feinstein always seemed puzzled by from his slight frown in response. Max had known the Feinsteins since he was a young boy, and he had never thought to ask after Frau Feinstein before he had glimpsed a future where something terrible had happened to her.

"She's well. Very good," Feinstein said now, sweeping. "But me? My sciatica is acting up." He stopped sweeping for a moment, put his hands on top of his broom, and looked around. "And I will tell you, Maxwell, I'm too old for this."

Max couldn't tell whether he was talking about his sciatic pain or about Hitler. Though technically they were supposed to, neither one of them had moved to salute the other. "You could close the shop," Max suggested. "Retire. Maybe leave Germany?"

"And why would I leave Germany?" Feinstein arched his eyebrows. "I was born in Germany. I've lived my whole life in Germany. I'm a German."

Max understood; he felt the same way. It was hard to imagine leaving everything he'd ever known, leaving his country. Why should they have to go? It was their home. But he didn't know how much longer staying would truly be an option for any of them either.

Herr Feinstein stopped sweeping and clapped Max gently on the shoulder. "Let me get you a loaf of bread, *mein Junge,*" he said kindly, just as he had so many other mornings. The gesture was so fatherly, and it suddenly made Max long for his own father. If only his father were still here, he could help Max sort out everything happening in Germany, help convince Feinstein and everyone around them to take the growing threats seriously.

But when Feinstein handed him the bread, what else was there for Max to do now but take it and return to his shop, alone? And life moved on still, just as it always had.

In May Hanna had a recital in Berlin with a quartet group she played with at the Lyceum. It was a concert in the public square to celebrate springtime, the coming of summer, and the end of the term at the Lyceum. Several student groups had been invited to play. Hanna had played in it the year before also, but Max hadn't thought twice about it then. This year he worried. Universities had begun firing Jewish professors, but so far Hanna's teacher had escaped being let go at the Lyceum because of his rare talent. It was not the same as a professor of mathematics or science, Hanna said, who seemed to be more easily replaceable. Herr Fruchtenwalder could not be replaced, and even Hitler cared about music.

"It's like you want to invite trouble in," Max said to her, as she tried to dismiss his concerns about the night concert in the city. This May was not the same as last May. Four students, two of them Jewish, playing in the public square, after dark? He couldn't imagine them being well received.

"Playing is inviting trouble? Oh, Max, really." Hanna sighed.

He tried to wrap his arms around her, hold on to her in a hug, as if his body could make her understand more than his words could.

But she shrugged away. "Music is different. No one cares if you're Jewish or anything else. They only care what you sound like. And I need to practice."

The train was crowded, almost buzzing, as Max got on to ride it into Berlin the next evening. There was something palpable in the air, a current of excitement. He took his seat, and then as he looked around, he noticed something odd. Almost everyone was carrying books, and not just one book, but stacks of them. Where had people gotten so many books? Not his shop, certainly.

"What's going on?" Max asked the man in the seat next to him, who had four books in his lap: H. G. Wells, Hemingway, John Dos Passos, and Heinrich Heine, all of which Max had read and sold in his shop.

"We're lighting them up." The man laughed, excited.

"Lighting them up?" Max pictured a stack of books illuminated, aglow in the street-lamps. But he knew from experience, people had not been that interested in books since 1929, before the market crashed in America, setting off an economic ripple all throughout the world. It didn't make any sense.

"There's going to be a big bonfire at the Opernplatz," the man said. "We're going to burn all the anti-German books."

Burn them? Books were treasures, his entire life and work. How could they be burning them?

Hanna's quartet was supposed to play not too far from the Opernplatz. His fear for her was not imagined, as she kept insisting, and not something far off in the future, either, but real. Right here. Here were these men, amped up at the idea of destroying ideas, stories. Beautiful books. They'd think nothing of doing the same with music, or hurting people making music. Max felt sure of it.

"You're welcome to come," the man said. "Doesn't matter if you haven't brought any with you. I hear they already brought the entire library from the Institut für Sexualwissenschaft out into the square. There'll be plenty for everyone." He stared at Max expectantly, as if waiting for him to say thank you for the generous invitation.

"I-I-I can't," Max stammered. "I have other plans tonight."

"Ah, well suit yourself then." He eyed Max up and down. "You're not a Commie, are you? Or a Jew?" As if his lack of eagerness to participate in burning books made him either one, or both.

"No," Max said. "I just . . . have other plans," he repeated. Then added, hoping to shut him up, "With my *Freundin*."

For a little while it did, until the train stopped in Berlin and they both stood to get off. "You know, you can bring her if you want," he said to Max. "It's a good night to be a German. You wouldn't want to miss it."

Max just nodded, as if he'd take it under consideration. The man saluted him with the *Hitlergruss* and Max saluted back. As he got off the train, the night air was warm, and the scent of diesel filled his lungs, and for a few moments he just stood there, unable to catch his breath.

When he did, he started running toward

the concert, which would be held outside, in the square just south of the Opernplatz. He could already see the smoke from the fire in the distance, and he wanted to cry. All those precious books going up in flames, all those awful people cheering it on.

He reached the square, and Hanna was standing with the other three members of her group, her violin in her hand, her back to him. Though there were chairs set up for a large crowd, only a few were filled.

"Hanna." He was out of breath, sweating from running so hard. He grabbed her arm, and he felt better once he touched her, as if by holding her, he could keep her safe.

She spun around, and she smiled. "You came!"

"You can't play tonight. We have to go."

"What? Max . . . ?" Her face turned; now she was annoyed. And she pulled out of his grasp.

"They're burning books in the Opern-platz. A lot of books."

She glanced off into the distance. "So that's where the smoke is coming from." She turned back to him, her face softened a little. "I know how much you love books."

It wasn't about the books. It was about their sheer delight, the number of people wanting to burn them, the horrifying energy

238

of the men on the train. And only because what, they believed some books to be *anti-German*? What else did they think was anti-German? Music, played by a beautiful Jewish woman?

"I can't just leave them here in the lurch." Hanna motioned with her head to the other three members of her quartet.

"You could cancel the concert," Max said. "It's not safe for any of you, and there's barely anyone here to listen."

"We have to play," she said. She jutted out her chin, put her hands on her hips, but her voice trembled a little as she spoke. "None of us will pass Chamber Quartet if we don't."

"Hanna, I'm sure your teacher will understand." He reached for her again, but she pulled away.

"Max, stop. I have to get ready. If you want to listen to the concert, then have a seat. I'll find you after. If you're so worried, then go home." She turned and walked off to go stand with the other three members of her group. There was no way he was leaving, so what else could he do now but take a seat?

The quartet began to play, and instead of closing his eyes, listening, enjoying the music as he normally would've, he could barely concentrate on it; as his heart pounded against his chest, adrenaline pumped through his veins. In the distance the noise of a crowd yelling, cheering, grew louder and louder. The quartet seemed to get softer and softer. The smell of smoke filled his lungs.

In Berlin tonight, all the beautiful books were burning; all the beautiful music was dying.

This is not my country, he thought. *This is not my Germany.*

Later that night, the acrid smoke still burning his lungs, Max exhaled loudly, relieved after walking Hanna safely home to her apartment. The train back to Hauptstrasse was quiet. Books were still burning in Berlin, and the men who'd rode the train out with him were still there celebrating.

When he got back to his shop, he looked around, running his hands across the shelves. How many of these would those men consider anti-German? He had English books. Books by Jewish authors. Books by American authors. His eyes lingered on a copy of *Buch der Lieder* by Heinrich Heine, the same book that the man on the train had been holding.

And then he remembered a play Heine

had written that his father had given him to read as a teenager. He couldn't remember the name, or even much of what the play was about, but he remembered a line that had chilled him even then, when he'd read it. He'd underlined it and showed it to Johann:

Where they burn books, Heine had written, *they will, in the end, burn human beings too.*

HANNA, 1948–1949

The new orchestra season began in September, and I was still not a part of it. Maestro Philip moved the second chair violin, Charles, into Stuart's old seat, and then rather than holding auditions for Charles's seat, he offered it to a man who'd had it before the war and who'd been recovering from his injuries for the past few years. He'd lost his right leg, below the knee, but he had a fake one now, and he was ready to play violin again.

"You are number one on my substitute list, Hanna," Maestro told me when I went to inquire about the seat, and inwardly I'd wanted to scream. I didn't want to be a substitute, a stand-in. I didn't want to be a sometimes violinist, only when the orchestra needed someone in a pinch. I wanted the violin to be my job, my entire life. I wanted my own seat.

I wrote to Stuart to tell him the news, and

then I eagerly checked the post each day, waiting for his reply, believing he would write me something back that would make me feel better. But for months, nothing came. And then I stopped believing I'd hear from him again. It seemed fairly clear: Stuart had given up on the violin, and on me. And I felt his absence as a loss, another missing piece in my world.

But I was used to that, and so I moved forward. I continued to practice my violin each day after work and picking up the boys. I had nothing specific to practice for, but not practicing would be giving up, and I was not going to do that.

I found myself wandering into bookshops that winter. The first time, it was on a whim. I was meandering through the West End on a Saturday. It still felt odd, even after a few years, not to be observing the Sabbath. Julia had put the boys on a football team, and they practiced on Saturday mornings. I usually walked them back and forth to practice while Julia and Friedrich were busy doing something else. And then I wandered around during their practice, having no interest in watching a bunch of boys kick a ball around. That's when I first walked into the Ivy Bookshop, a purveyor of new and used books that had opened up on Carnaby Street.

There was something about the place, when I first walked inside, that brought everything back. The smell of the paper or the binding glue, or maybe it was the rows and rows of books on high shelves, or the young man sitting behind the counter, offering to help me find anything I needed. When I was inside the Ivy Bookshop, for a little while, I felt that same thing as when I played violin with Stuart: *I was home.*

I browsed the shelves, week after week, and the young man behind the counter asked me what I was looking for. "I don't know," I told him honestly. He laughed and asked if I wanted a suggestion, but I told him I just wanted to look around.

I thought of Max, that day so many years ago now, when he showed up at the Lyceum with a biography of Beethoven, trying to win my affection. How I'd pretended to have already read it just to have an excuse to go to his shop, to see him again that very same night. How I kept accepting his books and his stories and his suggestions, just to keep coming and seeing him at first, and how in time, I eventually came to love them, to read them, to understand how books were to Max what the violin was to me.

"Do you have anything in German, Allen?" I asked the man one Saturday afternoon that February. I'd already come in enough times that I now knew his name and that the used section of the store was impossibly large. Finding a German book in there would be like finding a needle in a haystack. I only had an hour while the boys were at practice, and it was easier to ask than to continue to browse through myself.

Allen motioned for me to follow him. The shop was busy today, not like Max's shop, which was almost always quiet. And we had to walk through a crowd to get to the back of the used section. "I keep all the books in other languages here, but German books . . ." His eyes scanned the shelves, his fingertips brushing over the spines the same way Max's used to, and my breath caught in my chest. "Not many people looking for German anything these days," he said.

It was a strange thing, that in the years I couldn't remember, being German had come to only mean being a Nazi. *But Germans are the enemy,* Lev told me not too long ago when he heard me telling a friend of Julia's who'd come to the house that I was one. Julia had laughed uneasily and clarified to her friend that I considered myself a Brit now. But I wasn't officially,

245

and I didn't see myself that way either. In my heart, I was a German. I would always be a German.

"Ah, here's one!" Allen plucked a book from the shelf and handed it to me. Another customer clamored for his attention, and he told me to come up front if I wanted to buy it.

I turned the book over in my hands, a volume of poems by Erich Kästner. I'd never read him, but I knew they'd burned his books in Berlin after Hitler came to power because Max had told me; he had been a fan of his work. And then it, like so much else, went up in smoke. I was playing that night in an outdoor quartet, and we'd heard the cheers, watched the smoke rise. I'd never been more terrified, but we continued to play because stopping would've meant we were giving up, giving in. Letting the Nazis win. I didn't think the Nazis would ever win, but somehow, impossibly, they had.

Max had read this book once. He'd left it the first morning I met him at the Lyceum, and I'd tracked him down from the name and address of his shop stamped in the back. I'd thought Max was sort of cute, with his green eyes and his light brown curls and his impish smile. I'd never really noticed boys before him; I was too focused on my studies and violin to care. But then there Max was one morning, almost out of the blue, staring at me as if my violin had mesmerized him, enchanted him. It was instantly endearing.

I opened the book up now, wanting it to be the same one, looking for the Beissinger Buchhandlung stamp in the back, wanting to touch something again that Max had once touched. But of course it wasn't there. This was another copy, someone else's book. Still, I went to the counter and bought it, took it home, and then I read it secretively at night in my room. Not because I didn't want to explain to the boys and Julia that I was still a German and still needed to read my own language, but more because the poems made me think of Max. For the first time since I woke up in the field, I felt close to him, reading the same words that I knew he had years before. The poems made me weep. And I didn't want the boys to see me like that.

I read the poems each night before bed, and then I began to dream so many dreams of Max. We were always back there together, in his shop, among all the books, and then Max would grab on to me, he would implore me: *Please, Hanna. Please, you have to leave with me. We have to go. Now.*

I can't leave yet, I have the orchestra.

And then again, there was the man, the Nazi, holding the gun to my head, telling me to play. To play for my life. And then Max was gone. I was all alone.

I would wake up filled with fear, and regret. Why hadn't I listened? Why hadn't I left with Max when I'd still had the chance?

I'd resigned myself to this life in London, where my violin was just a hobby, but at least things were finally improving after the war. Clothes were no longer being rationed! And there was hope that food soon might not be too. Princess Elizabeth, Duchess of Wales, had given birth to a baby boy, Charles, a few months ago, and I, like everyone else, had been excited to see the photos in the paper, a fact that had made Julia smile, as if she finally believed that I might be recovering too.

But then, one night at the end of March, just before supper, I found a letter from Stuart in a pile Julia had left on the kitchen counter.

"When did this come?" I asked Julia, as I picked it up. She shrugged. She hadn't noticed it, or she couldn't remember. Friedrich was working late yet again, and I'd heard Julia complaining to him over the telephone earlier. *You should be able to eat dinner with your sons,* she'd said. And I wasn't sure what he'd said back, but now she seemed to be in a mood, so I didn't question her any further. I ran off with the letter to the privacy of my bedroom, not wanting Julia to stare over my shoulder as I read Stuart's words.

Dearest Hanna,
I'm so sorry it has taken me this long to write you back. I was waiting for my hand to improve, hoping that it would get better, and that I would write you then with the good news. But it is still very much the same as it was last summer, and the truth is, I might never play violin again. Then my mum took a turn for the worse, and I'm afraid that we lost her last month, so things have been hard for me on all fronts lately.

I stopped reading for a moment, feeling like I was going to cry. The letter continued much farther down the page, and I took a breath and read on:

But I cannot stay away from music or

249

the orchestra, and I've recently been offered the position as the maestro of a
new small orchestra starting up in Paris.
I'm going to try my hands, my good one
and my bad one (See, I'm making a joke
now, aren't I?), at conducting. And that's
also why I'm writing you. I will need a
first chair violinist, preferably someone
with passion. Unfortunately, it won't pay
very much, just 500 FF a week, and you
may have many other better prospects
by now. Even so, I had to write you to
ask if you had any interest in moving to
Paris and playing in my orchestra? (My
orchestra, what a strange feeling it is to
write this . . .)

The letter went on, but I put it down, my
hands shaking. Stuart was going to conduct
an orchestra in Paris, and he wanted me to
be his first chair violin? It was hardly any
money, and in a city where I didn't know a
soul. But I was so excited, I could barely
breathe.

"Hanni." Julia rapped on my door, then
opened it without waiting for me to answer.
She walked in and sat at the end of my bed,
and I held the letter up to my chest, defen-
sively, not wanting Julia to read it, until I
had a moment to absorb it myself.

Her eyes went to the letter across my chest. "What is it?" she asked.

"Stuart got a job," I exhaled the words. "Conducting a new orchestra in Paris and he wants to hire me to play in it."

"Paris?" Julia puckered her lips as if she'd eaten something sour. "But you don't even speak French." As if that would stop me.

I laughed a little. "Violin is the same in every language," I said. "And Stuart speaks English."

"So . . . what?" Julia asked. "You are in love with him? You want to marry him and move to France?"

I frowned at her. How had she gotten any of that from what I'd just said? It was as if love and marriage were to her the only viable options for women like myself. "Jule, no. It's nothing like that. He's offering me a job, playing violin in his orchestra. A real, bona fide job as a violinist." My voice rose with excitement, as if by saying it out loud to Julia, it had suddenly become more real. *There will be other orchestras,* Max had said once. *You will play in one someday, I know you will. I promise you. You can't give up the fire!*

"But where will you live? And what about your job at the hospital?" Julia was saying now, her face reddening. She was flustered

251

or annoyed. Or both.

"I'll figure it out," I said. "And Paris isn't really that far from London. There must be a train. I'll be back to visit. And the boys can come visit me, too, explore the City of Lights with me."

Julia bit her lip and looked down at the floor. "You've already made up your mind, haven't you?" she said softly.

She said it like it was a real decision, like something I might have to labor over, weighing out the positives and negatives in my mind. But here Stuart was handing me what I'd always wanted: a start at a life playing in an orchestra, a life as a violinist. There was no choice, no other option but for me to go. I loved my nephews. Julia had shown me enormous kindness over the past few years. But London, and Julia's house, was not my home. The violin was my home, and I would follow it wherever it would take me.

I didn't want to hurt her, though, and I knew I would, that she would take me leaving as a personal offense. I leaned over and hugged her. "This is what I've been working for, what I've wanted for my entire life," I said. "You've always known that about me." She stroked back my hair and then pulled back from our hug. She wiped at her eyes with her fingers. Was she crying?

"Don't be sad," I said. "Be happy for me. We'll still see each other."

"I'm worried for you," she said. "A woman all alone in Paris?"

"I won't be alone," I told her. I was going to say I'd have Stuart, but I wouldn't, not in the way she'd want me to. So instead I said, "I'll be with an entire orchestra. I'll make so many friends."

Julia frowned. "Oh, Hanni," she said. "It's just . . ." She tilted her head and stared at me like she was going to say something important and trying to find the right words. But then she finally said, "The boys are really going to miss you."

Max, 1933

It was remarkable how the sun rose each morning, set each evening, the earth still spinning on its axis, as it always had. How everything could change and nothing could change. In July, the Nazi Party was decreed the only political party in Germany, any opposition punishable by law. Most people in Gutenstat were not Nazis: not Johann and Elsa, not Herr Feinstein next door, nor most of the patrons who still came to his shop looking for books to read (some, even the banned ones). But now no one spoke of it in public; it was illegal and somewhat terrifying to consider what would happen if they did. Instead they exchanged grim expressions or shrugs or saluted with the *Hitlergruss* if they thought anyone was watching them.

Herr Fruchtenwalder had told Hanna that the principal violinist in the symphony was rumored to be retiring soon, and that he would be able to secure her an audition. It felt like they were holding their breaths for that to happen so she could make it in already. There would be a certain safety for her in the symphony that she did not have as just a music student. Max believed she would be excused for being a Jew due to her talent, her service to her country. Even Hitler enjoyed Beethoven, or so he'd read.

Then the fall came, and the leaves on the mulberry trees changed color, as they always had, turning the streets into shades of orange and red and gold. Germany left the League of Nations in October, and in November, Nazis won 93 percent of the vote in the Reichstag election. Of course, no other parties were allowed to nominate candidates, and so it came as no surprise. It seemed to barely even register with the people Max spoke with each day. Max wrote it all down in his notebook.

For months Max also thought about Johann's words, Johann's *legal advice* from last spring, that the best way he could keep Hanna safe would be to marry her. And every time he kissed her, every time she put her violin away for the night and collapsed into his arms in bed, he would stroke back her hair and be consumed by how much he wanted her to be with him always, wanted her to be his wife. Not because it would keep her safe (though that was important too) but because he loved her so much he felt a physical ache in his stomach when she left his shop in the morning.

He knew her mother still would not approve, and she had her ups and downs, good days and bad with her health. But by the end of November, when he hadn't seen Hanna in three days and he felt his heart might burst, he truly could not wait any longer. He had to ask her to marry him now. He would have to find a way to win her mother over.

He did what he had been putting off for months: he went into the closet in his bedroom and pulled the locked box down from the top shelf that he'd been avoiding since his father's death. The box contained his father's most personal things, and though he'd inherited the key to it, he had left it alone until now. He didn't want to invade his father's privacy, even in death. In fact, he felt sure his father wouldn't want him to open the box, the same way he would not have wanted him to walk inside the closet in the shop. But he had searched everywhere else he could think of for his mother's diamond ring to give to Hanna, and he felt certain that his father must have locked it in there.

As he put the key in the lock, he promised himself he would only look for the ring, take the ring if it was inside, nothing else. His father would want him to have that, want him to give it to Hanna. If his father had met Hanna, he would've loved everything about her and welcomed her with open arms. He wouldn't have cared about her religion, the way Hanna's mother cared about Max's. His father would've only cared that Hanna was wonderful, and that she made him happy. And a fresh wave of grief washed over him, making him miss his father in a way he hadn't remembered to in months.

He opened the box, and on top there were a few letters, his father's passport, a notebook, and then underneath it all, what he'd been looking for: the ring. It was gold and had a small round diamond in the center: a Beissinger family heirloom. It had once belonged to the grandmother he'd never met, then his mother. He held it in his palm, ran his finger across the smooth top of the diamond, and smiled.

He put the letters and the passport back in the box. He reached for the notebook but his arm bumped the edge of the night-stand and the notebook fell to the floor, opening a bit. As he picked it up, he couldn't help but see that the pages were filled with his father's handwriting. His eyes caught on the words: *Space-time continuum . . . One-dimensional tube (later, wormhole? Einstein, 1935).* 1935?

He quickly shut the notebook, put it back inside the box. If his father had wanted him to read his journal, wanted him to know what he'd written, he would not have locked it up like this.

Though he had locked his father's journal away, putting the box back up on the high shelf in the bedroom closet, Max couldn't sleep that night, still thinking about it. Hanna had come to see him late tonight, after supper, and he had the ring in his pocket. But he already decided he'd give it to her in a few weeks' time for Hanukkah. She loved the violin pin he'd given her last year; she wore it on the lapel of her coat. And he hoped with all his heart that she would soon wear his mother's ring and agree to be his wife.

But now she was downstairs in the shop, practicing. Usually her playing soothed him, put him in a musical dreamscape. When she finished, she'd come upstairs, and wake him with a kiss, her fingers tracing a line down his chest, toward his waist, and he would kiss her, half dreaming, half present, aroused. But tonight his mind went over the words he'd seen earlier in his father's handwriting.

He'd written those words about the closet in the shop. Max was certain, just from the few his eyes had caught on. *One-dimensional tube. Wormhole,* and perhaps most telling, *1935,* four whole years after his father would die. What if the journal explained everything? What if the closet wasn't what he believed it was, and the terrible future he'd seen wasn't real? Or what if this confirmed it was?

He got out of bed and paced back and forth, his body pulling him back toward the locked box, his mind telling him his father would want to keep it private. He wasn't at all sure he was ready to face the memories reading the journal would surely awaken, the feelings of great loss, and what if he learned something about his father he didn't want to know, that would change the way he remembered him? But he also knew that understanding what he'd seen when he'd walked into the closet might be the only way he could keep Hanna safe. More than marrying her.

And so he walked toward the bedroom

closet, reached up on the high shelf for the box, and found himself unlocking it again with the key. He pulled the journal out and held it to his chest, as if his father's words could warm him, comfort him, save him. Could they?

He took the journal back to his bed, lit the gas lamp, and opened the book to the first page.

April 2, 1915

Rebecca and I found the end of the war! November 11, 1918. Drank coffee in Feinstein's café. Gone approx. 96 hours. Rebecca and I both had head and body aches for two days following. Cannot remember all of what happened? But Gutenstat will survive the war.

Max would've been four years old in 1915 and had very few memories of that time, no suspicion at all that his parents had been involved in such a *trip*. Judging from the thickness of the journal, there would be many more trips, many more entries between 1915 and 1921 when his mother would die. He turned the page to read more:

November 10, 1915

Rebecca and I walked more quickly and went even further. 1925! Took the train to the city and people are happy again. There is so much new music and they play it so loud. Rebecca and I danced all night! Gone approx. 10 days. Suffered with head and body aches upon return.

August 11, 1916

We ran and found 1932! Everything is blurry when we come back. Rebecca can't remember anything, and I can only recall a feeling of sadness. Rebecca cannot get out of bed for nearly a week. I have head and body aches, but not quite as bad as her. Next time we should not run so fast? Detrimental effects?

"Max, you're awake?" Hanna's voice startled him, and he dropped the book. "What are you reading?" She reached for it, and he quickly picked it up.

"Nothing," he said. "Bookkeeping for the store." He quickly settled on the lie, knowing Hanna's disinterest in mathematics and accounting.

"Oh." She yawned, lay down on the bed

next to him, put her hand gently on his arm. "That can wait until morning, can't it?"

He shut the book and put it down on the nightstand. *Rebecca cannot get out of bed for nearly a week . . . Detrimental effects?*

"Max?" Hanna kissed him softly on the lips. "Where are you tonight?"

"I'm right here." He stroked her hair, traced her collarbone with his finger. It made a v, for violin, he'd once told her, and she'd laughed. But she was right, he was far away. He couldn't stop thinking about his father's words.

As soon as Hanna fell asleep, he picked up the journal again and read through the whole thing, devouring every little piece of it. His father's experiences — his mother, *oh, his mother,* experiencing it all with him. His father believed the closet in the shop to be a *wormhole,* what Einstein would use his theory of relativity to explain as a bridge through space-time, in two years from now, 1935. Max did not understand much about physics, but he understood that walking through the closet allowed you to go into the future. The faster they walked, the further they went. The further they went, the worse they felt upon return. But his parents had gone to the future, again and again and again. His father theorized at the end of his journal that their frequent jumping in time might have killed his mother. Max wondered now, if it eventually killed his father, too.

Still, he took it all in with a new understanding, a relief. He didn't need to convince Hanna to leave Germany, to move away from her symphony or from her mother. If things got really bad, *when* things got really bad, he had an escape for all of them, right here in the shop.

He tucked the book out of sight from Hanna in his drawer and closed his eyes. He climbed back into bed, and Hanna nestled into him. He slept better and more soundly than he had in months.

HANNA, 1949

I had imagined Paris as a city of lights and magic, a fairy-tale city I'd read about in one of the books Max had given me once, *Fiesta* maybe, by Hemingway. I'd envisioned the Paris of the wild '20s, of Jake and Lady Brett, and laughter in beautiful cafés. But when I arrived, Paris was also still recovering from the war, and in the middle of a housing shortage. Too many people were moving in, and there were not enough apartments for them all. In spite of what I'd told Julia, that my violin was *my home,* the reality was I still needed housing, and that was nearly an impossible thing to find. Even more so for a single woman with a meager salary.

As maestro, Stuart had been given a two-bedroom apartment on the rue des Fleurs by the orchestra's patron, Monsieur Le Bec. The apartment had been in Le Bec's family for generations, survived the war, and as Le

Bec had his own much more sizable apartment in the Fourth Arrondissement, he had no use for it. Stuart said it was also because Le Bec was barely paying him anything, and that otherwise he wouldn't have been able to take the job, much less afford to live in the city. Le Bec's son had played the cello and had been killed in the war, and ever since Le Bec had been wanting to do something to honor him. Hence the new orchestra would be named the Pierre Le Bec Symphony, in honor of his son. Stuart told me he'd known Pierre, who'd been a few years behind him at boarding school, which is why Monsieur Le Bec had come to him with the idea first. And my surprise at the thought of Stuart attending a boarding school reminded me just how little I actually knew about him. Not that he knew any more about me.

Still, our months having played violin together in London made us both feel a kinship toward each other. And Stuart offered to let me stay in his apartment's second bedroom until I found a place of my own. At first I resisted, thinking about how it might look to the other members of the orchestra, but after ten expensive nights at the Hotel Paris-Dinard that I couldn't really afford, I relented and moved into Stuart's second bedroom. I'd brought only my violin and one suitcase with me, filled mostly with old clothes of Julia's she'd given me in London. I could hold every possession I owned in both hands.

"It'll just be a few days," I told Stuart as I set my violin and suitcase down inside the second bedroom in his apartment and looked around. The room was small, much smaller than what I'd had at Julia's, containing only a bed and a nightstand and a very small chest of drawers. But it would be more than adequate. "I'm sure I'll find a place of my own soon," I said.

"Stay as long as you'd like." Stuart smiled kindly. "I don't use the extra room."

I already missed Lev and Moritz and our daily walks back from the Academy as they regaled me with stories of their school day. But I couldn't wait for orchestra rehearsal to begin next week. Stuart had been holding auditions while I'd been searching for housing, and he'd filled out the rest of the orchestra pretty quickly. There were enough struggling musicians in Paris looking for work that they were willing to accept the small salary of a start-up, and Stuart said they were a talented group. I was glad to see him smiling again now, even though his finger still looked oddly bent. I tried not to stare at it, but my eyes were still drawn toward it.

"I haven't tried to play in months," Stuart said, following my gaze. "But I can conduct." Conducting, choosing the orchestra's players and pieces excited him. His blue eyes shimmered in the last of the day's light coming in through his kitchen window. Then he changed the subject: "I was going to cook a shepherd's pie for supper. My mum's famous recipe. Would you like some?" he asked.

It was hard to breathe, the awkwardness of our arrangement hitting me swiftly, all at once. Stuart hadn't just offered me a room in this apartment, but a home, a life here with him. Shared meals and conversations. Temporary or not, I knew it was all terribly inappropriate. Julia would be beside herself, if I told her about it, which I didn't plan to. "I think I want to walk around, explore the neighborhood a little," I told him.

He smiled. "Of course. Suit yourself. I can save you some food, if you'd like?"

"I don't want to trouble you," I said. "There are so many cafés. I'll stop and buy something for supper." Stuart nodded and walked into the small kitchen. I heard him moving copper pots around, lighting a match for the stove.

Obviously, I couldn't do this every night. It would be a habit much too expensive for my small salary. But I needed time now to clear my head, to ground myself here in Paris alone.

I walked out of Stuart's apartment, down the two flights of stairs to the street, and then outside. There was a garden just next to the apartment building, and many of the flowers were still in bloom, even in the fall. I took a deep breath of the Parisian air: smoke, a hint of rain somewhere in the distance, and true to the street's name, flowers. Paris was my home now, but it didn't smell like home. Maulbeerstrasse had been lined with mulberry trees, and when they bloomed each year, the air felt thick and smelled like fruit. In the winter, the trees were bare and the air smelled like snow and coal.

It had been over three years since I'd woken up in a field outside of Berlin with no memory of the preceding ten, and moving here, moving in with Stuart, however temporary it might be, made it feel like I was giving up on that other life now. Moving on. Julia's house had always been a transition, a resting place before beginning my life again. I knew that from the second I'd stepped on the train with her in Berlin.

But now, here, on my own, with a real job in an orchestra, my life was finally moving forward again, no matter what had happened to me in the ten years I was missing, the three years since. No matter what had become of Max, too. And it felt strange and wrong and oddly dissatisfying to be beginning again, without him.

I bought a crepe from a street vendor and sat down on the curb in front of the apartment building, eating it for supper. Paris was supposed to be the city of love, and eating my crepe alone only made me ache for Max even more than I had in London.

Stuart and I mostly kept out of each other's way in my first week living at his apartment, before our rehearsals started. I explored Paris by myself during the day. I tried to learn the Métro, but many stations were still closed since the war and it was often easier to walk. So I did, my legs taking me everywhere, kilometers and kilometers. I took in all the sights: the Eiffel Tower, the Arc de Triomphe. Notre Dame. The Louvre. All this beauty and history had survived the war, even the paintings at the Louvre, as the docent told me that the curators had shipped them out in secret trucks, hiding them before Hitler invaded France.

I walked and I walked through the city. I stopped at street vendors and bought and ate crusty loaves of bread, so much tastier than anything I'd eaten in London and no longer rationed in Paris. As I walked and explored, everyone around me speaking an entirely unfamiliar language, I could feel my own heart beating in my chest, the sound echoing in my ears.

I was here. I was alive. I was all alone.

On the first day of rehearsal, I told Stuart to go on ahead without me, that I would catch up. I was ready to leave when he was, but I didn't want to arrive with him, didn't want the other musicians to know yet we were friends, much less that I was living in a room in his apartment.

"I'll see you there then," he said. It was quite early in the morning. The sun had barely risen; the light in the apartment was dim, a shadow cast across Stuart's face, but I could feel his excitement. It surrounded him, a new energy.

I felt it too. Coffee was still rationed, but I allowed myself a small celebratory cup in the half-dark kitchen, and my fingers buzzed. Here was my chance, at last! Not at all how I'd envisioned it, not at all what I'd expected and dreamed about and worked toward for so many years in Germany. But still, *here it was.* I was going to play in an orchestra, a position I'd be paid to do. This was my life and my job now. It still almost didn't feel real. But it was.

I finished off my coffee, picked up my violin, and walked the three blocks to the Cathédrale, where Stuart had secured rehearsal space. I hummed the Ravel Stuart had chosen for us to play first (a French composer to delight Le Bec) as I walked inside. There was a sign by the door, Stuart's handwriting: RÉPÉTITION D'ORCH-ESTRE, with an arrow pointing down the flight of steps. I followed it, and ended in a basement, which was somewhat small, a little dark. It didn't in the slightest resemble the hall where the symphony practiced in Berlin or even the stage where the Royal Orchestra had practiced in London. But that didn't matter. I breathed in the damp, musty air. This was it; this was mine.

I took my seat in the front of the orchestra, looked at the music in front of me on my stand, and took my pencil and etched today's date across the top. Then I took my violin from its case and started to tune. Stuart stood in front of me, at a podium, and as he tapped his baton against it, calling rehearsal to order, he caught my eye and he smiled.

MAX, 1933

It would be traditional to ask Hanna's father's permission for her hand, but her father had died when she was a baby, and if Max were to ask her mother, she would almost certainly say no. Though Max knew that he, and Hanna, would somehow need to gain her mother's approval before they actually got married, he decided it was better to ask only Hanna herself first. Then they could convince her mother together, a united front. He only hoped that Hanna wanted to marry him as much as he wanted to marry her. And as he sat upstairs in his bed and listened to her violin floating up from his shop, he silently prayed she did.

In two weeks' time, on the first night of Hanukkah, he would tell Hanna he had a present for her. Then he would drop down on one knee, tell her how much he loved her, how he didn't want to spend any more time without her, and he would pull the ring out of his pocket.

He was still nervous she would say no, like the last time he'd asked. But that was a long time ago, and they knew each other better, loved each other more. He jotted down notes about what he would say to her in his notebook, right next to the startling news he read in the paper. Now, Hitler had declared Germany and the Nazi Party one and the same.

Hanna was still practicing downstairs in his shop, and it was getting so late, he couldn't keep his eyes open. He put his journal away and closed his eyes, reveling in the music. He fell asleep and dreamed of placing the ring on Hanna's finger, the sound of her violin playing on in the background.

When she finally finished practicing, came to his bed, woke him with a kiss, it was nearly dawn. They made love, and he was still so hungry for her. He pulled her back into his arms when she began to get up again, to leave. "Max," she said, gently pulling away. "I have to go. Mamele will worry. And I have chamber orchestra rehearsal at nine."

"But I don't want to let you go." He held on to her arm, pulled her back toward him.

She giggled, fell back into bed, and kissed

him, a long, deep kiss that made him feel so much it was hard to breathe. "I'll try to make it back tonight. Or if I can't tonight, then tomorrow," she promised. She got out of bed, slipped her dress over her head, and leaned back down for one last kiss.

After she left, he got the ring out and ran his finger across the diamond. Once they married, he wouldn't feel so empty each morning as she left him, not knowing exactly when he would see her again.

The shop was surprisingly crowded that morning. People actually looking for books, German books, of course. He'd hidden the banned ones in boxes that he'd stacked in the storage room and had intentionally mislabeled (just in case his shop was raided), but he hadn't been able to decide what to do with them yet. He couldn't dispose of them, couldn't throw away all those beautifully bound words just because a madman made them illegal. But he couldn't risk displaying them in his store, either. He understood that much. The SA arrested people who disagreed with them publicly now, jailing them as political prisoners.

Midmorning, as he was trying to help Frau Schneider, a frequent customer, find a

German-approved book that would replace the American pulp romances she so adored but were banned now, Herr Feinstein stormed in through the front door of the shop. "You knew?" he spat at Max. "You knew and you didn't tell me?"

Frau Schneider dropped the book she'd been holding, then froze. *"Pardon!"* she said, leaning down to pick the book up. She eyed Herr Feinstein with suspicion, the way many in town, sadly, had since the brick incident. She handed the book to Max and quickly told him she'd come back for it later.

Feinstein didn't seem to notice he'd scared away a paying customer, and Max put the book back on the shelf. "Knew what?" he said. He could feel blood rush to his ears, though he wasn't sure what Feinstein thought he knew. He knew only that at some point in the future, things would not be well for the Feinsteins.

"You kept asking me about Frau Feinstein, and I kept saying to myself what a sweet boy, but why does he suddenly care so much about my Rachel?" Max opened his mouth to speak but Feinstein kept talking. "You knew about her pamphlets, didn't you?"

"Pamphlets?" Max shook his head.

"You asked me if I wanted to leave the

country and that is why, isn't it? But why couldn't you just tell me what you knew? What am I to do now when it is too late?" Feinstein held up his hands; they were shaking. His whole body was shaking.

"Come," Max said, gently leading him toward the steps up to his apartment. "Come upstairs with me and we can talk in private." He walked over and locked the front door of the shop, flipped the sign in the window indicating that he'd stepped out, and led Herr Feinstein up the steps.

Feinstein sat at the dining table and put his head into his hands and Max went to the stove and boiled water for tea. "I didn't know about the pamphlets," Max finally said, when the tea was ready, and he handed a cup to Feinstein. "Tell me."

Feinstein's hands were still shaking as they took the tea. "Rachel and her sister, Marta, have been making pamphlets, distributing them at the Lyceum and the Universität. Speaking out against the . . ." He paused and looked around, as if afraid to say the word out loud. "Nazis," he finally clarified, though he didn't need to. Max felt his stomach drop as he realized how bad this was. You couldn't speak out against the Nazis; you certainly couldn't put it in writing and distribute it. "Rachel didn't tell me, said she was afraid I'd tell her not to. And she's damn well right, I would have." Max nodded. "Then today she got a letter in the post, and she confessed everything to me. The SA is requesting an interview with her. Tomorrow morning." His voice cracked. "And we both know if she goes to that interview, she won't be coming home. If you had just told me earlier . . . I could've saved her. I could've gotten her out of the country. But now . . ."

Max closed his eyes, put his hand in his pocket, and ran his finger against the cool smooth diamond. He couldn't let Frau Feinstein go to that interview tomorrow. "You can still save her," he said softly. "I can help her. I can help both of you."

Feinstein laughed bitterly. "It is too late. Oh God," he cried out. "It is too late."

"It's not too late," Max said, putting his hand over Feinstein's to stop the shaking. "There is still a way. Come back tonight with Frau Feinstein and any gold and jewelry you can carry, okay? I will explain everything then."

Feinstein shook his head, like he believed Max had gone crazy, but then what other choice did he have now?

HANNA, 1950

The Pierre Le Bec Orchestra became my life so quickly, it was as if it had never *not* been my life. If all the days at Julia's in London with Lev and Moritz felt like only a distant dream now, then my life in Germany, my nights at the bookstore with Max began to feel like another lifetime. A life lived by someone else, a girl too young, too innocent, who loved too much. Now I was a woman, with the same violin, who didn't love at all. It hurt too much.

A few weeks living at Stuart's apartment turned into a few months, and then we both stopped pretending I was still looking for another place. I wouldn't have found one anyway. The housing shortage in Paris grew worse, not better, and I was quite comfortable at Stuart's. We went to rehearsal each morning, shared supper together each night, taking turns cooking it. I practiced afterward, and Stuart listened, often offering suggestions. My teacher, my partner, but not quite. We had a strange kind of happiness, an undeniable kind of domesticity. The neighbors believed us to be husband and wife — I could tell from their hellos and comments made in passing, even with my tenuous grasp of French. But it didn't strike me as strange, improper, because it didn't feel like any of those things, until Julia and the boys took the train to visit on the boys' spring holiday. And my first thought was, how was I going to hide my living arrangement from her?

Julia knew my address. I'd written her and the boys once a week since I'd left, regaling them with stories of the dazzling City of Lights, many of them (nearly all of them) madly embellished. I didn't mention the housing crisis, or the fact that I was quite slow to learn French and had trouble communicating with most of the musicians in the orchestra, other than Stuart, and Ling Li, the first chair cellist who'd been born in China and spoke Chinese but also English, like me. I was so grateful Mamele had enrolled Julia and me in the international school in Gutenstat where we'd both learned English as young children. But Ling was somewhat aloof and had come to Paris with her entire family, and she wasn't much interested in being friends with me. Stuart spoke fluid French, apparently learned in boarding school, but he translated important directions into English for me and Ling during rehearsal. Perhaps if he hadn't, I might've picked up the French more quickly.

Still, it didn't really occur to me that this life of mine was a strange and somewhat isolating life until Julia arrived. It was a Sunday morning — the orchestra's day off from rehearsal — and I went to meet Julia and the boys for brunch at their hotel, not wanting them at Stuart's apartment. I asked him if he'd mind leaving for the day so I could bring Julia back after brunch to see where I lived and pretend I lived here all alone. He'd frowned; he didn't understand. But his kindness overwhelmed his confusion, and he said he owed Monsieur Le Bec a visit anyway and would spend the day there with him. That I was free to bring Julia over and tell her whatever I liked about the apartment.

I walked into the Hotel du Paris that morning, a bit nervous to see Julia and the boys. Seven months had passed, and everything about my life and world was different than when I was in London. I was different. But as I walked inside the hotel restaurant,

I spotted Moritz first. He saw me, too, and he jumped up and waved. He was already so much taller, his shoulders a little broader, but he still broke into his funny little grin, revealing his two crooked front teeth, when he saw me. "Tante," he called across the breakfast room, waving his arm wildly.

I waved back and walked toward their table. Julia was sipping a tea and Lev was stuffing a croissant in his mouth, as if the flaky pastry were the best thing he'd ever eaten. I couldn't deny him that. I'd put on a few pounds in my midsection from all the bread I'd been eating in Paris.

I squeezed each of the boys' shoulders and kissed their heads. They smelled exactly the same, like gingerbread and sweat. "Ah, you have gotten so big in just a little bit of time," I said.

"Boys do that." Julia smiled a little into her tea. Her cheeks were sunken, her face gaunt, and she looked almost the spitting image of our mother. Even her hair looked much grayer than I remembered it in my head. But I kissed her cheek and told her she looked wonderful before taking my seat next to her at the table, folding the linen napkin in my lap and grabbing a croissant of my own from the basket on the table.

"How was your trip?" I asked. Moritz gave

me a thumbs-up to avoid answering with his mouth full of pastry. "And the hotel?"

"Quite lovely," Julia said. "The whole city, really; it's just as you've described it in your letters." I was struck by the ridiculousness of her observation, as my letters regaling her with the sights I'd visited had nearly all been a lie. But I smiled at her. "And look at you, Hannalie. You're practically glowing. Are you in love?"

"In love? Only with the orchestra," I said lightly. And that might've been the truest thing I'd told Julia about Paris yet. I got into bed each night both physically and mentally exhausted from my music-filled days. I immediately fell into a deep and dreamless sleep and awoke refreshed and ready to play again each morning. There was no time or energy left to dwell on what I'd lost. That, it seemed, was destined to be my version of happiness now. And I'd come to terms with that.

Julia shook her head. "Oh, Hanni, you and your violin." She began to cough, patted her chest, and took a long sip of her tea. I felt a tightness in my own chest. Mamele's bad heart had caused her to cough and cough for years before she finally died. Herr Doctor had given her medicine, before her health insurance was stripped away, and then there were no more doctors who would see her, help her.

"Are you all right?" I asked Julia now.

"Yes, quite. Just a little something in my throat." She smiled wanly and changed the subject. "Boys," she said, turning to them. "Finish up, all right? I want to go stop in and see Tante's apartment before we go to the Louvre. Apartment, is that right? Or is it a, what's the French word . . . *maset*? Pied-à-terre?"

"Le appartement," I said, having learned at least that much French in my search for housing. Julia knew no French, but knowing her, she'd studied up in a travel book on the train and she was showing off for me, or, for her boys, now.

"Ah, so you are learning French." She smiled approvingly, and I didn't correct her. "And you have friends here?"

"Of course," I lied. "Lots of them." If she pressed me for details, I would tell her about Ling, whom I would sometimes attempt small talk with over our lunch break, but Julia didn't. She took me at my word.

"Mummy," Moritz said, having finally finished chewing, "tell her about the man looking for her."

"The man?" My heartbeat quickened. *Max?* I pictured him standing on Julia's stoop in London, ringing the bell, asking for me. But Julia would've telephoned or at least written right away, wouldn't she have? No matter what she thought of Max, she knew how I felt.

"Oh, that's right," Julia said, delicately patting her lips with her linen napkin. "One of the doctors from the hospital."

I exhaled again. Of course it wasn't Max. *Of course it wasn't.* The only doctor I'd really spoken to at the hospital was Henry Childs and it had been quite a while, but it had to be him. "Henry?" I asked her.

Julia bent down and reached into her handbag, a ridiculous-looking, and I assumed, expensive, large black bag dressed with an enormous black bow. Did she carry this around London now? Or had she bought it special for this trip?

She beamed a little as she pulled a piece of stationery from her bag. "Oh, *Henry.* So you do know him."

I blushed. "Not like that. He was helping me . . . oh, never mind." I took the paper from her — it just had Henry's name and telephone line at the hospital written neatly in Julia's script.

"Yes, he came looking for you just last week and left his number. I promised I'd give it to you when I saw you." She raised her eyebrows again.

"Okay, I'll telephone him and see what he wants." I stuffed the stationery into my own small blue inexpensive and somewhat beat-up handbag. My guess was that since it had been a while, he was wondering about my memories. Except by now I was feeling sure they might be gone forever. And Henry would be disappointed to hear that.

But today we were in Paris, and I had a new life. I didn't want to think about Henry, or the past. "Come on. Why don't we finish breakfast, and then I'll show you my place quickly before we tour around the city?"

I was exhausted after a day of taking Julia and the boys around, playing tour guide, and after I ate a supper of coq au vin at their hotel with them, which had left me feeling way too full, I walked all the way back to Stuart's apartment, rather than attempting the Métro as I had done with Julia earlier.

It was dark inside. Stuart wasn't back yet. Today was the most Stuart and I had been apart from each other in months, and it felt kind of empty inside the apartment without him. I'd grown rather accustomed to his company. Julia had said that I glowed like I was in love. But it was a ridiculous notion, and I pushed it away.

I changed into my nightgown and brushed my teeth, and just as I was about to get into bed I heard the front door open, then slam shut. "Hanna?" Stuart's voice rose and fell in the entryway.

I stepped out of my room, into the hallway. "I'm here," I called back.

Stuart walked down the hallway, turned on a lamp, saw me, and smiled. "How was your day?" he asked. "Enjoy your time with your sister?"

I nodded. "Honestly, she's exhausting. She asks a lot of questions." He laughed. "But it was good to see her and my nephews. Especially the boys. How was Le Bec?" I asked him.

"Good, excited to hear us rehearse next week." Stuart had invited him to hear our progress, and he'd told everyone at rehearsal last week to play our best for the audience of one.

His eyes wandered down to my chest, and I realized that my nightgown was sheer, that it was freezing in the hallway. I folded my arms in front of my breasts, embarrassed. Stuart quickly averted his eyes to his feet. "Well, I should get to bed," Stuart said.

"Yes, me, too," I said. But neither one of us moved for another moment. We just stood there, inches away from each other in the hallway.

"Hanna." My named sounded sweet, familiar as it rolled off Stuart's tongue, and I looked back up at him. "Can I ask you something?"

"Anything," I said.

"That one time in London when I was upset about my hand and I . . ." His voice trailed off and I knew exactly what time he meant, that night when he'd kissed me, once, out of some sort of weird grief or desperation or . . . something. I nodded to show him I knew what he was talking about, that he didn't have to rehash it all in words. "You told me there was someone else. But there isn't, is there? You've been here with me all these months and I've never heard you so much as even talk about anyone else, much less visit him or telephone him or write him. That was your way of trying to spare my feelings, wasn't it? There isn't really anyone else." He paused, and I wanted to tell him everything about Max, everything about this girl I'd been once, and all the time I'd lost. But I also didn't want to talk about Max at all right now, because Stuart was standing here, so close, and I was feeling things I hadn't felt in so long. "Please," his voice cracked. "Just be honest with me.

We know each other well enough for that much now."

"Oh, Stuart," I breathed his name and took a step closer to him. I put my fingers on his face — he needed a shave, rough stubble dotting his chin. I ran my finger across it gently, and he shivered a little. I stood up on my tiptoes and kissed him softly on the lips.

He caught my hands with his, pulled back just slightly, so our lips were close now, but no longer touching. I was breathing hard and so was he. "But you don't want this," he whispered.

"I do," I said. And that was the truth. It really was. No matter how much I still missed and longed for Max, it was also the truth. "I do want this."

His breath caught in his chest. He kissed me. Slowly, sweetly. He tasted of wine, and I wondered how much of it he'd drunk at Le Bec's to have the courage to kiss me like this. But I didn't care; I kissed him back. His hands moved up under my nightgown, cupping my breasts, stroking them lightly, as if he were afraid he might break me, or I might change my mind. "I do want this," I said to him again, and I reached to unbutton his shirt, and pulled him into my bedroom, into my bed.

■ ■ ■

"I never answered your question," I said into the darkness a few hours later. We were both naked still. I lay on my side and Stuart lay behind me, his arm wrapped around me, his fingers splayed across my bare skin. He stroked softly with his thumb, playing pizzicato on my rib cage.

"Maybe I don't really want to know the answer," Stuart said softly. His thumb stopped for a moment, then started again.

"I think he's dead," I said, my voice wavering a little as the words, out loud, became like a strange sort of truth. "I was telling you the truth. There was someone else. His name was Max, and we were going to get married when I lived in Germany. But then . . ." I stopped short of telling Stuart everything because how would he understand it? Ten whole years gone. No memory of where I was, where I went, how I survived as a Jew. "But then I don't know what happened to him during the war. It's been . . . many years," I said.

"Oh, Hanna." Stuart kissed the top of my head, pulled me tighter against him. He wanted me again; I could feel him against my leg. And it was weird talking about Max with Stuart because I wanted him again, too, even though I knew deep down that I could never love anyone the way I loved Max.

Max, 1933

He waited anxiously for Hanna to arrive at his shop later that night as he was also expecting the Feinsteins, but supper came and went, the outside world turned dark, and Hanna didn't show. It wasn't unusual; she didn't come every night. She had said she might not be able to get away until tomorrow. But he'd been hoping she would. He needed to see her, needed to kiss her. And also, he wanted her to see the Feinsteins scared, in danger, if only so he might convince her that she needed to take everything more seriously. Consider her future more carefully, too.

But then the Feinsteins walked into the shop, and Hanna was still nowhere in sight. They held only one knapsack of belongings between them, and Frau Feinstein was pale, shaking. Herr Feinstein patted her on the shoulder but it seemed more rote than comforting, as his hands betrayed him —

they were shaking too. "I don't trust him," Frau Feinstein said, her voice breaking a little. "He could be a Nazi too."

It took Max a moment to realize she was talking about him. Because how could she not trust him? How could she really believe he could be a Nazi? She had known him since he was a little boy playing on the floor of this shop, wandering next door for a slice of bread. Her doubt stung, as if she had slapped him. Could she really not distinguish between the awful Nazis and him any longer?

"It does seem inconceivable." Herr Feinstein looked at Max and frowned. "Where could you possibly take us now?"

"Both of you, please," Max said. "I've known you my whole life. You were dear friends of my parents. I would never do anything to put you in harm's way. I need you to trust me."

Herr Feinstein shook his head. "I do not trust anyone anymore."

Max understood that feeling; he hated it, that this was what Germany had become. But he understood it. "What I am going to tell you is going to sound insane," he began. "But I swear to you, I'm telling you the truth." He explained to them about the closet, about everything he had read in his

293

father's journal. Then he told them what he remembered of his own trip last year, and how he'd seen Herr Feinstein in another time, distraught on the street, upset over something that had happened to Frau Feinstein.

By the time he was finished talking, Frau Feinstein had begun to cry. "He's going to rob us," she said to her husband, clutching the knapsack, the gold and jewels he'd told them to bring so they would have money to pay for a new life. "And then he'll put us in that closet and kill us."

Herr Feinstein looked at Max and frowned. "This sounds like a *mshuge* story you read in one of these books." He shook his head, sadly. "Max Beissinger, a Nazi?"

"But I can show you my father's journal," Max said. Proof.

"Your father was always writing tales," Herr Feinstein said. "Always wanting to write his own book."

"No," Max cried out. "This isn't a tale. Look . . . I'm going to go with you. And I'll go into the closet first, all right? You can just follow behind me, keep up my pace." Both of them stared at him, Their mouths slightly open. "I will take you to safety. I promise," he said. "You just need to trust me. I can save you."

He didn't want to go into the closet at all, but he felt certain they would not go without him. He desperately didn't want to leave Hanna, but he had to save the Feinsteins. It was what his father would want him to do, what his father would expect him to do. Max had a way to save them; he had a responsibility to do it that he could not ignore.

If he went with them, then he'd be gone a few days, and he'd return with a headache. But one more time in the closet would not be enough to kill him. It couldn't be. From his father's journal, he knew that he and his mother had gone many, many times. Max would not make that mistake.

He hastily scribbled a note for Hanna and left it by the register. He couldn't write anything in it about the Feinsteins (what if the SA were to visit his shop?), but he didn't want Hanna to worry or get upset again if he was gone when she returned.

Hanna, Had to do something urgent. Will be back in a few days. I promise. Don't be mad. I love you. Always, M.B.

The Feinsteins were whispering to each other as Max strode toward the closet and shoved the bookshelf out of the way. He took out his keys, undid the lock. "Come on," he said.

Frau Feinstein dug in her heels, shook her head. "And what if he is even telling the truth?" she said. "How do we know the future is better?"

Herr Feinstein looked from her to Max, then back to her again. He reached for his wife, grabbed her, hugged her hard to him, then pulled back, put his hands on her cheeks, and kissed her softly on the mouth. "I love you, Rachel," he said. "If we die tonight, then I want you to know that."

Her face softened. "I love you, too, Bertram."

His father had theorized the faster you went through the wormhole, the further in time you jumped. If they made it far enough, Hitler would have to be out of power, the world would have to right itself again. Max may be naive, and he had read far too many books, but still, he truly believed that good would always win over evil. Eventually. "Come," Max said, holding out his hand. "We're going to go quickly."

Herr and Frau Feinstein looked at each other again, and Frau Feinstein took her husband's hand. He placed his other hand in Max's, and then Max opened the door to the closet, holding on to them both, and began to run.

Elsa, 1950

Johann had been dead nearly an entire year when Max showed up on my doorstep. I had been counting my husband's absence at first in hours, then in days, weeks, and now it was months. Eleven of them. Soon, unbelievably, it would be a year. And still, I felt the hole each morning, the lack of him simply *being:* immediately upon waking, there was a sharp pain in my chest that made it hard to breathe. I might have been tempted to stay in bed all day, even all these many months later, if it were not for my Grace, who was still here living with me, and who at fifteen still desperately needed her mother.

Grace and Emilia both had grown up in a time of war. They'd spent a good part of their childhood being afraid of bombs and sheltering from air raids. Death and destruction were what they knew, how they came to be women. We'd relocated to the countryside for a bit when the girls were younger, living in Johann's father's fishing cabin, Johann refusing to be conscripted to fight for a government he no longer believed in, refusing to stay behind in Berlin and be arrested for it, too. But even in the country, the war had still been close enough to touch. One night an Allied bomber had fallen out of the sky, bursting into flames across our pond, and Gracie, at seven years old, had clung to me and refused to speak a word for three whole weeks. I still sometimes believed that she had not fully recovered. She was quiet, brooding; she had a darkness that Emilia never had, and making friends was difficult for her. Emilia had recently moved away to attend school in Holland, but sometimes I thought — or maybe I hoped? — that Gracie would live here with me forever. The only thing that made her happy was playing the piano, and on weekends, evenings, holidays, that was all she did, play and play and play. Her music was the only thing some mornings that got me out of bed.

I'd kept in touch with Hanna here and there, and I wrote her once about my Gracie and her piano. Hanna wrote me back: *Didn't we always know she loved music!* and in that exclamation point I saw Hanna's own happiness, that the orchestra she had joined in Paris was perhaps giving her what she always wanted.

Gracie was playing her piano when the bell rang that morning. And I called for her to get the door. I was in the kitchen, taking my brötchen out of the oven, a habit I'd forced myself to keep since Johann was gone, baking and cooking each day. Gracie needed to eat. And I supposed I did, too. Sometimes when I caught my reflection in the mirror, it surprised me to see how thin I was, how my bones protruded from my wrists, making my small arms appear bird-like. Johann would not have liked that. He had reveled in my roundness after I had the girls, but I still could not bring myself to eat.

"It's a strange man," Gracie yelled, upon opening the door. I nearly dropped the brötchen on the floor. Even all these years after the war, safely ensconced in West Berlin, this kind of thing still frightened me, and I ran to see for myself who it was.

And then there he was, like some sort of living illusion, Max, exactly as I remembered him: young, handsome, a winsome look on his face. In the second before I grabbed him in a hug, I thought the most ridiculous thing I had thought in the last eleven months (and that was saying a lot): *If Max could walk up and ring the bell, back from the dead, just like that, then maybe Johann could too?*

"Max?" I said. "Is that really you?" I hugged him to me hard, and he felt and smelled just as I remembered him, like mulberries and paper from his bookshop, before the war.

"Is Jo home? I need to talk to him," Max said, a note of desperation in his voice, and the words I needed to tell him caught in my throat.

So instead I said, "Why don't you come in. I have fresh brötchen. Tell me where you've been all these years. We'll catch up, hmm?"

Max ate my brötchen, saying he was starving, and it was refreshing to see that wherever he'd been, wherever he'd gone, he hadn't lost his appetite. It wasn't until I told him about Johann that he put the food down and stopped eating.

"How could this happen?" he asked, and it was a funny thing to say from a man who'd disappeared himself from our lives for twelve years.

But I told him as gently as I could about the double-decker bus that had jumped the sidewalk as Johann had been walking home from work last summer. "Wrong place, wrong time," I said, shaking my head. It was a phrase I had been repeating to myself. We had been lucky during the war, escaping relatively unscathed, and then when life was finally righting itself again, and we had settled into a nice life here in West Berlin, misfortune had finally found us.

"Where have you been all these years?" I asked Max. I wanted to change the subject. If I spoke anymore about Jo and what had happened, I would begin to cry, and I didn't want Max to see me that way. I especially didn't want Gracie to hear me from the other room.

"I was . . . traveling," Max said, wiping crumbs from his chin with a napkin, as if it were the most normal thing in the world to just desert your friends for twelve years and then show up again, on their doorstep, after all this time. Max had never handled grief well, and in the years after his father died, he had made a bad habit of leaving, running away. Johann had been quite worried after Hanna disappeared that Max would flee again, or worse, that he would bring harm onto himself. It was good to see him sitting here now, looking so very well.

"I have . . . missed some time," Max was saying.

"Just like Hanna," I mused, and it was the oddest thing that she had described her experience of the war to me once, in almost that exact same way. As soon as I said Hanna's name, his face changed. It lightened, and then he smiled. "She is safe? She is here?"

"Safe, yes," I said. "Here, no. She's in Paris now. Playing with an orchestra. She believed you were dead . . . we both did." It was only Jo who had believed that maybe Max was off somewhere, just being Max or perhaps convalescing. I wished he were here now, to see he was right.

"Paris," Max breathed. "Is there a train to Paris? I have to see her. She has to know I'm alive."

If seeing Max had been a shock to me this morning, I couldn't quite imagine what it would be like for Hanna. But then again, if Johann were to show up on my doorstep, after I believed him to be dead for only eleven months and seven days . . . I was overcome with emotion just thinking about it. "Of course," I told him. "Whatever you need, let me help you. Just promise me one thing, don't disappear on us again, okay? Gracie and I will want to see you now that

302

you're back in Germany."

Max looked down at the table, then back up at me. "I'm so sorry," he said, and I wasn't sure what he was apologizing for, disappearing, for what had happened to Johann, or for the fact that he already planned to disappear again. Johann had told me about Max's illness, about the way grief had disturbed Max's body as a child, and I'd long wondered if his disappearing was some sort of strange antidote to all that. The only way he understood how to survive in the most terrible of times.

"Come," I said. "Let me find Hanna's letter with her address in Paris, and then we'll get you some money and I'll get you to the train station, all right?" I stood, and then I realized, taking Max to the train would be the first time I left my house in months.

Hanna, 1950

We played our first concert to a packed audience, thanks to Monsieur Le Bec paying for advertising in all the city's newspapers, and because we held the concert for free outside in the Tuileries Garden. It didn't hurt that it was a lovely Saturday in April either; the sun was shining, and the air smelled like springtime: roses in bloom and freshly cut grass. Our pieces were polished from months of rehearsals, and we played a lovely and almost musically perfect concert of European classical composers (excluding the Germans, because everything German was still out of fashion): Ravel, Dvořák, Haydn, and Mahler.

The *Temps de Paris* published a review the following week, calling our little orchestra a *"grand accomplissement"* and as I read it over his shoulder, Stuart did not have to translate for me to know that they liked us. We were invited back to do a spring and summer concert series at Tuileries, eight different Saturday afternoons in May, June, and July, and Stuart told me in private that he believed if it all went well, we might be able to secure more patronage, better rehearsal space for the fall, and perhaps even a concert series next year where we could charge admission.

"You did it," I said to him, as he put the paper down on the kitchen table and poured himself a cup of coffee. He flexed and extended his fingers, what he did when he was tired or sore. I was used to his bent ring finger by now, so that I barely even noticed it, except in times like this, when clearly it was bothering him.

"We did it," he said, sitting across from me with his coffee. I smiled and didn't argue with him. We both knew that an orchestra's success or failure lay as much with the principal violinist as with its conductor. *If only Max could see this.* But I quickly tried to push the thought away. Max wasn't sitting here with me; Stuart was.

Stuart slept in my bed every night that spring, and even though we were both exhausted from long days of rehearsal, we would make love in the darkness. It was a weird, unspoken rule between us that during the day, we never discussed it, any of it. We were entirely professional at rehearsal, and even in the evenings when I practiced at home. We talked only about music, about the orchestra; we moved as we always had around the apartment. Except at night, when we got into bed, when we were together. Maybe Stuart understood that deep down I still grieved for Max; I still loved Max, too. Or maybe he was afraid that if he said anything at all, whatever we had would end, it would all fall apart.

That's why I didn't speak of it. Because I didn't want it to end. And sometimes, during the very long warm afternoons of rehearsal that spring, I would count the number of hours until the darkness would come, until Stuart would climb into my bed and touch me again.

By the time our final concert came around at the end of July, the orchestra had grown in great esteem. The concert series was, in fact, going so brilliantly that two other conductors had written to me about positions in their orchestras, one in the south of France and one in Vienna. And though they would both be better-paying, bigger orchestras, I didn't want Stuart to know other conductors were trying to poach me, and I didn't even mention the letters to him. I was content right here, in Paris, with him. My salary was still quite small, but I wasn't starving by any means. I was finally feeling something close to happiness. It was a delicate bubble, my forgotten past always hovering around the edges, threatening to pop it, but most days I did not think about the past. I thought only about the present and what might be my future.

And then, everything changed that final night in the park. We were playing, Saint-Saëns, and I stood for the violin solo, closed my eyes, and played it with my whole body and my whole heart. The night air was sticky, and when I was finished, beads of sweat trickled down my back, pooling underneath my curls in the nape of my neck. The audience applauded and I opened my eyes. And I saw him there, in the second row, clapping wildly: Max.

I blinked, not believing my eyes. It was nearly dusk, and my body was on fire from playing, from the July heat. When I opened my eyes and looked again he was still there; he saw me staring at him, and he smiled.

Stuart lowered his arms; the song was over, and the audience applauded for my solo. I was supposed to take a bow, return to my seat for the final number, but I could not move.

"Hanna." Stuart was whispering my name. I held on to Max's eyes in the audience. "Hanna," Stuart said again. Max averted his eyes first, turned, and began to walk away.

"I have to go," I said to Stuart, desperately trying to watch where Max was walking. But there were a lot of people. His head began to bob through the crowd, farther and farther from me. I clutched my stomach like I was about to be ill, and Stuart nodded. It wasn't a lie. I felt like I might vomit, or cry, or both.

I ran off to the side of the orchestra, following the path I'd seen Max take, and I heard Stuart announce our final number for the evening, our final piece for the summer, Debussy. They would play it without me. I might've felt a pang of sadness had I not been so frantic to catch up to Max.

I had lost sight of him, and I stopped, spun around. "Max," I called out. But the orchestra had begun to play again, the music drowning out the sound of my cries. Ling missed her entrance, her cello meandering in a beat late, and I sat down in the grass, put my head in my hands, and tried to breathe. Had I merely imagined Max here? Was I going insane?

Then I felt a hand on my shoulder, *his hand.* It had been so long since I had felt him, since he had touched me, but even after all this time, I knew, it was unmistakably him. I reached my hand up; his fingers laced through mine. "Hanna." *My name, in his voice.* How I had longed to hear that again. "What are you doing?" he asked. "Your orchestra is playing without you."

I stood and leaped into his arms, buried my head in his chest. "You're here. You're really here." I kept repeating the words, not believing them, so I said them again, and again. "You're really here?" His shirt still smelled the way his shop had once, earthy, like wood and books, and for a moment I was back in Gutenstat, nearly twenty years ago, a young girl with a whole heart and a faraway dream I completely believed was within my reach.

I stood back and looked at him. And he was exactly as I remembered. I reached up and touched his face, and every line, every crevice, felt exactly the same.

"Will you come with me?" he asked, holding out his hand. I glanced back to the orchestra. Stuart's back was to me; he was conducting, and I had never viewed him from this angle before, the way the music poured from his shoulders, mirroring the same passion I felt in my fingers as they rode my violin. *Preludes* was half finished, no one in the audience noticing my missing part, but me. "Hanna," Max said. "I don't have much time."

And though playing in an orchestra was all that I'd ever wanted, and though I had been happy just an hour ago, I turned away from the music and took Max's hand.

I could not take Max to my apartment, to my home I shared with Stuart. Not because he would be angry that I had been with another man, but because it wasn't fair to Stuart. None of this was. But I tried not to think about Stuart, and instead I took Max to the Hotel du Paris, where Julia and the boys had stayed in the spring. I paid for a room — Max did not have any francs with him. Never mind that I couldn't really afford such a nice hotel. Max was here! Nothing else mattered. I had so many things to ask him. Where had he been, and what had happened to him, and me, during the war? But then we opened the door to our room. I put my violin down on the settee, and we did not bother to turn on the light before we were embracing each other, before Max was unzipping my black dress, and I was pulling at the buckle of his belt, his pants.

My body, my hands, knew these things, this man, and they took over for my mind, which might have been feeling something akin to alarm if I'd stopped to allow it. But I didn't stop.

My skin was hot and feverish, and so was his. It was this fever, this fire, that consumed me, that kept me from asking all the questions I should've been asking, and just kissing him instead, touching him. Max lifted me up, placed me gently on the bed, kissed the center of my collarbone, *my true heart,* the place where my body formed the *v for violin,* as he used to tease me.

I ran my hands across his back, my fingers knowing his body as well as they had ever known the violin. Max was Beethoven's Concerto in D Major, the first concerto I'd ever played onstage by heart.

"What did you mean, you don't have much time?" I asked him later, lying in the darkness, our bare legs entwined, my head against his chest, listening to his heart beat softly in my ear. "I am never letting you go again." I turned on my side and wrapped my arms around him, kissing his neck.

He kissed the top of my head. "Tell me what happened to you . . . how you got here? Elsa told me a little, but tell me all of

311

it." *Elsa.* So that explained how he had found me. Elsa and I had written a few letters over the years. She knew I was here; I'd invited her and Grace to come to the concert series in Paris this summer, but she'd politely declined, saying it was too far to travel and they were saving money to go visit Emilia in Holland at the end of the summer. In truth I believed she was depressed since Johann had passed, not that I blamed her for it.

It had been a while since I'd recounted the whole story to anyone, even since I'd really thought about it myself. But then I began again, my voice ringing out in the darkness, telling it all to Max. How I awoke in the field, the kindness of Sister Louisa, the doctor in Berlin who told me I had experienced a trauma and Henry Childs who'd tried and failed to help me remember it. The ten years missing and the entire war I couldn't remember! Julia bringing me to London. Stuart bringing me here.

Stuart. My betrayal to him took my breath away when I said his name, and I stopped talking for a moment. Max stroked my shoulder with his thumb, not seeming to notice that part. "Ten years," he mused quietly.

"Do you know what happened to me in

longer than a week, even two; the realization hit him hard and swiftly, a punch in his gut that made it momentarily hard to breathe. He needed to find Hanna now.

He walked outside, and the brightness of the sunshine blinded him. He squinted, inhaled the scent of mulberries, and noted the feeling of the air on his face: warm, humid. It was spring, at least, maybe summer. Next door, there were people inside Feinstein's shop, the smells of fresh baked bread wafting out onto the street. But Feinstein's name had been painted over on the awning above the glass storefront, and now it just said: *Bäckerei.* His stomach rumbled, but he didn't stop in to satisfy it. If he had been gone awhile, Hanna would be worried. His hunger now was a penance for whatever pain or stress he'd caused her.

At the train station, the date was posted up above the ticket booth: *July 2, 1934.* He blinked, looked at it again, praying he'd misread January for July. But anyway, it could not be January. It was much too hot. It was, despite his disbelief, actually July. He'd not only missed Hanukkah entirely, but he had been gone for six months.

He took the first train to Maulbeerstrasse, barely able to stand the ten-minute train ride — it felt like forever. The interminable field rolling by outside his window was no longer covered in snow, but it was brown, dead, as if it hadn't rained the entire time he was away. He put his hand in his pocket and felt it there still: the ring he had planned to give to Hanna last December.

A memory or a dream came to him in a flash: *We can finally get married now,* Hanna had whispered to him in bed.

They could finally get married. He would go to her now, apologize, explain that he had been helping the Feinsteins get to safety, and she would understand that. She would still love him here, in 1934, though he had left her for so very long. She had to. He ran his finger over the cold, smooth diamond and clasped it in his palm as he got off the train.

In the summer, Hanna didn't always have classes at the Lyceum, though she did keep up lessons with Herr Fruchtenwalder each week. Max decided to try her apartment first. It was more likely she'd be there and also, it was closer to the station.

He ran toward her building, then stood outside her apartment door a few seconds before knocking, listening for the sound of the violin, or even her mother's cough. But when he heard nothing at all from inside, he knocked, softly at first, then louder. Finally the door opened, and Julia, not Hanna, stood there on the other side. She frowned deeply and folded her arms across her chest. "My sister doesn't want anything to do with you," she said, sharply, moving to close the door.

He held up his hand to stop her. "Wait," he said. "Please. I just need to talk to her." He squeezed his fist tighter around the ring.

"You think you can leave her for months and come back whenever you want?" Julia demanded.

"Hanna," he yelled past Julia into the apartment. "Hanna, please. Just come out and talk to me."

"Ssssh." Julia put her finger to her lips. "She's not even here. And Mamele's sleeping."

"Where is she?" Max asked. "The Lyceum?"

"And why would I tell you?" Julia said.

"I love her," Max's voice broke, understanding as he said it, how impossible that must look to Julia right now. But it was the truth, and he said it again.

"You have a funny way of showing it." Julia frowned.

"Please, just tell her to come to the shop and see me later. Please," Max implored her. But Julia swung the door shut, slamming it in his face before he could say another word.

He took the train back. He wasn't going to listen to Julia, or give up. If Hanna wasn't home now, she was likely at the Lyceum, practicing, and he didn't want to interrupt her there. It would only make her angrier with him than she already was. But she would go back to her apartment for supper. She always had unless she was eating with him. He would return to Maulbeerstrasse later that night, armed with flowers, apologies, food . . . anything else he could think of to get her to forgive him.

He got off the train back on Hauptstrasse, his hunger nearly capsizing him, and he doubled over in the street, clutching his stomach. He walked the block to Elsa and Johann's and knocked on their door. They, too, would've noticed his long absence, worried about him, but he hoped they would be less angry and more willing to offer him some food.

Elsa opened the door, and she opened her mouth, then held up her arms. But his eyes had already gone to her large, protruding belly. *Grace,* he thought. Apropos of nothing. *Playing the piano.*

Elsa grabbed him in a hug. "Max, really, I should string you up by your toes, running off like that. Johann and I have been worried sick." As he hugged her, he felt an odd sense of déjà vu. They had just done this. But they hadn't, had they?

Johann walked up behind Elsa now. "Jesus, Max. Where the hell have you been?" But he stepped past Elsa and clapped him on the back. Max hugged him, too, and he felt so happy to see Johann. He hazily remembered something would be wrong with Johann, in the future, but he couldn't put his finger on what.

"I'm sorry," Max finally said to both of them. The simplest and best thing he could say. "Please, can I come in?"

Johann opened the door wider and gestured for Max to follow him inside. "Have you been ill?" Elsa asked him. "You don't look well."

"No . . ." Max said. "But I am starving."

"I have some brötchen in the kitchen," Elsa said, and she brought him a basket of it, setting it in front of him on the table. He gobbled the brötchen down, slightly embarrassed about the crumbs he was leaving on their table, which he tried to gather into a pile with his fingers as he ate.

"So where did you go?" Johann asked,

leaning forward in his chair. "And why didn't you tell us like you promised? Or write to us . . . or anything?"

"I was traveling," Max lied. The lie came so easily off his tongue; he didn't even think about it. It was just there, as if he'd already made it up in advance.

Johann frowned. "Hanna was a wreck with worry. You left her a note that you'd be gone only days. She thought you'd been killed." *Killed.* Max saw the worry in his oldest friend's eyes and it sunk in his gut. He remembered in a flash: Johann had been *killed* in the future. That was why Elsa was so very sad.

He pushed the basket of bread aside. He'd eaten too much, too fast, and now he felt like he might be sick. "Oh, Jo," he said.

"Come on, Max," Johann said. "Where the hell did you go that you couldn't even send a telegram?"

He wanted to tell Johann the truth desperately, but he had tried that one summer when he'd first gone into the closet and he and Elsa hadn't believed him then. They would believe him even less now. He would sound crazy and they would worry about him even more. But maybe he could explain that he'd been helping his neighbors, which was also the truth. "You know the Feinsteins from next door to me?" he finally said.

"Yes," Johann said. "They're not there any longer. There was a rumor that the SA chased them off in the middle of the night or arrested them . . . There's a Christian baker who runs the shop now. Elsa doesn't like the brötchen half as much, so she's been making her own." Elsa sighed and folded her arms across her round belly. It wasn't the bread she disliked as much as the idea of Jews being driven out.

Emilia called for her mother from the other room, and Elsa excused herself, walking out to attend to her daughter.

As soon as she left, Johann leaned in closer and lowered his voice. "Things have gotten so bad while you were away, Max. Jews are being arrested for nothing, taken away in the middle of the night. And not just Jews, but anyone sympathetic is in danger. A lawyer at my firm was arrested last week for 'aiding criminal activity.' He simply had a Jewish client he'd been working with. That was his crime. Helping a Jew with legal matters!"

Max opened his mouth to speak, to tell Johann that the Feinsteins hadn't been arrested at all, that he had helped them escape instead. But if everything was as bad as Johann was saying, he also didn't want to put his oldest friend in any danger.

Johann was still talking: "On top of that, Jews no longer have health insurance and they're being banned from things left and right. I fear it is only going to get worse."

They no longer had health insurance? What about Frau Ginsberg and her heart problems? How was she being treated without insurance? Hanna must be devastated, and he hadn't been here for her.

"You need to get Hanna to forgive you," Johann was saying now. "Then you need to marry her. And get her out of Germany." He laid it out matter-of-factly, like it would just be that easy. That Hanna would forgive him quickly and consent not only to being his wife but also to leaving her country, her orchestra, her mother.

Max nodded, but took comfort in knowing now that he had another way to get Hanna out. "It'll be okay," he assured Johann. And Johann frowned, as if he believed Max wasn't taking him seriously.

"Well," Elsa walked back in, holding Emilia against her hip, "did you find out all the details of his trip?"

Johann smiled at his wife and tickled Emilia's toes. She giggled a little and rubbed her eyes. "No. Max, why don't you tell us both."

"I was, um . . ." He thought of his father's old lie, where he'd always believed his father to be when he left for weeks at a time. "Going around Europe. Book buying."

"Book buying?" Elsa raised her eyebrows. Emilia let out a little cry and Elsa turned her attention back to her daughter. "I have to get her a snack, excuse me, Max." She kissed Johann on the head and walked back into the kitchen with Emilia.

"Elsa loves you so much," Max said to Johann. "You know that, right?"

"I'm a lucky man," Johann said, but he stared at Max, his blue eyes brimming with worry.

Max spent the afternoon cleaning up his shop, wiping away the dust, and looking at what books still remained. Mostly it was volumes of poetry that had been sitting on the shelves for years, books his father had ordered and he hadn't been able to bring himself to clear away even though his patrons weren't interested in poetry these days. He wasn't sure what happened to all the other books, as he'd locked the shop before he'd left, and only Hanna had a key. But when he opened the cash register, it was also flush with reichsmarks, more than he'd seen in one place in a long time, so he couldn't believe anything had been stolen.

He got his answer in the middle of the afternoon, when the shop door opened, the bell clanged, and there she was, so beautiful as always. Hanna stood in the doorway, her round green eyes wide open, staring at him, disbelieving. "Max, is that really you?"

He ran to her, hugged her, held her to his chest, and breathed in the molasses smell of rosin on her skin. They stood like that for a moment, until Hanna pulled back, put her hands on his chest, and pushed him away. "Where have you been? I thought you were dead," she yelled at him.

"I know," he said. "I'm so sorry. I didn't mean to worry you." He reached for her, grabbing her shoulders gently, but she pulled away again. "Hanna," he said. "Come on. Please don't be upset with me. I love you."

"Six months," she said. "What could you possibly have been doing for six months that you couldn't send a telegram or write a letter to let me know you were okay? Were you arrested?" He shook his head. "Held against your will? Imprisoned?" Her voice rose, and she began shaking a little. Her face was red, her eyes bright and hot with anger.

"No, no," he said. "Nothing like that." The truth was right there, on the tip of his tongue. He had helped the Feinsteins, touched the future, and she was in it, she was safe. He would rescue her, at some point. She would go into the closet with him. Eventually he would have to tell her everything. But he would wait until they needed to leave. He didn't want her to be in any danger by knowing what he'd done before that. He reached out for her again, but she pushed him away, harder, so he lost his balance a little. A searing pain shot across his forehead, in a line above his eyes, and he reached his hand up to rub it, to attempt to quell the ache.

"We're done," she said. Her voice was calm, even. It wasn't the anger talking; she actually meant it. The words cut him; his chest felt tight, and it was hard to breathe.

"You don't mean that," he said. "Julia told you I was back and you came to see me. Why else would you come here, if you didn't still love me?"

"Julia?" She shook her head. "I'm not here because of Julia. I've been coming here a few times a week, opening the shop for you. I didn't know what else to do . . . or when you were coming back. If you were ever coming back."

So that explained all the missing books, all the money in the register. "Oh, Hanna," he said, loving her even more, if that was possible. He tried to take her hand.

But she wouldn't let him. "No," she said. "Now that you're back I have no reason to be here. I want nothing more to do with you." She turned and ran out.

"Wait," he called after her. "Please! Let me try to explain!" He ran out after her into the street, but she kept running and refused to even turn back to look at him.

An agonizing week later Max's headache had finally gone away, and he understood that he was not going to die. Not now, anyway.

He used all the money Hanna had made in his absence to order more books for his shelves, and as he'd caught up on all the news in his absence, writing it all down in his journal, he also calculated a plan to win back Hanna's love. He would visit her every evening and every morning until she agreed to talk to him, until she listened to him.

"Just give her time," Elsa said kindly. "She'll come around."

But how much time did they have?

He rode the train to Maulbeerstrasse each morning and then again each evening, only to have her slam the door in his face twice, and not even open it up the other times.

But he would not give up, and eventually she would have to listen to him. She would have to.

And then, two weeks had passed, and she came to his shop one evening before he had set out on the train himself. She didn't use her key to open up the door, but she knocked on the glass. He opened the door, and she stood shaking, crying on the sidewalk. "I'm done," she shouted at him as she walked inside his shop. "Everything's done. Ruined!"

He opened his arms and was both surprised and relieved that she ran into them. He wrapped her in a hug, kissed the top of her head, smoothed back her hair.

"What happened?" he asked, wiping away the tears from her cheeks with his thumbs. "Did the SA threaten you?" He looked around on the street, but it was empty tonight. Quiet. The new Christian baker next door was friendly enough but closed his shop down much earlier than Herr Feinstein used to. "Is your mother okay?" Now that Jews no longer had health insurance, he had been so worried for Frau Ginsberg's health.

"My audition," she said between sobs. "I was so mad at you . . . and I didn't wear the lucky pin . . . and I messed up my audition. I'm done."

"Ssh." He rubbed her back, wiped away her new round of tears. She buried her face against his chest. He saw a flash of her, playing a solo. A humid summer night in Paris. The music like a sudden rainstorm. "There will be other auditions. You will have other orchestras," he told her.

"There are no other orchestras in Berlin." She pounded her fists against his chest in frustration, and then suddenly exhausted, she just put her hands up in the air, sat down on the floor.

He sat on the floor next to her, pulled her into his arms, and let her cry for a little while. "I promise you," he told her again. "There will be other orchestras."

When her crying subsided, she finally kissed him. "I can't lose you and my violin," she said. "I'm still mad at you . . . but I can't lose you."

It felt like it had only been two weeks to him, but for her months had passed. And all her anger and fire and love and disappointment and passion entwined in her kiss as she pulled him to her again, and he could suddenly think of nothing but her, feel nothing but the hotness of her skin against his.

"You're not going to lose me," he said

fiercely. And maybe if he said it like he believed it, he could make it true.

Hanna, 1950

I showed up on Julia's stoop in London two days after my night with Max, without even telephoning her first. And when Lev opened the door and saw me standing there, his mouth formed an O of surprise, quickly followed by a frown.

"What? Are you not excited for a visit from your tante?" I asked him, forcing a cheeriness I didn't quite feel.

"Mother's not feeling well," he said, staring at his bare feet. I picked up my suitcase and violin case from the stoop and pushed my way inside. The air inside the house felt stale, the foyer dark, as if someone hadn't thought to pull the shades or open the windows all summer.

"I should've telephoned," I said.

Stuart had waited up all night for me the other night, had telephoned the hospitals looking for me. I hadn't been able to look him in the eyes, as I apologized for alarming him, as I promised him I was completely fine. I lied and said I'd just been feeling ill and had spent the night at a hotel to avoid infecting him.

Then I quickly packed all my belongings and told him I needed to go to Julia's for a visit. The orchestra was on break for the month of August. I hadn't had the heart, or the courage, to stay and tell him the truth. Stuart deserved better; Stuart deserved someone who would love him and only him. And if Max was still alive, then that was never going to be me. I'd gotten on the first train to London, needing time away, space, to figure everything out.

"Julia," I called out into her darkened house, now.

But Moritz walked out from the kitchen, and his eyes lit up when he saw me. He ran up and gave me a hug. He may have been bigger, looking more and more like a small man now, but he was still the same mischievous little creature I adored. I kissed his head and ruffled his hair.

"Where's your mother?" I asked both him and Lev, who'd shut the door and walked up behind me. "And what's wrong with her?" She'd been coughing when she visited me in France a few months ago but had passed it off as nothing. Now I was genuinely concerned. "Has she been ill?" I asked the boys.

"Not exactly," Moritz said at the same time Lev said, "Yes."

"Boys, you're worrying me," I said. "Where is she?"

Simultaneously they pointed up the winding staircase, toward her bedroom. "I'm sorry," Moritz said. "She made us promise not to tell you."

"Tell me what?" Both boys looked at the floor, and I dropped my bags and ran up the staircase. The illness that had killed our mother had been terrible, the coughing, the weakness. But if Julia had the same thing, she could at least get good medical care here in London, unlike Mamele who'd had that ripped away from her by Hitler. Friedrich worked at the hospital for heaven's sake; she would have access to the best doctors.

Her bedroom door was shut, and I knocked on it. "Julia, it's Hanna. I've come for a visit." She didn't answer. "Can I come in?" She still didn't answer, so I turned the knob and walked inside.

The room was dark, the air smelled musty, and Julia made a lump underneath the covers in her giant messy bed.

"What are you doing here?" Her voice was

hoarse, raspy. "Did the boys call you?"

"No." I'd forgotten my own worries for the last few minutes. "The symphony is on break, and I missed you and the boys." It was only partly a lie — I had missed them. "I've come for a little visit."

"Without calling or writing me first?"

I switched on the table lamp and sat down on the edge of her bed. Her hair, which was curly like mine, but which she usually had pulled back in a proper, neatly coiffed bun, was a mess, like a great wind had come and thrown curls everywhere. I pushed a few away from her face. "Are you sick?" I asked her gently. "Like Mamele was?"

She sat up, pushed my hands away from her face, and pulled her hair back with her hands. "Goodness no, Hanni. I'm healthy as a horse."

"You don't look healthy as a horse. You look horrible," I shot back, finally honest with her in a way I hadn't been when I saw her in April. She hadn't looked great then, either, but I'd thought she just wasn't aging well. Or she was tired from the trip. "And how long have you been in this bed? It smells stuffy in here." I ran my finger across her nightstand and it came back dusty. "It looks like you haven't cleaned in ages."

"He's gone," Julia said, her voice breaking

335

on the word *gone,* as if she couldn't quite get it all the way out without choking on it.

"Someone died?" I was genuinely confused about who she meant, and why she hadn't telephoned to tell me. And why she made the boys keep it from me.

"Not died," Julia choked out. "Gone. Friedrich left me."

"Friedrich?" I was still confused. I didn't know my brother-in-law all that well. We hadn't ever been close or really even talked much, not in Germany, not when I lived here. But he and Julia had been together since I was ten years old. It had never occurred to me that they might be having problems, that he would *leave* Julia. "Oh, for heaven's sake." I was still thinking it was just a misunderstanding, that Julia was being overly dramatic. "Why would he leave you?"

"He fell in love with someone else." Julia held her hands up in the air. "A young, pretty British nurse who works at the hospital."

"Dumme Arschloch." I felt a wash of such sudden and deep anger on Julia's behalf that I slipped back into our native German for the insult.

She shook her head. "I didn't want you to know."

336

"Why not?"

"You have your life in Paris now. You're finally happy. After all these years! The boys and I are just fine. You don't need to concern yourself with us."

"Yes, I can see that. You look fine indeed." There were so many times I'd been frustrated with Julia for not understanding me, my passion for violin, my love for Max. But maybe she had only wanted me to be happy all along? She'd just had a different idea of happy than I'd always had. Now that she believed I had it, that she'd seen me in Paris, *glowing,* as she'd called it, she didn't want to do anything that might take it away from me. Not even ask for the help that I could see she so desperately needed.

I climbed into the bed next to her, got under the covers, and wrapped my arms around her. "I'm not fine either," I told her, perhaps the most honest thing I'd ever said to her. "Max is still alive," I said. "He came back and left me again, just like he always did." Julia squeezed my hand under the covers. "And that's not even all of it," I said. "I've also been having this . . . affair with Stuart."

"Oh, Hannalie." She sighed, and I wasn't sure if she was frustrated with me, as always, or relieved that she wasn't all alone. "Leave it to you to make sure your life is more of a mess than mine. So what are you going to do now?"

I wasn't exactly sure of the answer myself until I said it out loud to her: "I'm going to follow my greatest love," I told her.

"Max?" she asked.

"My violin," I said.

I spent three weeks in London with Julia and the boys, but then it was time for me to go. I had a train ticket to Vienna for the following morning; I had accepted the first violin position there, and orchestra rehearsals would begin in three days' time. I was both nervous and elated about starting over again, about moving to a new city where I understood the language. In a weird way I already believed it would feel like home.

I'd managed to get Julia up and out of bed during my stay; I'd helped her clean up the house and shop for food and cook meals. She said she could no longer afford Betsy without Friedrich's handsome salary, and she wasn't sure whether she could afford to keep the house forever either. Friedrich was still making the payments, and giving her a small monthly allowance, because she'd told him it was the only way he could continue to see the boys on weekends. *But who knows how much longer he will even care about them?* she'd said to me, holding her hands up in the air. And suddenly it didn't seem so silly that I had always loved my violin so much. Julia had never loved anyone or anything besides Friedrich, and now, she told me, worst of all, she wasn't at all sure what she would do with herself.

"Typing at the hospital wasn't so bad," I said with a false air of cheeriness, but Julia quickly shot back that she didn't want to work anywhere near the hospital. Friedrich and his *Flittchen* both still worked there.

"You'll find something else," I told her, though I honestly didn't know how easy it would be for an older woman with no real skills to find something in London these days. "You could always move to Vienna with me." Though it wasn't like I had anywhere for her to stay. I'd already gotten a place to live — the conductor's daughter and her husband had offered to rent me the extra room in their home, a duplex in the French-occupied quarter of Vienna just a few blocks from where we would rehearse.

"I wouldn't uproot the boys," Julia said with a frown. "London is the only home they've ever known. I'll figure something out. I always do."

■ ■ ■ ■

On my last day in London, I was out buying groceries for Julia, making sure she would have a supply for the rest of the week after I left, and on the way there, I found myself walking that familiar path toward the hospital, walking inside, and then taking the lift up to the fourth floor. Henry's office was still right there, looking as it always had. I had forgotten to call him after Julia's visit in the spring. My excuse was that I'd been consumed with the orchestra, but the truth was I hadn't exactly wanted to call him either. I wasn't sure I still wanted to revisit the past. But then the past, Max, had shown up anyway. Now I had even more questions, and even fewer answers.

I knocked gently on the door, half hoping he wasn't inside. But he opened up, straightaway. "Hanna!" he exclaimed. "What a lovely surprise. Come on in. What are you doing here?"

"I'm visiting Julia while the symphony is on break," I said. Henry frowned, and I remembered he and Friedrich were friends. Or they used to be, anyway. I quickly brought the subject back to me. "Actually, I'm moving to Vienna tomorrow, to play with a new symphony. I couldn't leave London without stopping in to say hello to you. It's been a while."

"Vienna?" Henry raised his eyebrows in surprise. "But I thought you loved Paris?" Julia must have mentioned how happy I'd seemed when he'd come to her house, looking for me last spring.

I cast my eyes down to the floor. "It'll be a bigger symphony," I said. "Better paying, too. And besides, I'll understand the language. French was proving impossible for me to learn."

"Ahh," Henry said, as if he understood. But I wasn't sure how he could, when I couldn't exactly understand it myself. I already missed Stuart, and I'd been such a coward; I'd written him a letter rather than telephoning him to tell him about Vienna. I'd told him exactly what I'd told Henry, better pay, speaking German again. But no matter what I wrote or said to Henry now, part of me longed to return to Stuart and the comfort of our apartment, our orchestra there. But I also held on to the note Max had left me on the hotel pillow. He would come back for me again. And when he did, I would go to him. I always did. It was something I hated about myself, but it was also something I knew in my heart as truth.

I would forgive and love Max, no matter how many times he left me, whether it made logical sense or not. And that wasn't fair to Stuart.

"So," Henry was saying now. "Back to a German-speaking country. You are confronting your past in a way then, aren't you?"

I shrugged. "I don't know. Maybe? I still don't remember it."

He nodded. "Are you still having the same dreams?" he asked.

"Not really," I told him, though I wasn't sure if I was or not. Stuart used to tell me I'd wake up screaming sometimes, and even though I no longer remembered the dreams the next morning, if Stuart said it happened, I trusted him that it had. The last dream I remembered was the one I had the night I spent with Max, but now, a few weeks later, I almost believed that entire night was a dream. Max was here, and then he was gone. Max was alive, or was he dead? Everything had changed, and nothing had changed. I had been waiting him for so long and was more confused than ever.

Henry sipped from a mug of coffee on his desk. "I asked your sister to have you telephone me a few months ago," he said.

"I know. I'm sorry. I was so busy with the orchestra and then . . ." I held my hands up. My excuse sounded as flimsy out loud as it had felt in my head.

"Perhaps you weren't ready to hear from me then?" Henry smiled kindly and offered me the familiar chair inside his office. I sat down.

Though I was different than I was when I'd come here a few years back, older, more confident, a real bona fide violinist, I couldn't help myself: I still felt like a lost little girl in this chair. "I really can't stay long," I said, moving to the edge, ready to jump up and run out at any moment.

"Of course," he said. "And I have an appointment as well. But I have something I've been wanting to tell you." I smiled nervously and waited for him to continue. My hands were shaking, and I clasped them together in my lap. "I came across someone a few months ago who thought they could've seen you during the war." His words tumbled out in a rush, as if he believed I might run out of his office before he could finish. He would not be wrong to think that. Part of me wanted to.

"Seen me?" I could barely breathe.

"Do you want to hear this?" Henry asked kindly. "Do you want me to tell you more?"

"No," I said quickly. Then: "Yes. I don't know . . . How did you meet this person?" I asked. "What is their name?" Max Beissinger was on the tip of my tongue, though I knew it wasn't him. He didn't know where I'd been in that time either.

"I've been working with some survivors of the camps at the hospital. Talking through their trauma with them."

I thought of all my Jewish friends in Berlin: Gerta and Fritzie, and Herr Fruchtenwalder. I had kept them in a space in my mind, where I only remembered the happy things about them, where I never let myself consider what had become of them in those ten years, during the war. It was quite warm in Henry's office, and I began to sweat.

"I have been working with one woman," Henry said, "who told me there was a women's orchestra in her camp. When she mentioned it to me, I immediately thought of you and your violin. I asked her if she remembered any of the women who played the violin there." He paused, and stared at me, trying to judge from my face if he should keep talking. My entire body felt frozen, suspended. "She didn't know their names," he said tentatively. "But she described one violinist who maybe looked like you . . ."

I shook my head. "No," I said quickly. "It

wasn't me." It couldn't have been. I couldn't have been in *a camp,* in a women's orchestra? I would've remembered that. The first orchestra I'd ever been in was in Paris. And Herr Doctor even said it, I was too healthy to have been in a camp, of such good weight in 1946.

"Well, it very well might not have been," Henry said. "But what if it was?"

"I have to go." I stood suddenly, bumping into his desk. His coffee tipped, spilled over the side of the cup, and Henry lunged to catch it, keep it from falling over entirely. "I'm sorry," I said to Henry. "I can't . . . I don't want to."

"Hanna," he called after me. "Please don't run away."

But that's exactly what I did. I ran the whole way back to Julia's. When I got there, I ran into the bathroom and I vomited, barely making it to the toilet in time.

Max, 1934

In the beginning of August, President Hindenburg died of lung cancer. Hitler quickly announced that he would be combining the positions of president and chancellor into one, and that he would now be everything to Germany, Führer. Soldiers were required to take a personal oath of allegiance not to Germany anymore, but to Hitler himself. *Die Führer* was their country and their country was him. It made Max sick to his stomach to think about it. And Elsa, whose belly seemed to be growing larger and larger by the day now, announced to him and Johann and Hanna one Saturday night over supper at their house that *her* country would never be Hitler's country.

"If none of us believe it, then he will not be Germany. *We* will be Germany," she said. Johann shushed her, telling her it was dangerous to even say such things out loud. And Elsa said, "So what are they going to

346

do, arrest a woman with child?"

"I wouldn't put it past them," Johann said quietly, lighting a cigarette after dinner and leaning back in his chair. He offered a smoke to Max, but Max declined. Hanna didn't like the smell of it on his clothes or the taste of it on his breath and she would complain when she kissed him after he spent a night out with Johann. He did not want to do anything to upset her tonight, as he had already decided that later, after dinner, he would finally give her the ring in his pocket. In these last few weeks, they had fallen back into their old routines. All the anger she'd had for him had finally subsided. And with not even the kindly old gentleman Hindenburg to temper Hitler now, Max wanted Hanna to move above his shop with him, so they would be close to the closet, able to leave at a moment's notice.

"I don't know," Hanna chimed in now. "I tend to agree with Elsa. There are more of us than there are of them. Chancellor? Führer? Why does that matter?" She still did not believe that Germany had become something terrible, unsafe for her, despite all evidence to the contrary. It was easier for her to believe she wasn't in danger, no matter how much Max had tried to convince her or read to her the same developments in the news he was reading.

Elsa smiled at Hanna now and asked if she would play something for them. "The baby likes music." Elsa put her hand to her stomach. "He kicks to and fro whenever you play for us. Dancing." She laughed a little. She had already told them she believed this baby to be a boy with all her heart. Max knew it was a girl, but he didn't tell her that. They would find out soon enough.

Max hadn't seen Hanna with her violin since her failed audition last month, and he was surprised when he'd met her at the train tonight, and she'd been carrying it. *Elsa asked me to,* she'd said with a shrug. And he had smiled, happy to see her looking like herself again. She seemed more relaxed, more happy tonight, than she had in weeks too.

Hanna took her violin out of its case now and stood in front of their fireplace. "What shall I play?" she asked them. "Something happy or something sad?"

"How about something German?" Johann took another puff of his cigarette and blew the smoke out in a circle in front of him. "It would do us all good to remember what is still German and beautiful."

"Brahms it is then." Hanna put her violin

under her chin, closed her eyes, and began to light up the room with her music.

Later as Max and Hanna walked back to his apartment, Hanna was still humming Brahms under her breath. She held on to her violin case in one hand, his hand in the other. "Did you know that Brahms wrote that concerto for Clara Schumann? He loved her desperately but could never be with her. It's a song about their unrequited love."

"What a sad story," Max said. "The song was so beautiful when you played it. I never would've guessed it."

"Love is always beautiful," Hanna countered. "It just doesn't always have a happy ending."

The night was quiet, but the swollen August moon illuminated their pathway home. It was easy to feel what Elsa and Hanna still felt about Germany on this starry summer night. It was their home, their country, more than it was the führer's. The familiar Hauptstrasse, where Max had spent his entire life, the mulberry blossoms that lined the sidewalk, turning his shoes yellow as he walked, the glint of moonlight on the window of his shop that illuminated the *Beissinger* on the sign: all that felt more real than the news erupting in the papers, day by day, worse and worse. But he could not be sentimental and naive. He knew that, but still, just for the night he wanted to pretend that the world was all right, that being in love was the only thing that mattered.

Just as they got in front of the shop, Max stopped, put his arms around Hanna, kissed her gently, and then stepped back. "We are going to have a happy ending," he said. His hands were shaking, but, at long last, he pulled the ring from his pocket and held it out in front of her.

"Max?" She said his name softly, and it was hard to tell whether she was happy or sad.

"Hannalie Ginsberg," he said, using her full name. "I love you. I want to spend every minute of my life with you. Would you make me the happiest man in Germany and marry me?"

She didn't move for a second, and neither did he. They stood suspended, as if time and the world had stopped. But then she nodded and Max took her hand, slipped the ring onto her finger.

Hanna stared at the ring on her finger, then at him. "I love you, too. But I also love my violin," she said softly. "There will be another opening in the symphony in the summer. I will audition again. I won't ever give up."

"My wife will be a world-famous violinist," Max said. He forgot about everything he knew, everything he worried about. It was only here and now, him and her. And he wanted her to have everything she wanted and had worked tirelessly for.

Hanna stood up on her toes and kissed him, and he pulled her inside the shop. As he was locking the door behind him, she was already reaching for him. A new desire had come over them, and they couldn't even make it up the stairs to his apartment. They made love right there, on the floor of his shop.

The next morning, Hanna slipped the ring off before she left and put it in his palm. "I'll come back for this tonight," she promised. "Just let me tell Mamele. Let me talk to her about it first before I go home wearing a ring."

Max frowned, knowing that her mother and Julia wouldn't approve, especially not now. Julia hated him more than ever, and Frau Ginsberg was growing sicker and weaker without any medical care. "They'll try to change your mind about us," Max said now.

"No, no," Hanna insisted, stubbornly. "My mind is made up. You're stuck with me forever, Max Beissinger." She kissed him one last time, grabbed her violin case, and then she was gone.

Hanna did not come back that night. He waited for her after he closed down the shop, and once it grew dark, he began to worry. Recently he'd made her promise not to come see him too late, not to ride the train at night alone. Jews were often harassed by the SA, and worse, sometimes beaten for seemingly no reason. The *Fischmarkt* across the street had apparently been vandalized in his six-month absence, not with a brick like Feinstein's had been but with a bright red Hakenkreuz painted across its door in the middle of the night, the windows smashed out from the street with sticks, and then the owner, Herr Sokolov, who was not even a Jew but a Russian whose family had emigrated to Germany after the war, had disappeared. He'd always kept to himself and Max hadn't known him well, but he had noticed his absence on the street and had to ask Elsa and Johann what had happened to him. They weren't sure. He might've been arrested. He might've gone back to Russia. It became less and less unusual for someone to just disappear into what seemed to be thin air.

It was his biggest fear now that something would happen to Hanna before he could take her into another time. He had seen her, in the future, and she was safe. But that didn't feel like any sort of guarantee. He didn't believe that anyone's future was certain, unmalleable.

Max waited as long as he could stand it, and when it was half past eight, he ran to the train station and rode the train to Maulbeerstrasse. He got off and ran through the mulberry-lined streets to Hanna's apartment, and he was out of breath, sweating by the time he knocked on the door.

Hanna opened the door, her eyes red and puffy. She must've told them, and they fought. Maybe they had talked her out of it? "Oh, Hanna, no," he said, unable to help himself.

As she said: "Mamele is dying and no one will help her."

"What?" It wasn't what he was expecting at all, but as soon as she said it, guilt washed over him. He should've come sooner.

"She needs a doctor. She can't even open her eyes. But no one will come. Julia went down the street and tried to telephone almost every doctor in Berlin. But we have no medical insurance. And even if we did . . ." Hanna held her hands in the air, and suddenly it had all become real to her, everything he'd been trying to convince her of since Hitler had begun to come to power.

"Maybe I could help," Max said. He wasn't Jewish and he still had quite a nest egg from his father. Even in Hitler's Germany, gold still meant something.

"How can you possibly help?" Julia had walked up behind Hanna, put her hands on her sister's shoulders. Friedrich stood there, too, a little off to the side. Even married to Julia, he appeared somewhat out of place, maybe even a little scared of the force that was Hanna and Julia together. "Did you acquire a medical degree when you abandoned my sister for six months?" Julia asked snidely.

Max grimaced. *He didn't abandon Hanna.* He would never abandon Hanna. But he wasn't going to argue with Julia, not at a time like this. "Friedrich, don't you work at a hospital?" He knew very little about Julia's husband, other than he worked in some kind of lab.

"I was fired months ago," Friedrich said, frowning. *Of course.* That's why they were waiting on the visas for London, where Jews could still work in hospitals. How easy it was to forget that he'd missed months, not days, when he'd gone into the closet.

"But you must know a lot of doctors."

"None of them will treat a Jew with no medical insurance," Julia said, exasperated. "Don't you think we've already tried?"

"Which one is the most in need of money?" Max asked Friedrich, ignoring Julia.

"We don't have any money," Julia spat at him.

"But I do," he said.

"No," Julia said, firmly. "We can't take your money."

Hanna put her hand on Julia's arm, and her face softened. "Jule," she said. "Max and I are going to get married. He's going to be family. We need his help. We should take his money."

"Married?" Julia sputtered. This was the first she'd heard of it. Her surprise stung Max. Maybe it shouldn't have. Hanna's thoughts had obviously been consumed by her mother's health today. But still.

But then Hanna reached across the doorway and grabbed his hand, squeezed it. "Yes," she said, quite firmly to Julia. "Married."

Friedrich grabbed his hat and stepped

outside, ignoring Julia's anger. "All right," he said calmly to Max. "Hector Bergameister likes to bet on the horses at the Hoppegarten, and he almost always loses. He lives in a *stadthaus* near the hospital. We can take the train, you and I." Neither Julia nor Hanna protested, and the two men left.

It was the first and only time Max and Friedrich would ever be alone together, and the silence between them was a little uncomfortable as they rode the train into Berlin. "Those Ginsberg girls," Friedrich finally broke the silence. "They're a lot to take sometimes, aren't they?"

"Hanna feels deeply for the people and things she cares about," Max said. "But that is what I love about her."

Friedrich shook his head a little. "You've got it all worked out somehow, don't you, Beissinger? Best of both worlds. You travel all over, probably have girls all over Europe, and then you got Hanna waiting for you at home." He raised his eyebrows and elbowed Max.

"It's not like that," Max said.

"Sure," Friedrich said. "If you say so."

Neither one of them said anything else until the train stopped in central Berlin, and they got off. "It's too late, you know," Friedrich said. "Hedy's been off her medicine for months. Hasn't seen a doctor in a long time either."

"Don't say that," Max said. He thought about his own mother, lying in bed in their apartment, Herr Doctor telling his father that all they could do was make her comfortable, but at least he'd come, at least there'd been comfort and morphine for the pain. *Death and comfort were one and the same.*

"I'm just telling you the honest truth, before you waste your gold," Friedrich said. "The girls don't want to hear it . . . but whether we get Hector to come with us or not, she's never going to make it through the week."

HANNA, 1950

Vienna, and Austria, had been divided into four occupation zones by the Allies after the war: American, French, Soviet, and British. I was living in the French occupation zone, but it felt nothing at all like France. Everywhere I went, there was the glorious cadence of my German language again, and it comforted me, even overhearing it in bits and pieces on the street. Though much of the arts district of Vienna was still being rebuilt, war rationing had mostly ended, and you could get meat more easily again. Frau Schmidt made a wonderful schnitzel on the night of my arrival, to welcome me to their home and to their city. And it tasted so much like the Gutenstat dishes of my girlhood, I almost cried.

The Orchestra von Frankreich was larger than Le Bec's — the violin section alone having twice as many players — and we rehearsed on an actual stage. Not in a concert hall, since the grand ones were still being renovated after being bombed in the war, but inside a school that had been closed down after the Anschluss. The orchestra rented the space from the French government now, and the former school auditorium was the orchestra's home, both for rehearsal and concerts. This orchestra had started up only a year before Stuart's but our maestro, Herr Krauss, was older than Stuart and had been a well-respected cellist, then maestro in Vienna even before the war. I wasn't sure what had happened to him during the war exactly, and I didn't ask either, though, whatever it was, he was missing his middle finger on his right hand, which did not fail to remind me of Stuart each time he raised his arms to begin, and his four good fingers dangled precariously close to my head.

As the Orchestra von Frankreich charged admissions and wanted to appeal to people in all sectors of the city, we rehearsed music by French, British, Russian, and American composers in equal measure. Some of it was new to me, having never played much music by American composers in Germany, or in Paris, and I threw myself into learning it, practicing so much, so many hours, that in my first few weeks in Vienna I had to ice my fingers before bed each night. But then I would fall into a deep sleep, without the time to think or breathe or live anything else but the music. Which was just the way I wanted it.

I received weekly letters from Julia, and once a month, on a Sunday, she would telephone me to catch up. But we would only talk for five minutes, so as not to run up the charges too high. She had gotten a job minding the neighbor's children, which seemed like a bad fit to me, but she claimed she enjoyed it, since they were little girls and she'd never had any of her own. Her letters contained anecdotes of taking care of the girls, and about the boys' accolades in school and sports. She barely mentioned herself, or Friedrich. But when I wrote her back, I did much the same, telling her only about rehearsal and Frau Schmidt's cooking, and how it reminded me of Mamele's before she got sick.

Stuart wrote me only once the whole fall, and really, I wouldn't have been surprised if he hadn't. He included nothing personal, only of the pieces they were working on in Paris: I was missing Holst's *The Planets,* one of my favorite orchestral suites, and I felt a little jealous, thinking of them rehearsing it in the basement without me. But when I wrote him back, I told him only about our first concert, which we played to a sold-out audience. And how Maestro said it was nearly unbelievable, given that not too long ago people were still struggling to buy food. And about the American composer Barber's *Adagio for Strings,* which was completely new to me, but which I could now play from memory.

I wrote to Elsa, too, letting her know of my new address and asking her to let me know if she heard again from Max, but she wrote back, saying she hadn't heard from him in a while.

I tried not to think about Stuart, about Elsa, about Max, nor about what Henry had told me in London. If I didn't think about it, didn't believe it, didn't remember it at all, then it could not have happened.

The past was still an infinite blank, but most days I did not dwell on it. I lived and breathed music. And when I slept, I dreamed only of the adagios I had practiced too many times before bed, and the new American symphonies that awaited me when I awoke in the morning.

We played a concert in December, just before Christmas, our last of the fall season.

The entire auditorium was decorated in red and silver garland, and a large ornamental tree sat just behind the violin section onstage. I might have been the only member of the orchestra who was Jewish, but I might not have been. Though many of them spoke German and English, like me, I hadn't become close friends with anyone in the orchestra. I knew them all by name and waved and said *guten Tag.* I engaged in small talk from time to time, especially with the older Austrian gentleman, Hanz, who sat right next to me. But I never would've told any of them, not even Hanz, that I did not celebrate Christmas. I wondered if all the Austrian Jews had disappeared during the war, just like the German ones, or if people just didn't talk about such things anymore.

The Christmas pieces were easy, requiring very little practice on my part, and for the first time since I'd moved to Vienna, I began to feel a tremendous longing that December: for my sister, for Stuart, for Max, for answers about my past. I had trouble sleeping again; my dreams were restless. And when, during the Christmas concert, I gazed into the audience and my eyes caught on Stuart's face, I thought for sure I was imagining him there, the way I might have imagined Max in Paris. An apparition of my wanting. But then I found him waiting for me backstage, afterward. He raised his good hand to wave, smiled sheepishly, and I knew he was real.

"You're here?" I breathed it as a question, still not certain it was him. I reached up my hand to touch his face; his cheeks were rough with gray stubble, which also made him look older than he had only a few months ago, when I'd left him in Paris clean-shaven.

"Should I have written?" he asked, gently removing my hand from his face. "I was worried you would tell me not to come if I did." I probably would have.

"Hanna, *Fröhliche Weihnachten.*" Hanz wished me a Merry Christmas in German and tapped me gently on the shoulder on his way out. He eyed Stuart with suspicion.

"You, too, Hanz," I answered back in German. "Don't eat too much stollen." He'd been telling me at rehearsal yesterday about his weakness for the Christmas pastry, and it had made me long for Mamele's jelly doughnuts, which she used to make from scratch for me and Julia for Hanukkah when we were little girls.

He walked out and I turned back to Stuart. "I'm glad you're here," I said to him, in

English, now. "Would you like to get a drink? Or are you hungry?" I reached my hand out, grabbed his, more out of habit than of anything else. Now that Stuart was near me, I wanted to touch him, to hold on to him.

"I am a little hungry." He gently extricated his hand from mine, clenching his fist and holding it firmly at his side. My fingers stung a little from the rejection, or maybe they were just still sore from too much practicing.

"There is a place, a few blocks away," I told him, forcing a smile. "The strudel almost tastes like home." Though as soon as I said it, I thought of Herr Brichtman's bakery near the Lyceum, the first time Max and I ever kissed, eating strudel there together, and I quickly looked down at my feet.

"You know I am never one to turn down pastry," he said with a chuckle, and I suddenly felt so homesick for him, for our apartment in Paris, that I had to bite my lip in order not to cry.

Stuart and I walked outside into the frosty December air. The street was bustling with people, shopping for last-minute Christmas gifts. Twinkling lights hung from storefronts, illuminating the dusting of snow on the sidewalk that had fallen while I was playing the concert, and the air smelled hopeful, like pine, fresh snow, and chimney smoke. I buried my hand that wasn't carrying my violin in my coat pocket to keep it warm, and also to keep it from reaching for Stuart again.

We walked inside the dimly lit bakeshop, sat across from each other, and for a few moments, we ate our strudel, not talking at all. There were so many things I wanted to say to him, not the least of which was how much I missed him, and how sorry I was for hurting him. Not knowing what to say at first, I picked at my strudel with my fork, saying nothing at all.

"Ling left the orchestra," he finally spoke. "She's with child and says she's too big to play the cello right now."

"Oh no," I said, not sure whether I felt sorrier for the orchestra or Ling's baby. She was not the warmest person. "Did you have trouble replacing her?"

"I don't know," he said. "I mean, I suppose they won't. It was quite easy to replace you." He stopped talking, opened his mouth, then bit his lip. "I didn't mean it that way."

"No, I know, of course." I imagined

someone beautiful, and decidedly French, who took my place, not just in the orchestra, but in Stuart's apartment. I stared at my strudel, moving it around the plate with my fork, but I was no longer hungry for it.

"I just meant that . . . . there was a lot of interest. A lot of people auditioned for your seat. Le Bec's little orchestra has been doing quite well. I'm sure they will replace Ling easily too."

It hit me that he said *they,* and now he was calling it Le Bec's orchestra, not *ours* or, more rightly, his. "And what about you?" I asked.

"I was getting other offers last summer too," he said. He put his fork down, his strudel barely eaten, folded his hands in his lap. "I wouldn't have taken them. But then . . ." His voice trailed off.

"But then I left," I said.

"Yes, I mean, I don't blame you. This job will be better money for me. *On ne peut pas vivre que de pain,* as the French say."

"You cannot live on love alone?"

"Bread," he corrected me. "On bread alone."

I began to blush furiously at my bad translation, my assumption that he was leaving because of me, not because of the money. "Of course, yes," I said. "I'm glad to

366

hear you have something better, too."

"That's actually why I came," he said. "I got an offer in America. In New York City. It's a second-tier orchestra, for now. But if they like me, if everything goes well . . . the conductor of their first-tier symphony plans to retire in a few years' time, and they might move me up."

"Wow," I said. "America. Stuart, that's . . ." I couldn't come up with the appropriate word, because I was thinking only of how far it was, how it would take days and days on a boat across the ocean to get there, not merely hours on the train. "Will I never see you again?" I said softly.

"I hope that's not the case," he said. "That's why I came to talk to you now. If things go well and they do move me up in a few years . . . I'll have complete hiring control. I'll want to make it the best orchestra in the world, and the only way to do that would be to hire you."

"Oh, Stuart, you don't have to say that."

"It's true," he said. "No one plays with your passion, Hanna. The Le Bec Orchestra isn't the same without you. Nothing is," he added. I stared very hard at my strudel, trying to avoid Stuart's eyes. "It will be a little while." Stuart was still talking. "A few years. So just think about it. Keep it in the back of your mind. Mull it over." He paused. "And there, of course, would be no strings attached."

"No strings, in your orchestra?" It struck me funny and I chuckled. He laughed, too, and the tension between us eased. I finally looked at him. He smiled a little.

"I just mean —"

"I know what you mean." I reached across the table and put my hand on top of his. He didn't immediately pull away, and I suddenly wanted to tell him that I missed him, that I wanted him, still. That I had never ever wanted to hurt him. But the night I'd been with Max, I hadn't really thought of Stuart, and I knew the best thing I could do for him was to let him go. To tell him that maybe in America he would find someone who loved him, whose heart didn't still belong to someone else. But neither one of us said anything at all.

He pulled his hand back, and my palm hit the table. "Your orchestra played quite well," he said. "You made the right decision to come here. Paris was never going to be forever, for either of us." He made it sound like he was still talking about the orchestra, but I knew in my heart he was talking about us.

"No," I murmured. "Of course not."

Because if there was anything my life had taught me, blanks and all, it was this: nothing was forever.

MAX, 1934–1935

Grace Eliza Wilhelm was born during a blizzard at the end of November 1934, and Max and Hanna were the first people, other than Elsa and Johann, to meet her. They walked through the snow from Max's shop, arriving freezing, and wet up to their knees. Hanna carried her violin case above her head, to keep it safe and dry. And inside, the Wilhelm house was warm, and they put their boots by the fire. Elsa brought a sleeping Grace out to the sitting room in her arms. Grace was bright pink, with blue eyes and a full head of coal-colored hair.

"What a beauty," Hanna said, stroking Grace's little fingers, glancing at Max, as if she were envisioning their own future, their own child. Max smiled at her, though inwardly he felt sad. He knew they would not have a child together. At least not in the future he had seen. "A future violinist, perhaps?" Hanna said.

Elsa laughed and asked Hanna if she would play something for them. "Maybe she will love your music as much on the outside as she did on the inside?"

But Hanna played only a few notes before Grace began to wail, scrunching up her tiny pink cheeks, raising her clenched fists in the air. Hanna stopped playing and laughed. "I know how you feel, *meine Liebling.* Sometimes I hate the sound of it too."

Emilia ran in circles through the house, declaring herself a big sister, and as happy as Elsa looked, Johann looked the opposite: exhausted, pale. "You all right?" Max asked him quietly, away from all the girls.

"Are any of us all right these days?" Johann said.

Max clapped his friend on the back. "You'll feel better once you get some sleep," he said. But he knew Johann spoke the truth. Just last week the Nazis had won the election in *Freie Stadt Danzig,* a semiautonomous German city-state, where other parties had still been permitted to run. And the Nazis still won. So what did that say about their country, about the good people who lived here, freely choosing the Nazis, even when they weren't forced to?

Frau Ginsberg died before the ground froze,

and without Max even being able to bribe one single doctor with gold to come and help her. He had let Hanna down, and he apologized to her and Julia, saying he wished he could've done more. Hanna told him that their mother's heart had been on borrowed time for many years, and that he shouldn't take any of that on himself. But she lost her usual light for a little while after her mother died, playing the saddest songs on her violin, night after night after night in his shop.

By March of 1935, Julia and Friedrich had secured their visas and were readying themselves to move to London. They tried to convince Hanna to move away with them, but she believed she'd be able to get another audition in the symphony that summer. Nothing was more important to her than to do well and finally secure her spot, and it blinded her to everything else that was happening in their city, their country. Max understood why Julia wanted Hanna to leave so badly, but selfishly, he wanted her to stay with him for as long as possible. He knew that he would save her when it was time. With this peace of mind, he did not try to convince her to take her sister's offer. Not that she would've listened, even if he had.

He and Hanna were also making their wedding plans. Max wanted to marry Hanna right away, but she insisted they do it after Julia left the country and after she made it through her audition. She said she was exhausted from fighting with her sister about everything, about him, about her violin. Julia's disdain for him was palpable. He disliked being in a room with her, even when Hanna asked him over to Maulbeerstrasse each Friday for the Sabbath, in the weeks before Julia and Friedrich left. He wanted to spend their holiday with them, to understand it, to be a real part of it. But Julia glared at him through dinner, and Friedrich kept to himself, if only to be loyal to his wife it seemed. Max dreaded going each Friday, though he never thought of *not* going, not being with Hanna, not learning the rituals of her religion.

And then, Julia and Friedrich moved away, and Hanna spent the next Sabbath above the bookshop with him, lighting only two candles, whispering a brief prayer, before they enjoyed their supper together.

By spring, it felt as if they really were married. Hanna spent days at the Lyceum, nights practicing in his shop, and then she would walk upstairs and reach for him in bed. He made space for her clothes in his closet and chest of drawers, and she had moved many of her things in. She still kept the apartment on Maulbeerstrasse because it would be too hard to sell now (her mother had owned it outright), and from time to time, if she had to practice or stay too late at the Lyceum, she would still sleep there. But for almost all intents and purposes they lived above Max's shop, together, as if they were husband and wife.

At night sometimes, when it was just the two of them in the darkness, in his bed, Max could forget about the impending feeling of doom that hung on him like a heavy blanket in all waking daylight hours, the growing hatred for Jews in his country, his worry that Hanna was in danger every time she left his shop. His creeping fear that he would wait too long to take her into the closet, or, that even now with her mother dead and her sister gone, she would refuse to go with him. Military conscription in Germany had just been renewed, violating the Treaty of Versailles, and he knew that things were growing dire, that a war was coming again. But unlike the last war, this would be Hitler's war, a war against Jews. A war against Hanna.

"I will protect you," he whispered to

Hanna at night, after she fell asleep, sometimes midsentence, her body and mind weary from her extensive practicing. "I will save you," he promised. Next to him, she murmured something unintelligible in her sleep, rolled into him, and he held on to her tightly.

In late May one night, there was knocking on the glass window of the shop. Hanna was practicing at the Lyceum, and though he'd stayed downstairs waiting for her for hours, he knew she wasn't coming. It was already too late, too dark out. Too dangerous for her to ride the train by herself. He'd just shut his book, blown out his candle, and resolved himself to going upstairs when the knock came on the glass, softly at first, then, louder.

"Herr Beissinger," an unfamiliar woman's voice called. "Open up. Please."

He opened the door just a little bit at first and saw that a woman and her child stood outside. They looked terrified, and also harmless. But then the child, a boy of maybe ten or twelve, saluted with the *Hitlergruss,* and Max quickly saluted back. The woman shook her head and lowered the boy's hand. "I'm sorry, the shop is closed," Max told them, moving to shut the door again. They did not look like Nazis, nor SA, but he could not risk letting strangers into his shop at night.

"Please," the woman said, putting her hand up to stop him from closing the door. "I am Rachel Feinstein's sister, Marta, and this is my son, David." He remembered what Herr Feinstein had told him, *Rachel and her sister, Marta, making pamphlets, distributing them.*

He looked around at the street to make sure it was empty, ushered them both inside the shop, and quickly closed and locked the door behind him.

"My sister told me your name. She said you were going to help her, and I don't know if you did. I haven't heard from her since. But I didn't know where else to go." Her face was white, and she gripped her son's hand tightly. "The SA came to arrest me tonight, and we escaped out the back window. I didn't know where else to go," she repeated, her voice breaking on the words. "Please, if you helped my sister. Can you help me? I brought this." She held out a large round diamond in the palm of her hand and tried to give it to him.

But he did not take it from her. He didn't want her valuable possession.

"Please," she said again. Marta began to

sob softly, her small shoulders shaking from the weight of her fear. Her son patted her shoulder awkwardly and Max thought of his mother, lying in bed, dying. How much he'd wanted to save her, wanted to breathe for her, and he couldn't. His heart broke for them.

He glanced at the closet. Maybe he could give them instructions for how fast to run to get to safety, send them in alone? He didn't want to leave now himself, didn't want to leave Hanna. But how could he not help this woman and her son?

"All right," he said. "What I'm going to tell you is going to sound crazy, but I promise you this is how I helped your sister." He told them about the closet, Einstein's theory about wormholes, about how he'd taken the Feinsteins and left them in another time where Jews were safe.

Marta stared at him wide-eyed with disbelief. David's face turned white. "Come on, David." Marta grabbed her son's hand and began to back away from Max very slowly. "Please." She held up her free hand. "Don't hurt us."

"I don't want to hurt you," Max said gently. And he understood no matter what he told them, no matter what he said, they were not going to go into the closet, not without him. And if they left his shop, went back outside, Marta would be arrested. David would lose his mother.

"You can have the diamond." Marta held it out again, her hand shaking. "Please just don't hurt us."

"I don't want the diamond," he said. "Keep your diamond. You will need it." He sighed. "Look, I will go in first," he said. "You only need to follow behind and keep my pace. Your sister was skeptical, too, but she trusted me, and she is safe now."

He could take them through the closet very quickly. And he should only be gone a few days, a week or two at most, if he turned right back around. He had to help them. Otherwise they'd be arrested or worse.

He walked to the counter, scribbled a quick note for Hanna, then walked back to the closet and held out his hand. Marta shook her head. But David looked at his mother, then at Max, and he let go of his mother's hand and walked to the closet.

HANNA, 1951

I returned to London in April when the orchestra went on a short break, and it happened to coincide with Passover. Julia wrote me that she wanted to make dinner to celebrate the holiday, that it was time for the boys to understand where they came from now that they were getting dangerously close to being grown men. I hadn't celebrated Passover in so many years and I was actually eager to visit and share it with them, to spend a few days with people I loved.

On the train ride there by myself, without a day of violin practice to consume me, I was hit by an overwhelming sense of emptiness. It reminded me of the way I felt in Berlin, just before I auditioned for the second time and Max had disappeared on me again.

Max and I had been engaged then, and for a little while, I'd worn his mother's ring, felt its extra weight on my finger each day when I practiced. It reminded me that I loved two things: the violin and Max. The violin had my heart all day. Max had it all night.

I was so angry when I saw the note he'd left for me on the counter in his shop. I'd taken the ring off my finger, left it there. I had one love, only one love. My violin had never left me, never hurt me, never let me down. I practiced and I practiced and it behaved the way I wanted it to. But after I took the ring off, I longed for it back again. I noticed its missing weight, every single time I played.

This past year in Vienna I had felt so much the same, though I did not allow myself to fully feel it until I took a day away from my violin and sat on the train. I missed Stuart, and it pained me not to know when, or if, I'd ever see him again. And I still longed for Max, too. I didn't know where he'd disappeared to, or if, or when, he would find me again like he'd promised. Another note, another city, another time. Everything had changed and nothing at all had changed. Except I still had my violin.

And my sister and my nephews. I had them now, too, I reminded myself. That was why I'd been so excited for this break, for this trip back to London. Things were not the same as they had been before the war. I was a concert violinist now; I had a family.

But still, it was hard to shake the feeling of loneliness. It rode with me, all the way to London.

Lev and Moritz met me at the train station in London by themselves, and I felt better as soon as I saw them. Lev, at fourteen, looked so much like a man, much like the young Friedrich I remembered courting Julia in Germany that when I stepped off the platform and saw him there waiting for me, I gasped. At almost twelve, Moritz was taller than me, but he still had the face of a little boy, thank goodness.

"Where's your mother?" I asked, as Lev took my suitcase, and Moritz offered to carry my violin. There weren't too many people in the world I'd let carry it, but Moritz was one of them. "She's not hiding out in her bedroom again, is she?"

"No," Moritz answered, inspecting my violin case to see if it still looked as it had years ago, then tracing his forefinger over the *Orchestra von Frankreich* sticker I'd pasted on near the handle. "She's cooking. Matzo balls for soup."

"Ah." It had been many years since I'd

eaten a matzo ball, not since Mamele had passed, or maybe longer, as matzo was not easy to find in Germany after Hitler came to power.

"And I'm old enough to go everywhere alone now," Lev informed me. His voice was deep. He even sounded like Friedrich.

"Of course you are." I ruffled his hair a little just to annoy him and make Moritz smile. He did not disappoint. Even an almost twelve-year-old Moritz still found me amusing.

"I have to tell you something." Julia accosted me as soon as the boys led me inside their new home. It was a flat, not a house, in central London, not the West End. Much smaller and less fancy than their old place, but I felt immediately more comfortable here. It reminded me a little of the apartment we'd grown up in on Maulbeerstrasse, with its small front parlor between the front door and the kitchen. "Boys," Julia said. "Go put Tante's stuff in Moritz's room. The boys are rooming together while you're here," she said to me, and I shrugged, really not caring where I slept.

She wiped her hands on her apron and grabbed me in a hug. Then she stepped back and looked at me, pushed a wayward curl behind my ear. "You look wonderful," she said. "Vienna agrees with you."

She appeared to have gained a little weight back, and her color was much better than when I'd seen her last. Her hair was messier, out of her usual bun, framing her face, but surprisingly, the messiness suited her. "So do you," I told her. "I'd say the unmarried life agrees with you."

"Well . . ." she said. "That's actually what I need to talk to you about. I've met someone."

"Julia! That's great news. Why didn't you write to me about him?"

"I wanted to tell you in person. It's sort of a . . . well, you know him."

I didn't know anyone in London except for her and Friedrich, as well as some of the musicians in the Royal Orchestra, and then it dawned on me. "Henry Childs?" I asked, surprised.

She bit her lip a little and nodded. "He came to see me after you first left for Vienna because he was worried about you, and then, well, we started talking and we have a lot in common."

I had no idea what on earth Julia and Henry Childs had in common — Henry wasn't even Jewish for one thing — but then, I didn't know very much about Henry at all. The majority of the time we'd spent together had been spent talking only about me and my foggy past. But he had always been so very kind to me, and I was glad that Julia seemed happy. "Good for you," I said.

"Henry was worried that it might upset you . . . He's coming tonight, for the Seder; I mean, if that's all right with you?"

"Of course. Why wouldn't it be?" I forced a smile. I liked Henry, and I wouldn't mind seeing him. But I didn't want to try to talk about my past, or the things he'd told me the last time I'd seen him, and I hoped he wouldn't bring it up.

She hugged me again. "Come on," she said. "I need your help to roll the matzo balls."

It was just like when we were kids. Only then, Julia and I stood at Mamele's apron, staring up, watching her roll the balls in her large palms.

I washed my hands and dug my fingers into the bowl of cold sticky matzo meal, my past soaking in through my fingers. It was still here, whether I wanted it or not.

It wasn't until Henry rang the bell a few hours later that Julia told me the rest of the story. "We have a few other guests coming for dinner too," she said nonchalantly, as she seasoned the soup, like she hoped I wouldn't notice if she slipped it in right along with a pinch of salt and grind of pepper.

"Friends of yours?" I asked.

"Not exactly . . . a few Jewish women Henry has worked with. They didn't have anywhere else to go." Julia was talking fast. She knew it was more than that. Henry must've told her everything.

I opened my mouth to protest, but it was too late. One of the boys had already answered the door, and Henry was walking in, three unfamiliar women with him. "Hanna." Henry smiled when he saw me. I lifted my hand to wave, but my eyes drifted to the women behind him. They were all young, maybe younger than me, and I was certain I had never seen them before in my life. *Or had I?*

"Everyone, this is Bernie . . . Franciszka . . . Adelle." He pointed to each woman, left to right, each of them lifting an arm to say hello. Bernie had a number tattooed on her wrist; she fiddled with it self-consciously when she waved. *Is she the one who told Henry about the orchestra?* But I didn't see a flash of recognition on her face as Henry introduced me, nor on any of their faces. I was a stranger to them, as they were

385

strangers to me.

"Come," Julia said. "Everyone have a seat. It is almost sundown."

"It has been so long since I have had Seder," Franciszka said. Her English was stilted, her accent unfamiliar. Not German, nor French. "I was little girl," she said. "The youngest one. I sang questions. *Czwórka.*" She held up four fingers.

"Four questions," Adelle corrected her kindly, in English. "But when we sing them in Hebrew we all speak the same language, yes?"

"Moritz is the youngest tonight," Julia said. "And we've been practicing, haven't we, darling?" Moritz grinned, still not too old to adore being the center of attention. He was a performer, just like me.

Julia arranged the Seder plate in the center of the table and passed around the very same Haggadahs we had used so many years ago in Germany. She must have taken them with her when she fled, and I ran my fingers across the worn leather cover, the familiar Hebrew letters on the front, grateful that Julia had gone when she had, that she had saved something, however small, from our childhood.

Dusk came outside Julia's front window, and she lit the candles on the table. The curtains were open, and our Seder was in full view to anyone who might be walking by, no one giving this exposure a second thought the way we had last time we'd done this in Gutenstat, before Mamele had died. That year we had pulled the curtains tight, and I'd been reminded by Julia to whisper-sing, so there was no chance that anyone passing by would hear us.

"Louder," Julia said to Moritz, as his voice wobbled a little on the first question. "Sing it out darling, the way Tante plays the violin."

At the mention of my violin, I looked down at my plate, but when I raised my eyes again, no one was looking at me. All eyes were on Moritz, singing the words loudly, off-key.

After dinner I escaped onto the balcony off Julia's kitchen with a cup of tea. I wasn't trying to be rude, but talk over dessert had turned to the war. Henry shared about how his younger brother had been sent to the front lines, and how worried he'd been for his safety until he'd returned remarkably unscathed. I never knew he had a brother, but Julia nodded like she already understood all there was to know about him. Then Franciszka began speaking of when her family was arrested in Poland. And my head started to hurt in a way it hadn't in years, since I'd first come to London, trying so hard to remember. It was easier not to try, to let the past linger hazily behind me. The air outside on the balcony was damp, but springlike. I took a deep breath and looked out at the building next to Julia's. Across the way, through the window, another family was having their own Seder.

"Do you mind if I sit with you?" Adelle had opened the door and noiselessly stepped out while I'd been spying on the neighbors.

"No, of course not," I lied, gesturing to the empty chair across from me. She didn't say anything for a moment, and then she said, "I played the violin as a little girl. I wasn't very good, though." She laughed a little, twisted her fingers together in her lap.

"You are the one," I said softly. "You told Henry about the orchestra in the camp?" She looked down at her hands. My heart beat wildly in my chest; my skin felt hot the way it did when I closed my eyes and played a solo. I stared at her fingers, twisting together. "You do not have a tattoo," I said, and I did not mean to doubt her, though it might have come out sounding that way.

"They only did that at some of the camps," she said softly. "I guess I was lucky then, eh? I had a number pinned to my shirt as they tried to work me to death."

Lucky? I felt ashamed for questioning her. "I'm sorry," I said. "I didn't mean to —"

"Yes," she interrupted me. "You don't remember the war. Henry told me."

"Do you remember me?" I asked, though the words felt impossible even as I said them. "Did we know each other?" How could she know me, when I did not know her? How could she remember me in a time when I could not remember myself?

"No," she said. And I exhaled, not realizing I'd been holding my breath. "We did not know anyone but the girls who worked with us. And hunger. Oh, we knew hunger so very well." Her voice broke a little. It was a struggle for her to speak about it, to remember it again, now. "The women in the orchestra, they had it much better than us, you see. A warm place to sleep, more food to eat, less work. We didn't intermingle with them. But we heard their music. They played when prisoners came in and when prisoners came out. And I hated them." She shook her head a little. "But you do not know what kind of person you will be until you are truly starving, no?" She said it to me like I would understand it. I nodded, but I didn't. Or if I did, I couldn't remember.

"Tante." Moritz opened the door, interrupting. He sounded out of breath. "Mother wants you to play violin for us. Will you, please?"

"Oh, I don't know," I said, suddenly uneasy about playing in front of Adelle, who had felt hatred for the women in the orchestra at her camp.

"Yes," Adelle said, her tone sounding more pleasant, as she was no longer talking about her past. "Please do."

"I'll come in a moment," I told Moritz, motioning for him to close the door and go back inside. I grabbed my teacup and saucer from the wrought-iron table and stood to go inside myself.

"She had curls like you," Adelle said, putting her fingers on my arm. "I remember because we were all shaven, and the girls in the orchestra weren't. And the violinist . . . her hair . . . I could see her off in the distance sometimes, from behind. She had such beautiful, beautiful curls."

"A lot of people have curly hair like mine," I said curtly. Julia had almost identical hair to mine.

"Yes," she agreed with me, reaching up to

touch her own short curls. "I guess a lot of us used to."

Back inside Julia's apartment, I did not realize my hands were shaking, until I picked up my violin. I tried to breathe deep, to steady myself. "Play us all those delightful songs you used to play as a little girl," Julia said, and it surprised me, because it was the first time she ever admitted that she thought my playing back then was *delightful.*

I closed my eyes, put my violin under my chin. I remembered them all so well: Beethoven, Bach, Handel, even Mendelssohn, and yet my fingers were frozen. I could not play a single German song of my youth. My mind knew all the notes, but my fingers would not allow it.

"Go on," Julia was saying. "Don't be shy."

My mind was blank for a moment, not able to think of anything else, but then it came to me: the Saint-Saëns solo I was playing the night I saw Max in the gardens in Paris, and I exhaled and began to play a concert, just for them.

When I finished, I was breathing hard, and I opened my eyes. But I would not look in Adelle's direction. I could not meet her eyes.

Max, 1935

It was worse than before, coming back. Max's mind was numb, nearly blank. He had gotten Marta and David to safety, he felt that much was true. But when he returned to the shop, he'd been painfully dizzy, his head too heavy to hold it upright, and he slept fitfully for days and days. The closet had affected him, changed him, the way it had once changed his mother, then his father. He could not go back again until he would take Hanna, no matter what. He could not risk anything happening to him before he got her to safety.

Once he finally slept off most of his headache, he found his mother's ring sitting on the counter downstairs in the shop, a note from Hanna scribbled on the same paper he'd left her. At the bottom she'd written only: *Wir sind fertig. We're finished.* He felt defeated as he picked up the ring, put it back in his pocket. He would have to win her back all over again, and it made him feel so weary, his body and his head still aching from the trip. But what other choice did he have? He loved her. And she would play in another orchestra, in another time, because he would get her out of this one, the same way he had gotten Marta and David and the Feinsteins out.

Hanna refused to talk to him for weeks. It didn't matter how many times he showed up at her apartment door on Maulbeer-strasse or waited for her outside her lesson at the Lyceum. He wrote her letters, left books on her doorstep. German books, of course, just in case anyone else should see them sitting there. Love stories, with happy endings. And when he would return the next day, the books would be gone, but whether she read them or his notes, who could say?

And then one night, in the middle of August, she appeared at the entrance to his shop, carrying a stack of books and her violin. And though she frowned when he opened the door, his first thought was that she had finally forgiven him.

"Hanna," he breathed. "I've missed you."

"I just wanted to return these." She walked inside and put the stack of books on the counter.

"Please." He put his hand on her shoulder; she yanked away. They'd been here before, and he hated it. Hated having Hanna angry with him. Hated that he couldn't find the words to make her understand why he'd left and how he hadn't meant to. "I'm never leaving you again. I promise," he said now. "Just please, sit down and talk to me. We can go upstairs, I'll make you a cup of tea."

"You've said that before." She did not sound angry, more, tired. "I can't be with someone who's always running away from me."

"I'm not running from you." He pulled her close, kissed the top of her head, and for just a moment she let him hold her. "That's not the way it is," he said. "I was helping people . . . Don't you trust me?"

"I did," she said softly.

"Well, can you believe me when I tell you I didn't want to leave you?"

"That doesn't even make any sense. You're a grown man. If you don't want to leave someone, you don't leave someone." She stepped out of his embrace and held up her violin case. "There has only been one thing in my life that has never left me." *Her violin.*

"Your audition?" he asked tentatively, reading her face for any signs of whether it had gone well, or badly.

"It's in two weeks' time," she said. "Actually, that's the real reason why I came . . ." She looked down at her feet, not daring to meet his eyes again, as if she were afraid to forgive him, to love him still. "Could I practice here in the shop? The acoustics are better and I practice better here."

"Of course!" He could barely contain his joy, to be able to hear her play again, just for him, the notes seeping up through the floor of his bedroom, a lullaby and a love song, both at once.

"This doesn't mean I forgive you," she insisted. "Or want to be with you. It only means that I like to practice here. And I really need to practice." Her voice broke a little; she was nervous. She didn't want to mess up this audition like she had the last one. And somehow that was more important to her than everything else.

"Whatever you need," he said. "I love you. And I'm here."

But she was no longer looking at him, no longer listening. She was already taking her violin from its case, rosining the bow. She held it up to her chin and began to play. And his entire body grew warm, standing so close to her, listening to her play.

The day of her audition, Max was so nervous he could barely breathe. He closed the shop early, rode the train into the city. She was auditioning at the symphony hall, and he waited for her outside on the sidewalk. Whether it had gone well or gone badly, he wanted to be with her afterward. He wanted all the stress and worry and anxiousness about the audition to fall away, and then for her to put her arms around him, to whisper in his ear that of course, she forgave him now. She would be with him now. She trusted him. She loved him.

He paced out on the sidewalk in front of the hall. The afternoon was quite warm, and thunderclouds swelled above him, gray and heavy with moisture.

At half past two, Hanna finally walked out, the sun glinted through a cloud, turned her face into a yellow blur for a moment. He could not tell, at first, whether she was elated or devastated.

"Hanna," he called out, waving. She turned to find the sound of his voice and then she ran to him, jumped up and hugged him. "It went well?" he asked, but he was certain from her reaction that it had.

"It was perfect," she said. "I didn't miss a single note."

"So you made it?" Max asked.

"I'll find out in a few days."

"Well, come on, let's go get something to eat to celebrate." Hanna hesitated, but only for a second before she took his hand.

They took the train back to Gutenstat, got off at Maulbeerstrasse, and walked to Herr Brichtman's shop. "Strudel is my favorite way to celebrate," Hanna said, clinging to him as they walked, and he thought of their first kiss there.

"Mine, too," he said.

But as they approached the shop, three SA stood outside the front entrance, and Herr Brichtman was arguing with them, his voice rising with anger.

Hanna handed Max her violin case and ran toward them before Max could stop her. "Is everything all right? Herr Brichtman, are you okay?"

"You should not be here," he said to Hanna. He caught Max's eyes, and Max understood instantly that everything was not all right. That he needed to get Hanna away from here now.

"Hanna, let's go." Max grabbed her elbow and gently tried to pull her down the street, away from the SA.

But one of the men turned to look right at Hanna. "Another dirty *Jude*? Is she yours?"

"No, I don't even know these people," Herr Brichtman lied. "They are just wanting a pastry. That is what I do, I run this shop. I told you, I've run it for thirty years." His hands shook as he spoke, but his voice was resolute.

Max pulled Hanna across the street. "Max," she said, ripping her hand away. "We can't just leave him there. What if they arrest him?"

"And how are you going to stop them?" Max asked. She opened her mouth, then closed it again.

They watched for another minute, from relative safety across the street. Until the SA finally left Herr Brichtman alone, and he walked back inside his bakeshop. Max and Hanna both exhaled. But neither one of them was hungry any longer.

Back at the bookshop, Hanna was still angry. "I hate this stupid Hakenkreuz flag you hang out front." She yelled at Max like it was his fault, but they both knew, if he didn't hang the flag, the SA would be here harassing him, just like they had been with

Herr Brichtman.

"I hate it too," Max said gently, locking the door to the shop behind them and leading her upstairs to his apartment.

She kissed him, and he could feel her anger in the intensity of her lips on his. Or maybe it was just her fire, her passion. They made love and spent the rest of the afternoon in his bed, naked. He wasn't sure if Hanna's forgiveness was from her fear at seeing Herr Brichtman accosted on the street or her joy and relief at having her audition go so well. Or simply because she loved him, that she could never stay mad at him forever.

"If I am to make the orchestra," she said, sometime after the darkness of night had overcome the bedroom — she stroked his bare arm with her finger, the way she might play a love song on her violin — "you will need to be my husband to move into the city with me, to travel around with me for concerts."

He got out of bed and searched his pants' pockets for the ring — he'd been carrying it around ever since she gave it back to him. He took it out again now, slipped it on her delicate, strong finger. She held it up to admire it, the diamond glinting in the candle he'd lit on the table.

"Please don't ever take it off again," Max said.

"Please don't ever leave me again," Hanna answered back.

Hanna received her acceptance letter to the symphony in the mail, two weeks after her audition. She ran into his shop, waving it in the air and screaming in the middle of the afternoon. She was being invited to participate as a third chair violinist for the 1935–36 orchestra season, on a one-year trial basis. It was the most tenuous of acceptances, but it was an acceptance nonetheless.

That night they celebrated with a bottle of Sekt and whispered wedding plans. They had no family or friends nearby other than Elsa and Johann, and so the ceremony would be small. It would be too dangerous to ask a rabbi to officiate, so they were going to find a magistrate to do it as soon as they could. Johann would know someone.

When Max awoke the next morning, he was still smiling, and not even the slight headache from too much sparkling wine dulled his mood. Hanna was still sleeping, past the sunrise, which was something she hardly ever did. He kissed her bare shoulder, got up and quietly got dressed, and went into the kitchen to make her breakfast.

He switched on the radio to listen to the news as he made coffee, humming under his breath while he worked. But then the words he heard crackling through the air stopped him, midstep: Hitler had convened a special Reichstag session at a rally in Nuremberg yesterday. They'd passed two new laws: the Law for the Protection of German Blood and German Honour and the Reich Citizenship Law. By order of the Law for Protection, Jews were no longer allowed to marry, nor even have any relations with non-Jews. And by the Citizenship Law, neither were Jews considered citizens any longer.

"Max?" Hanna said. She'd gotten out of bed, wrapped herself in his shirt, and stood at the entryway to the kitchen. He could tell from the expression on her face — a mix of fear and sadness, of anger and disbelief — that she had heard the radio too. But she walked to him, put her hand on his cheek.

She gently pulled the ring from her finger and tried to put it in his palm. But he closed his fist tightly, refusing to take it back. "No," he said. "It's yours. Keep it somewhere safe. I don't care about Hitler or some stupid law. I am going to marry you, no matter what, some . . . time." He pulled her close, held her tightly, breathed in the rosin of her skin and the lemon of her hair and kissed her.

"It'll be all right," she murmured, more for her own sake, than for his. "I still have the symphony."

But three days later, Hanna received a second letter in the post. This one informed her that her original offer had been rescinded. Due to the Nuremberg Laws, Jews were no longer citizens of Germany and thus could no longer hold positions in a German symphony.

"What am I going to do now? What am I supposed to do?" Hanna was so angry. She waved the letter in front of his face as they stood in his shop, and he glanced nervously out at the street, hoping no one would choose this particular moment to come in for a book.

She didn't wait for his answer, but ripped the letter into shreds, tiny unrecognizable pieces. She was breathing hard, her face bright red. He thought she might cry, but she was too angry for tears.

Max went to her, wrapped his arms around her. "I am going to take you far away from here," he said.

Hanna, 1951–1952

Even back in Austria, I had trouble forgetting Adelle and the things she had told me at Passover. I tried my best to stop thinking about the past, even about being Jewish, passing the fall holidays with barely any notice except when a phone call from Julia came, for the sole purpose of her wishing me *shana tova.*

"I wish you could join us for Rosh Hashanah," Julia said on the other end of the line. And I said that I wished that, too, murmuring excuses about not having any time off from rehearsal, which wasn't exactly a lie. But it was not the real reason I wasn't going to London for high holidays.

I fell into bed most nights, thankful that I was too tired to dream, and most days I thought only about the music, about my fingers on the strings. I had no time or room in my mind for nightmares, or what-ifs, or wondering about the war. I barely even had the energy to think about Max, to worry if he was alive or dead, if he would find me again or not. If our night in Paris had been real or my imagination. Or about Stuart, either, building a new life in America without me.

On Sundays, our one day off, I busied myself as a tourist in Vienna, sometimes alone and sometimes with the company of Frau Schmidt, who constantly wanted to be my hostess more than my landlady. I appreciated her kindness, but often I found it was easier to be alone.

She took me to the Wiener Staatsoper, the opera house, and pointed out that it still had a temporary roof, though reconstruction was under way. Bombs had nearly decimated it. "But once," Frau Schmidt told me, "Father played his cello here, and I came to see him as a little girl. It was the most beautiful place, and now . . ." She held up her hands. I still didn't know what had happened to Maestro or how he'd lost his finger during the war, but I bit my tongue and didn't ask, not sure I wanted to know.

"It will be beautiful again," I reassured her, though even as I said it, I thought it was like so much else. And like all of us. It would never be quite the same as what it was before the war.

■ ■ ■ ■

In January of 1952, we had just begun the new year rehearsing for a Tchaikovsky spectacular. And one chilly morning, I received a telegram from Henry Childs, letting me know he was in the city and asking if I might be free to see him that night for dinner. I had already planned to spend the orchestra's spring break in London again, but that was still months away. I'd put it in the back of my mind, and I felt strangely nervous to get Henry's note, to know he was here. I hoped he hadn't brought Adelle with him.

"What brings you here?" I asked him, sliding into a chair across the table from him at the Lehár Restaurant in his hotel, the Ambassador. Frau Schmidt had told me this morning that this restaurant had been named after Franz Lehár the composer and that he'd played a concert here long ago. That was before the war, and also before much of the hotel's facade had nearly crumbled after being hit by aircraft bombs. I wondered if Henry had chosen it simply for its musical connection.

He stood to kiss my cheek and sat back down. "I'm in the city for a medical conference," he said. "Julia insisted I check up on you." He smiled kindly, and I was pretty sure he'd check up on me, Julia or not.

"Oh, how nice," I told him. "Well, I am off from rehearsal on Sunday if you want me to show you around. I've learned a lot about Vienna. I have a chatty landlady who likes to take me around." He thanked me, saying maybe he would take me up on it.

We ordered dinner and made small talk. Henry asked what the orchestra was playing now, and I told him all about Tchaikovsky, the "1812 Overture," which was my favorite of his pieces and nothing at all like the romance most people associated with his work. Henry smiled, but his eyes seemed far away. "Henry?" I snapped my fingers. "Henry? Is everything all right?"

"Oh yes," he said. "I just . . . to tell you the truth I only decided to come to this conference so I would have an excuse to see you."

"Me?" Had Henry learned more from Adelle? My heartbeat quickened.

"I wanted to talk to you about Julia."

"Oh?" I exhaled. "Is she all right?"

"Oh yes, quite all right. In fact, I want to ask her to marry me."

I was confused. "And you are asking me . . . my permission?" Henry nodded.

"Henry." I patted his hand gently across the table. "You do not need to ask my permission. Do you love her?"

"Yes," he said. "Very, very much."

"And you will never leave her for some young . . . *Flittchen.*" I couldn't think of the right English word to express what Friedrich had done to Julia. But Henry nodded, understanding all the same.

"I will never leave her," he said solemnly.

"I know," I said, and I really did know that. I genuinely liked Henry. He had always been kind to me, so willing to listen and help. And I knew he would be that same way with Julia, as her husband. That was who he was not only as a doctor, but also as a man. "I could tell when I was there last spring, you make her very happy," I told him.

"Do you really think so?" he asked. I nodded; I did.

Henry finished off his glass of Riesling, we ordered dessert, and then over chocolate cake Henry suddenly looked up at me. "Hanna, will you play for us, at our wedding?"

"Play for you?" I thought about Julia's last wedding. She had walked down the aisle in silence because the piano player had quit the day before, citing illness, though we had all suspected that was a lie, that it was more anti-Semitism than anything else. But no one had ever considered asking me to play, least of all Friedrich who'd never had any appreciation for my violin. "I don't know if that's what Julia would want," I said.

"She would. She loved it when you played for us at Passover." He took a bite of his chocolate cake. "She is quite proud of you, you know?"

My eyes stung with tears at his words, and I bit my lip to keep them from falling. I didn't want to cry in front of Henry. "That is very sweet of you to ask," I told Henry. "But maybe you don't know my sister as well as you think?"

He took another bite of cake, and then he smiled at me. "Maybe you don't know her as well as you think," he said.

Max, 1936

After Hanna lost the symphony, Max thought it would be easy to convince her to leave with him. She had nothing left in Germany, after all. Her mother was gone; her country and her symphony had abandoned her. Her teacher was fired from the Lyceum, but then Hanna was no longer allowed in as a student either. Max slowly exchanged all his reichsmarks into gold over the course of a few months, so as not to arouse too much suspicion, and when Hanna snuck into his shop early one cool morning in February, he was ready to tell her his plan. They would leave all this behind; they would be together in another time. They would get married and Hanna would play in a symphony in Paris. And all he had to do was convince her to walk into the closet with him.

But she removed her head scarf and pulled a letter from her violin case. She smiled and held it up. "They want me in Holland," she said, the words coming out in a rush.

"Holland?" His mind was still on the closet, on what he would tell her, how he would explain it to her. He'd taken his father's journal out and had already decided he would hand it over to her as proof when she questioned him, as she most certainly would.

"Yes, there's a symphony in Amsterdam who heard about me and would like me to come there. I just have to get a visa. You could apply for one, too, and we'll go together. Jews can still marry anyone they want in Holland."

Max stood there, his mouth open, not sure what to say. Everything he'd planned to tell her now sounded even more ridiculous in his head than it had moments earlier. "But it might be hard to get a visa and . . . we don't speak Dutch," he finally said.

She laughed as if it were the silliest thing she'd ever heard, then stood up on her tiptoes and kissed him on the mouth. They were in full view of the window, and he pulled back. "Hanna, stop. We cannot be stupid." If someone saw them together now, like this, they could both be arrested.

"The street is empty," she said, glancing over again now. And she was right, it was.

But her letter from Holland had given her hope, and her hope had made her suddenly careless.

He glanced at the closet at the back of the shop. "Hanna," he said, "I need you to promise me something. If ever you're in danger, or if the SA bother you, I need you to promise you'll come straight here, to me. I have another way for us to leave." She tilted her head, looked at him funny. "We could even go right now," he said softly.

"Go where?" she asked, confused. "Holland?" He shook his head. She waved her letter in the air and smiled. "It's all going to work out." She breathed deeply. "I can feel it. And soon we'll have a wonderful Dutch life together, you and I."

"What if I told you that I knew the future?" Max said to Johann a few weeks later, after having drunk two ales. They were sitting on Johann's porch, late one evening. Hanna was spending the night at her apartment, where she said she could practice more hours, more freely, as she was among Jews and would not arouse unusual suspicion simply for playing her violin. Elsa and the girls were already asleep inside the house.

Johann was working on getting visas for Max and Hanna through some connections at his law firm. Max had stopped by to check up on that, and then they had begun drinking, and two ales in, Max had blurted out what was really on his mind. If he could get Johann, his oldest and closest friend, to believe him, maybe Johann would help him convince Hanna to believe him too.

Johann took another swig of his ale and he shrugged. "None of us know the future, Max. We can only hope for the best while preparing for the worst, right?"

"But I have seen it," Max told him. "Gone to it. My parents did, too. My father wrote it all down. I found his notebook." The truth had been rolling around in his head for such a long time, that it was something of a relief to say it out loud, to share it with Johann now. It sounded absurd; he knew it did. But if someone had told him even five years earlier about Hitler, about what their country was becoming and what it was like to live here now, he wouldn't have believed that, either. Nothing was certain anymore. Nothing was true. The entire world was upside down and backward.

"Your father was always writing down stories, telling us stories." Johann shrugged. "He had quite the imagination. You got that from him."

"But it is real, Jo. I swear to you."

Johann cocked his head to the side, gave him a funny look. "I know this has all been hard on you. It's not fair and it's not right. But you have to stay strong for Hanna. You can't go back to that . . . place." Max knew what place he meant, though they hadn't spoken of it in so very many years. After his mother died and his grief had turned into a physical illness, Max had almost died too. He'd been hospitalized in Berlin, unable to breathe right for months, and no official diagnosis was ever determined other than grief.

But this was different. Max knew it was. How could he make Johann understand? "What if you knew you were going to die?" Max asked him. He thought of Elsa in another time, of sadness and silver spider-webs in her hair. Of a much older Grace playing something haunting on the piano.

"Max." Johann put a hand on his shoulder. "We all die sometime. But you need to hang in there, a little while longer. For Hanna. My contact at the embassy believes the visas will come through by fall."

And then from inside the house, Grace began to wail, and Johann jumped up quickly. "I should get her before she wakes Elsa," he said to Max. "We'll continue this another night."

Max nodded, watched his friend walk inside the house. But they never would continue their conversation.

HANNA, 1953

The week before I left for Julia's wedding, a letter came from Stuart. He would be taking over the first-tier orchestra in the fall, and he anticipated he would have a spot for me. *Let me know,* he wrote. *If you want it, the seat is yours. If not, I will have to begin auditioning soon. Please want it. Remember what I said, no strings attached.*

I smiled, remembering how the tension had eased between us when he'd said that to me the last time I saw him, over strudel. And the truth was, as a violinist I did want it. The first-tier symphony in New York City? I might never get a chance this amazing again. But then, as a woman who felt something for Stuart I couldn't hide, I wondered, how could I be near him every day? How could I be with him and continue to breathe? But what if Max never returned again? Then why shouldn't I be with Stuart? Why should I deny myself whatever happiness I could find?

I wrote Elsa: *Did we both imagine Max? Did we both need him so badly that we conjured him to us?*

Elsa wrote back: *He will find his way back to you again. If there is anything I know in the world, it is that Max loves you. Max will do whatever he can to be with you.*

If Max truly loved me, why had he left me alone for so long? Whether it made sense or not, I knew I would continue to love him, continue to take him back if he popped back into my life again. That wasn't fair to Stuart. But what was fair to myself? I'd told Julia once that my violin was the greatest love of my life, so why was it so hard to do what I knew would be best for my career?

I couldn't decide what to say, and so I put off writing Stuart back until I would return from the wedding, hoping that after a week away in Wales the right answer would come to me, somehow.

Julia and Henry were getting married in a small ceremony, only a handful of guests. Henry's mother owned an estate in South Wales, and the wedding would be held there, in her rose garden. On the train ride in, I thought about Stuart, who'd also grown up in Wales, and how he'd retreated to Wales when he could no longer play his violin. The misty green pastures rolled by outside my window, and they seemed to be the only thing in Europe completely untouched by the war. It was so beautiful here; I could see why Stuart needed it when he'd been hurting. And suddenly I allowed myself to miss him, more than I had in a long time.

But I shook it off as I got off the train. This weekend was to be about my sister and about Henry. Not about me or Stuart. Lev had driven Henry's mother's large black automobile to the station to pick me up, and Moritz sat in back with me on the short ride to her estate.

"Can he really be old enough to operate this thing?" I asked Moritz, skeptical that my oldest nephew was nearly a man, though, it was true. He looked the part. And he was driving very slowly, like I made him nervous.

"Tante, *I'm* almost old enough," Moritz said. His voice cracked a little, reminding me that at thirteen, he was caught between being a man and being a boy.

"No way." I ruffled his hair. "You are staying young forever."

He laughed and asked if I'd practiced my violin for the wedding. "I hope so," Lev chimed in from the front. "Mother has been quite nervous about everything going off without a hitch."

Julia's request was simple: she wanted me to play Wagner's "Bridal Chorus," which she knew as the more popularly named "Here Comes the Bride," as Lev and Moritz walked her down the aisle. She'd always imagined she would hear it at her wedding, she said, and that didn't happen for her in Berlin when she'd married Friedrich. I told Julia I would play whatever she liked, not sharing with her the song's history or that Wagner was known for his anti-Semitic beliefs. Herr Fruchtenwalder never assigned his pieces because of this. Julia had no idea and I'd thought it silly to mention all that and spoil her wedding dream. I would play what she wanted. I truly wished great happiness for my sister and for her to have a long and loving marriage with Henry.

"Yes, of course I practiced," I told Lev and Moritz now. But it was a lie. I hadn't practiced at all. I usually overpracticed until my music was like breathing, until I could play it without even thinking. And it wasn't that I hadn't wanted to or hadn't tried to practice. It was that I hadn't been able to. I had stood there in the rehearsal room last week, my fingers freezing on the fingerboard, refusing to move. I'd chalked it up to exhaustion. The piece was easy enough. It would work out fine. I didn't need to practice. Really, I didn't. "My violin," I told the boys, "should be the least of your mother's worries."

But I realized how much of a lie it was as I stood with my violin the next afternoon, behind a small cadre of folding chairs, and in front of a trellis of pink roses. I was so nervous, my hands shaking in a way they usually did not, even in front of a large crowd at the hall in Vienna. It was silly; this would be a crowd of only thirty, family and friends, and a simple song, too. But I had tried to rehearse it quietly before I walked out, and my fingers would not budge.

I should've suggested something else, "Ave Maria" or Mendelssohn's "Wedding March." But Julia had been so insistent: no one had played "Here Comes the Bride" for her in Germany. She wanted it this time around. What would she do if I played something else? Knowing her, she'd probably stop and yell at me; her entire wedding would be ruined. I had to play what she wanted. I would. It was only one song. One simple silly song.

"They're coming," Henry's mother whispered to me. She was a tall woman with a kind face, her hair a red tinged with silver, and seeing her made me think I was glimpsing Henry in the future. I raised my violin to my chin, set my fingers on the fingerboard, took a deep breath. *I can do this.* It was one song. But my hands were shaking so very badly, I could barely hold my violin in place. *What is wrong with me?* "Go ahead, darling," Henry's mother said.

Julia turned the corner, Moritz on one arm, Lev on the other. Both of them were dressed in cream-colored suits, looking startlingly grown. Julia, too, wore cream, which she had said was more fitting for a second wedding, though I wasn't sure anyone cared but her. All three of them stopped walking, looked at me expectantly. Julia smiled.

I raised my bow, and for a moment I still could not play. Julia nodded at me, as if to say, *Go on, I'm ready.* And when I still didn't play, she glanced up the aisle expectantly at Henry who stood up front, waiting for her with both the rabbi and the minister.

"Go on." Henry's mother nudged my elbow. "They're waiting on you, darling."

I was shaking still. But I could do this. I could. I had to. The first note came out wobbly, but it came out. And everyone sighed collectively and began to move again. Julia floated toward Henry. I moved the bow, but with so much effort, it felt as if I were dragging my arm through a thick trough of mud. I played with my eyes open, forcing the song out, note by note. I was shaking, sweating, crying.

Play something German. Play for your life.

And suddenly it was no longer a dream, but a flash, a memory: an SA held a gun to my head, and he told me to play, to play something German, to play for my life.

HANNA, 1936

It was a crime to love Max in Germany now, and yet, I did not care. Every kiss, every touch between us was illicit, forbidden. I wanted him even more. I only loved him more.

Johann said we had to be careful, that if anyone knew we were still together they might turn us in, and we could both be arrested. But I could not stay away from my Max just because Hitler wanted me to. Hitler had already taken my symphony. And Herr Fruchtenwalder had been fired after the passing of the Nuremberg Laws, so now I didn't even have my lessons with him. All I had was Max. And this: a letter I'd received in the mail from a symphony in Holland. They had heard about my audition in Berlin, and they were still accepting Jews. I was waiting for my visa to come through, and I clung to that hope. Johann had a contact at the embassy that he knew through his law firm, and he was working on getting the visa for me, and for Max, too.

In the meantime, Max and I could not be seen together in public. I would sneak into his shop at suppertime when the streets were mostly empty, as if I were a common criminal, trying to thieve from him. And then I would hide out in Max's apartment, waiting to come and go again only when the shops and the streets were empty very early in the morning.

Time moved slowly then. I could barely even practice in the shop, except at night, when the Christian baker next door was sleeping, and not too loudly, either — we didn't want him to hear me, to ask too many questions. It was silly because of course he had heard me before the Nuremberg Laws were passed, but now it seemed everyone asked more questions, noticed more. You could not be a Jew and slip quietly through Gutenstat, shopping or minding your own business anymore. In fact, you could not be a Jew and be much of anything in Germany now.

In the summer, the Olympics were coming to Berlin, and things seemed to get better for a bit that spring, an odd flicker of hope in an otherwise very dark year. Hitler did not want to risk losing the Olympics and so he relaxed the rules for a little while. Arrests eased up. People were not blatantly hating Jews as much. Some of the JEWS NOT WELCOME signs came down around the city. People stopped saluting each other all the time. And I felt like I could breathe again.

Elsa and Johann secured tickets to the track events through Johann's firm but Elsa did not want to go and leave the girls, so Johann invited Max instead. "Why don't we watch the girls?" I suggested. "Let Elsa and Johann have a date." Everyone thought that was a grand suggestion, and Max and I became child minders for an entire weekend while Elsa and Johann were in Berlin at the games.

I watched Max play on the floor with Emilia, his long body stretched out as Emilia fed him pretend cookies and pretend tea in a doll-size teacup. He drank her tea, proclaiming it delicious, and I held on to Grace's hand as she toddled around the sitting room, wobbling to and fro. Max caught my eye, and we smiled at each other. I wanted this, with him. For the first time in my life I understood I needed more than my violin. I wanted more, with Max.

It was a breezy summer afternoon, and after Grace napped, Max and I decided to take the girls for a stroll to the park where they could run around and play. We might not have considered such a thing only a few months ago even, but the whole world was watching Berlin and the Olympics, and nothing bad was going to happen to us. Everyone was on their best behavior, even Hitler.

Who was going to notice a Jewish woman and the man she loved, holding hands, walking down the street with two little girls? Who was going to care?

But a week later, the games had ended, and I was in Max's shop late one night, practicing softly. I didn't have lessons anymore, and I wasn't sure when I'd get a visa for Holland. All I knew was that I had to keep playing. Playing was breathing. My violin was life.

Then suddenly there was a knock on the door. I stopped midnote, my bow suspended in midair for a second before I put my violin down softly in its case.

More knocking. This time banging, louder, harder, and on the glass, too. *"Öffne die Tür!"* They were shouting for us to open the door.

My entire body began to shake and I looked at Max, who had been sitting behind the counter, but now had run to the back of the shop. He was pushing on a bookcase, moving it out of the way.

"What are you doing?" I hissed as I ran back toward him.

"We need to go," he said. "Now." He was breathing hard, pushing the bookcase still, until a closet was exposed; a sign saying ACHTUNG! hung crooked just above the handle. This was where he'd hidden the banned books?

"We can't hide in the closet with the books," I said. "They'll find us, and the books, and you'll be in even more trouble."

He took out a key, unlocked the door. "We have to go," he said.

The banging was getting harder, the yelling louder. It sounded like they were kicking the door now, and I felt the walls shake as the door moved, inching forward. *They were going to kick it down.* "Hanna," Max said, "we're going to go in the closet and run as fast as we can." He was so scared, he wasn't even making any sense. "We'll be safe in the closet."

The door bulged and sunk. They kicked and yelled and it bulged again.

We were both about to be arrested, maybe killed, and I understood that so completely that it overtook my body in the same way a sonata did, when my fingers hugged the fingerboard without me even thinking about their motion. It was Chopin's "Marche Funèbre," its minor key resonating in my brain. I was shaking, paralyzed. I could not move.

Max grabbed my hand and pulled me into the closet with him. But as he went to shut the door, I remembered: my violin, sitting in its case. I couldn't leave it there for the SA to steal. "Wait!" I ripped away from his grasp. "I have to get my violin."

"Hanna, no!" Max cried out. But I ran away from him, toward my violin.

Just as I grabbed my violin case, the front door broke, the men flooded in. There were only four of them — how had it sounded like so many more? But I only had a second to think before they were grabbing me and Max.

"You are under arrest," they said. "For violating the Law for the Protection of German Blood and German Honour."

HANNA, 1953

By the time Julia and Henry exchange their vows, so many of my memories have come back to me. Not all of them, not ten whole years in ten whole minutes. But the flashes are bits and pieces, like one of Moritz's old jigsaw puzzles, enough of them arranged so I can see the full picture almost clearly.

Max and I were both arrested that night in 1936, and I had been clutching my violin. They asked me to play it for them at the police station, and then they had separated me from the others, put me on a train. I became a prisoner and I was taken to one camp, then a second one. But even the Nazis loved my violin. And as my playing was always considered valuable, I was never forced to work, forced to starve. My violin saved my life.

Adelle had been right; I had played in an orchestra. Forced to play my violin in a group, held against my will, and yet I was spared from death and hunger. I played and I played and I played. My violin was breath and life and light, even in a terrible darkness.

I sit down on the ground, squeeze my eyes tightly shut, not wanting to remember all the horrible things: the hideous sounds, screaming and the smell of burning flesh, the ash that fell from the crematorium not too far from the barracks where the orchestra slept, ensconced in an odd and tenuous safety.

But now I cannot forget them. As much as I try, I cannot make my mind forget again. The images come, rolling through my head like a film reel that will not stop, that will not turn off.

The guilt twists in my stomach now, foreign and familiar all at once: I had despised being a prisoner, but a part of me could not help myself from enjoying the music, even as we were forced to play when and what the Nazis wanted us to. I think about what Adelle said, that she *hated* the women in the orchestra: my beautiful curls while she was shaven, me having enough food to eat while she had none. And now I hate myself too. I had played and played, and I had closed my eyes and felt the same passion I always feel playing my violin, even as other Jews, no different from me, were starving to death, being murdered, all around me. And that is the truth that my mind had buried most: Am I not so different from the Nazis after all?

Until the very end, the very last day, when I almost died, too. It comes to me in another flash, right when Julia and Henry say *I do,* and everyone around me begins to clap.

The guards had lined us up, all the women in the orchestra. There were eight of us: three violins, three violas, a cello, and a bass. They had told us to take our instruments, stand against the wall, turn away from them. It was a firing squad; they were going to shoot us.

I held my violin in one hand, the cellist's hand with the other. I was going to die. All these years I had played and played and thought, well, at least I was practicing, keeping up my skills for after when the war would end. I had found hope while everyone else had been suffering. Maybe I deserved to die.

And then somewhere a bell began to chime. People were screaming? Or crying? Or were they cheering? I couldn't remember the difference between happy and sad any longer.

The guards lowered their guns. The gates opened. The camp was being liberated.

What happened next is still something of a blur. But I eventually made it back to Gutenstat, I remember that much now. I saw that it was all gone. I walked and I walked and I stumbled into the field. And eventually I lay down, cradled my violin, and closed my eyes, wanting to die, wishing I had died. And then while I slept, my mind grew a cocoon around all that had happened.

When I awoke again, the sky was black. A million stars glittered above me. And the night was diamonds and Beethoven's Concerto in D Major.

"Are you all right?" Henry comes up to me an hour into the reception. They'd hired a band for this part, and everyone is dancing and laughing in the garden, while I have been on the ground, clutching my violin, my back against the trellis. I've been sitting here, ever since I'd made it through the march. Henry sits down on the ground next to me, loosens his tie. "What are you doing on the ground all by yourself? I bet Moritz wants a dance with you."

"It is all true," I whisper. "I remembered it. The 'Bridal Chorus' . . . Wagner. I played it for them when they told me to play something German. It saved my life . . ." But I cannot tell him the rest of it. I don't want to say any of it out loud, and I especially don't want to ruin Henry and Julia's wedding with all these awful memories.

"You finally remembered?" Henry's voice rises. He's surprised, or delighted. I nod. I know where I have been, what happened to me. I hadn't missed or escaped the war; I'd just blocked it out as my mind was trying to recover. "So Adelle was right?" He sounds surprised. He hadn't really believed it. "You were actually with her in the camp?"

"I think so," I say. I wish it were not true. I don't want to be a victim, like Adelle. I want to be the first chair violinist, fearless and passionate and brave. But now what does it say about me that I played violin for the SA at their command, while they murdered and tortured other Jews all around me and I did nothing to stop them? That I blocked it all out afterward for so many years, convinced myself even that the war had never happened, that I had never even existed during it? "People were being murdered. And I was just . . . playing violin. And then I forgot," I finally say. "All those people. I should have done something to help them."

Henry pats my hand kindly and looks over at Julia who's dancing with Lev. "And what would you have done? You were a prisoner, too. Your violin saved you. Thank goodness you have such a gift, or you might not be sitting here now." He squeezes my hand.

But Henry's words feel empty. "They murdered so many people," I say. "And I played music for them. I gave *them* a gift. Maybe I should quit violin." It seems only right, a penance. A punishment. I can stay here in the UK with Julia and Henry and the boys. Forget Stuart and America. Forget Vienna, too.

"And why on earth would you do that?" Henry asks. "You are enormously talented. You have accomplished great things since the war. And Julia told me you have a new opportunity in America."

"But I don't deserve it," I say.

"You're exactly right," Henry says. "You didn't deserve any of what happened to you. But it happened and you did what you had to do to save and protect yourself. And tell me, what good will it do for you to give it up now?"

"I feel like a monster," I tell Henry.

"No," he says. "You are a survivor."

433

Max, 1937–1938

Max blamed himself for everything, for all of it. If only he had taken Hanna into the closet earlier, days or weeks or months earlier. He could've talked her out of the symphony or for trying for the visas. He could've convinced Johann of the truth if he'd really wanted to. He had been so stupid to believe that he would just take her into the closet when the time came. Now Hanna was gone. He hadn't saved her, and he blamed himself for all of it.

The SA let him go after a few weeks in jail, having no use for a Christian shopkeeper, even one who had broken the law by loving a Jewish woman. (Thankfully, they had no idea about the Feinsteins or Marta and David.) Max was bruised a little, but worse, his soul felt broken. It was a crushing pain to know he hadn't kept Hanna safe. It overwhelmed him so that he couldn't breathe properly. And as he stumbled out into the street and caught the train back to Hauptstrasse, he gasped for air and began to cry.

That was how he showed up on Elsa and Johann's doorstep, crying, barely breathing, his eye encircled in a purple bruise, his nose crusted with blood from having been punched by an SA who had called him a traitor to his country. Elsa opened the door, and when she saw him, she put her hand to her mouth and let out a sob. "Hanna's gone," Max said. "She's gone."

Johann brought him in the house, and Elsa got a warm wet rag to clean his face, some meat to put on his eye. He felt guilty taking it from her; meat was scarcer and scarcer these days, but Elsa insisted, and it felt so good that he couldn't refuse.

"They let you go," Elsa said, hopefully. "Maybe they will let Hanna go, too?"

Maybe Elsa was right, and for the first time since they'd been arrested, he felt the air flowing into his lungs. In another time — he'd seen it with his own eyes — Hanna was safe, missing years of her memory. Maybe she would still come back to him and he could still take her into the closet? Maybe it wasn't too late?

He waited for days, and weeks, and then

months. He wrote letters to the SA, to the Reichstag, trying to get information about Hanna's whereabouts, and that resulted in him being arrested again. Why should it be a crime for him to love her, to want to know if she was safe?

After another few weeks in jail, they let him go, but they promised him that next time, he would not be so lucky.

Max smelled the smoke first. Just a wisp, like a cigarette lit out on the street. But it quickly intensified, filled his nostrils, an acrid burning sensation.

Something came flying in through the front window of his shop, breaking the glass, a firebomb with a note: *Judenliebhaber.* Jew lover. As he took a second to look at it, he didn't notice right away that the flame had leaped onto a book, that the book was burning, and that it was touching another book, which also quickly became engulfed in flames.

Where they burn books, they will, in the end, burn human beings too.

The books were going to burn, the shop was going to burn. He would burn, too, if he stayed put. And the closet. *What would happen to the closet?*

He hesitated for a moment, but then he

made a choice. If he didn't leave now, he might never leave. And if the future he'd seen once was real, Hanna was there, alive, okay.

He opened the door to the closet and ran through it as fast as he could, faster than he had ever run in his life.

HANNA, 1958

I have played the violin since I was six years old, and it has always felt a part of me, another limb, one that is necessary and vital to my daily survival. My violin connects my present and my past, my dreams and my reality. My fingers move nimbly over the strings, my mind forgetting all I've lost or misbelieved or imagined. There is only the music that is my constant companion. Nothing but the music. Not Stuart. Not Max. Not now. Not the past, either.

"Hanna," Stuart interrupts me today. I've etched the date, November 6, 1958, in pencil at the top of my music, so I know it is real. I do this every single day and have since I was living in London with Julia. While I sometimes still forget how old I am now, my fingers do not move as they used to. Some days my knuckles swell, and I must cover them in bags of ice when I get home after practice. But Stuart doesn't know this;

"I am never going to leave you again," Max says, holding me, pulling me closer. "Never." And maybe I am still naive, but he says it so forcefully that I really truly believe him.

I lead Max to my bedroom, and as he unbuttons my shirt, I feel self-conscious about my body, which is different than it was the last time I was with him, much different than when I was such a young girl in Gutenstat. My hips are fuller, my stomach rounder. But Max doesn't seem to notice any of that. "Your neck still smells like rosin," he whispers in my ear, and then slowly he kisses a trail down my naked body, from my neck to my calves, and then back up again.

We make love, slowly, sweetly. Our bodies move together, keeping time perfectly. And afterward I lie in his arms, and we whisper to each other. I tell him about everything he has missed, everything I have done: all the orchestras, all the solos. Julia and Henry. My grown-up nephews. The only part I leave out is Stuart. And not because I think Max would be mad but because I don't know how to describe Stuart to him exactly. Stuart and I are just friends here in New York, but sometimes, some nights when we need each other, we are more than that.

"What have you been doing all these years?" I ask him.

He kisses the top of my head. "If I told you, you wouldn't believe me," he says.

"Try me," I say.

"Well," he begins. "I have . . . lost many years. Skipped ahead in time. One minute it was 1938 and then it was . . . when is it now?"

"November 6, 1958," I say, recounting the date I'd written on my music only a few hours earlier.

"You must think I sound crazy," Max says.

"No," I tell him. "I don't think that at all. For me it was the . . . trauma. I blocked it out." I repeat the explanation I had been told myself. "Is that what happened to you, too? Did something terrible happen to you?"

"Yes," Max says. "I thought I'd lost you forever."

"No," I tell him. "I'm right here." I turn my body into his, snuggling in closer, entwining our legs as we had done so many times, so many nights. Those early days of our time together are far away, but also, it still feels so close.

"I'm so tired," Max says.

It is still the middle of the afternoon, and I'm not tired at all, but I don't want to leave

444

my bed, leave him, so I tell him we can sleep if he wants.

"I love you, Hannalie Ginsberg," Max says, his voice lazy, his words, slightly slurred.

"I love you, too," I say.

"Will you play me something? What was the song you played the night we got engaged?"

"The Brahms concerto. His love song for Clara Schumann." I remember that night perfectly. Everything was still possible, and hopeful. I'd thought that Max and I would be together forever, not like the unrequited love Brahms had been writing about.

I kiss his chest, kissing over his heart, feeling it thump slowly beneath my lips. And then I get out of bed, pull my robe from the bathroom, and grab my violin from where I'd left it on the front table.

I stand at the foot of my bed, close my eyes, and begin to play: the Brahms I'd played that night by Elsa and Johann's fireplace is in my mind and in my heart, and it pours from my fingers, the way rain pours from a thundercloud, sudden, almost violent.

When I finish the song, my whole body is shaking, and I open my eyes again. "Did you enjoy it?" I ask, breathing hard. Max doesn't answer and I turn to see if he's fallen asleep. His head is to the side; his nose is bleeding a little. I put my violin down and run to the bathroom for a washcloth.

"Max, are you all right?" I sit on the bed next to him, dab at the blood. He doesn't respond, and I grab his shoulders and try to shake him gently awake. But his shoulders feel limp in my hands. His skin is cold to the touch. "Max?"

I put my head on his chest, and where his heart had beat beneath my lips ten minutes ago, now there is only silence.

HANNA, 1959

The concert hall in Berlin has been rebuilt since the war, and as everyone else in the symphony exclaims how stunning it is, to me it looks all wrong, not nearly as beautiful as it once was. But then I am the only German-born of the group, the only one whose zayde brought her to hear the symphony here as a little girl.

Berlin in general looks entirely different, everything so new that it is almost hard for me to walk around the city, to explore the streets and the plazas I used to walk and know and love as a girl. But I force myself to walk them, anyway, and to walk them alone. I break off from the rest of the orchestra who go in search of monuments and museums, and by myself, I retrace the familiar and unfamiliar steps of my past.

I have invited Sister Louisa and the nuns to come to the concert tonight, Elsa and Grace, too. Elsa and I have plans to go to dinner tonight after the performance. I have tried many times to write Elsa about Max and to tell her what happened, but every time I started to write it, it felt all wrong, confusing, unbelievable. I will talk to her tonight, in person, and I both long for the comfort of sharing the news with someone else who knew and loved Max and dread giving Elsa more heartache.

Though it has been almost five months, I have not quite accepted all of it myself. The doctor at Mount Sinai told me that Max most likely died of a massive stroke, fairly unusual for someone in his twenties, and he asked if I knew Max's medical or family history. *Max only looked young,* I'd told the doctor. *But, really, he was in his forties, like me.* As for his family history, I knew only what he had told me, that his father had died fairly young himself one day in the shop, in the middle of a conversation with a patron. And that his mother had died of illness, even younger. Too soon. At the wrong time. And then the same had happened to Max. His history and his destiny. It felt unbelievably cruel that Max had finally come to me again, and then, just like that, he was gone for good.

I grieved Max silently, inwardly, for a few months. I didn't tell anyone else or speak of it. I immersed myself in my practice, in my violin. But then at night I would get into bed and it would come back to me again. Knowing he was dead, truly dead, that he would never again wander into my life whenever it suited him, made my head and my body and my soul ache. But it also felt a strange relief that I was no longer waiting, no longer hoping for him to reappear, just like that.

Henry and Julia had taken a transatlantic flight (their first!) to come visit me last month in New York, now that Lev and Moritz are both at university. And when I saw them in person, I couldn't help myself; all the details about Max came rushing out of me. It was the first time I'd said it all aloud, and I felt better, in a weird way, to have it out there, outside of my head. A real, spoken truth. Max was dead.

Henry said that he was so very sorry for my loss. And Julia bit her lip for a moment and then said, "Well, if you want to look at the good side, you are free now. You can love someone else. What about that handsome distinguished Stuart? I always thought you'd end up with him."

"Sweetheart," Henry said, patting Julia's leg. "Maybe now is not the time?"

Julia apologized, said she hadn't meant to

be harsh. I enjoyed the way Henry tempered her. In fact, I liked her so much better married to him than when she was married to Friedrich. "I'm glad you two found each other," I said.

"See," Julia said. "That's only what I meant. We all need second chances."

"I have my violin," I said, and I shrugged her off.

"Well . . ." She touched my hand. "Henry and I are going to get front-row tickets when you come play in London. Mamele would've been so proud," she gushed.

It was the strangest and the nicest conversation we had ever had. I glanced at Henry and then I glanced at her. Her life was far different from how she'd ever thought it would turn out, but she had survived a lot, raised two wonderful boys. "She would've been proud of you, too," I said.

I finally told Stuart everything, just before we all got on the plane to fly to Europe. I went to him last week, after rehearsal, and then I couldn't keep it to myself any longer. As if talking to Julia and Henry had caused this great dam to break inside of me, and everything flooded out. I told him about all my missing years, and how I found them again the night Julia and Henry got married. About missing Max and finding him again too. In Paris and also, last year, in New York.

"I'm so sorry," I told him. "I hurt you, and I wanted you to understand why. But now you know how broken I am. Why I could never really be with you the way you want."

"It's all water under the bridge," he said, kindly. He put his hand gently on my shoulder. "And you are not broken," he said. "You have lived through so much, and you have come through so beautifully."

And he looked at me in that way he had once in his apartment in Paris, as if to say he was here, he was waiting. Whenever I was ready.

It is both exhilarating and terrifying to be on the stage in Berlin. I stare out into the crowd, looking for Elsa and Grace, but the lights are so bright, the audience so big, that all I can see is a sea of gray and yellow tinted faces staring back at me.

Tonight we are beginning with Bartók's "Six Dances in Bulgarian Rhythm," in 7/8 time, and Stuart stands in front of us counting it off quietly, reminding us to pay attention to the time signature. The time is everything in this piece, in this concert. In Berlin.

The date handwritten at the top of my music reads March 16, 1959. Here I am again, in Germany, playing my violin for a country that raised me and loved me, that cared for me and destroyed me. *I have lost so many years. Skipped so much time,* Max said, just before he died.

But here I am again.

Then Stuart lifts his arms, catches my eye the way he always does. I put my violin to my chin, stare at him for a moment. His blue eyes shimmer in the stage lights, and he smiles at me.

I lift my bow, smile back at him to say that *yes, I am ready now.* And then I close my eyes and play.

AUTHOR'S NOTE

I had just started writing this novel when I went to speak to a Holocaust survivors' group about my last book. One woman there shared with me what it was like to be a little girl in Germany as Hitler was coming to power, and she told me how her family didn't leave because they were Germans. It was their country, too. And no one truly believed how bad it would get. That stuck with me, and I thought about it as I created Max and Hanna and their world in the 1930s in Germany. Though all the characters in this novel are fictional, as are the orchestras Hanna plays in throughout the book and the suburb of Gutenstat, all the events going on around them are based on historical facts, both before and after the war. I tried to re-create Germany during Hitler's rise and London, Paris, and Vienna after the war, sticking as close to the facts and true time line and landscape as I could.

The orchestra and the unnamed camp Hanna plays in during the war are also fictional, but I got the idea based on what I read about the real women's orchestra in Auschwitz. I read that the musicians were treated better than the other prisoners but that many of them grew depressed and despondent as they were forced to play as other prisoners were marched to death. I also read that the orchestra was scheduled to be shot to death on the day the camp was finally liberated, which is where I got the idea for the scene Hanna finally remembers, near the end of the book. Richard Wagner was known for his anti-Semitism and his music was revered by the Nazis. His "Bridal Chorus" still, even today, is sometimes not used in Jewish weddings because of his anti-Semitic history. The idea for Hanna came also from multiple real stories I read about musicians who survived their time in concentration camps because of their musical ability, in one way or another, and who went on after the war to become professional musicians.

Though I never played the violin, I grew up playing music, spent most of my teenage years at band and orchestra rehearsals, and even fell in love with my husband when we played in a band together. Music has stayed a large part of my life, though now I listen to it rather than play it. I first thought of Hanna's character as my family attended a symphony concert during the contentious 2016 election season. As I listened to the symphony play that afternoon, I thought to myself, *No matter what happens in the world we will still have this beautiful music.* And Hanna's character came to me later that afternoon. I became fascinated by the role music had played before, during, and after World War II. And though my orchestras are fictional, the fact that the orchestras in Europe lost many of their players in the war and had to rebuild like everything else is true.

The US Holocaust Memorial Museum site was an invaluable resource in helping me to understand the events in Germany in the years before World War II. In 1933 there were more than five hundred thousand Jews living in Germany. About half left by 1939. I read *In the Garden of Beasts* by Erik Larson, which really helped me get a sense of what Berlin was like in 1933 and 1934, and *Gone* by Min Kym, which helped me understand what it would be like to grow up as a violin prodigy, and how deeply connected a violinist is to her instrument. I highly recommend both for further reading, in addition to the soundtrack that goes with Kym's book. I took some fictional liberties in giving Hanna a Stradivarius and allowing it to survive the war in playable condition.

Max's bookshop is, of course, fictional. But in 1935 Albert Einstein and Nathan Rosen posited a theory about wormholes, using the theory of relativity to explain the existence of bridges through the space-time continuum that could allow people to travel into the future. Neither Max nor I quite understand the physics, but we both agree with the line from *Hamlet:* "There are more things in Heaven and Earth, Horatio, / Than are dreamt of in your philosophy."

ACKNOWLEDGMENTS

With deepest thanks, first and foremost, to the entire Harper Perennial team. Laura Brown, I am deeply indebted to you for falling in love with Max and Hanna's story, and for your wise editorial vision, which helped me make their story shine. Thank you to Sarah Stein for taking over and seeing them through to publication. Thank you to copyeditor Laurie McGee for your wonderful attention to detail. Extra special thanks also to Emily Taylor, Mary Sasso, Emily VanDerwerken, Jennifer Civiletto, Amy Baker, and Doug Jones for your unwavering commitment to this book.

I am lucky to have the best agent, and I'm forever grateful to Jessica Regel for her undying support and always sage advice. Thank you for always telling me to write what I love and for believing I can figure out a way to pull it off. Your faith in me means everything! A huge thanks also to the entire team at Foundry, with special thanks to Kirsten Neuhaus, Heidi Gall, Colette Grecco, and Michael Nardullo for taking Max and Hanna around the world.

Thank you to my amazing parents, husband, and kids for their love, support, belief in me, and continued willingness to read the earliest drafts of my work. Thanks especially to Gregg, who is always up for takeout when I'm consumed in a fictional world, and always willing to talk through plot problems — I love you! Thank you to my group of mom friends who invited me to the perfect weekend to finalize the first draft of this book and who also toasted with me right after I finished. Thanks also for all the mah-jongg! Thank you to all my writer friends who are always willing to talk, text, email, complain, and/or rejoice with me. Special thanks to Laura Fitzgerald for always giving me great advice and for the celebratory margarita the day this book sold. And to Maureen Leurck and T. Greenwood, who keep me sane on a daily basis and continually remind me just to keep on writing. Thank you to Mary Kubica, Brenda Janowitz, Pam Jenoff, and Fiona Davis for support and friendship.

I am so grateful for the support from so many in the book community. Thank you to

Andrea Katz and Robin Kall, who are dynamo book influencers and whom I am also lucky enough to count as friends. Thank you to Emily Homonoff for the advice, doughnuts, and always, the ice cream tacos! Most of all, thank you to all the readers, booksellers, and librarians who continue to support me and my books and help spread the word — I'm so grateful for all you do.

ABOUT THE AUTHOR

Jillian Cantor has a BA in English from Penn State University and an MFA from the University of Arizona. She is the author of award-winning novels for teens and adults, including, most recently, the critically acclaimed, *The Lost Letter, The Hours Count,* and *Margot.* Born and raised in a suburb of Philadelphia, Cantor currently lives in Arizona with her husband and two sons.

The employees of Thorndike Press hope you have enjoyed this Large Print book. All our Thorndike, Wheeler, and Kennebec Large Print titles are designed for easy reading, and all our books are made to last. Other Thorndike Press Large Print books are available at your library, through selected bookstores, or directly from us.

For information about titles, please call:

(800) 223-1244

or visit our Web site at:

gale.com/thorndike

To share your comments, please write:

Publisher
Thorndike Press
10 Water St., Suite 310
Waterville, ME 04901